FLYING

FLYING

CARRIE JONES

TOR
TEEN

A TOM DOHERTY ASSOCIATES BOOK
NEW YORK

This is a work of fiction. All of the characters, organizations, and events portrayed in this novel are either products of the author's imagination or are used fictitiously.

FLYING

Copyright © 2016 by Carrie Jones

All rights reserved.

A Tor Teen Book
Published by Tom Doherty Associates, LLC
175 Fifth Avenue
New York, NY 10010

www.tor-forge.com

Tor® is a registered trademark of Tom Doherty Associates, LLC.

The Library of Congress Cataloging-in-Publication Data is available upon request.

ISBN   978-0-765-33659-0

Our books may be purchased in bulk for promotional, educational, or business use. Please contact your local bookseller or the Macmillan Corporate and Premium Sales Department at 1-800-221-7945, extension 5442, or by e-mail at MacmillanSpecialMarkets@macmillan.com.

First Edition: July 2016

P1

For all the girls like Emily Ciciotte . . .
girls who know they can save the world.
Let's do this!

FLYING

CHAPTER 1

I wake up scared. Chills shudder down my body and my mouth tastes bad, like old sandpaper mixed with—what? Spaghetti sauce? Diesel oil? Rancid sour cream? I shut my lips tightly and try not to smell or taste or breathe, just fall back asleep, but my heart beats too hard, too fast, too crazy quick from whatever nightmare it was that woke me. It feels like when Dakota Dunham goes ballistic on the bass drum when someone gets a three-pointer at a basketball game.

The moment I think of Dakota Dunham, I know it's no use. I'm not going to fall back asleep. My hands are clutching my quilt as I open my eyes. My glow-in-the-dark stars have faded into the ceiling, which means it's past midnight—way past midnight.

Something thuds downstairs. I reach out to turn my light on and then think better of it. Because what if it's some sort of demonic serial killer who attacks the single women of Milford, New Hampshire? What if he's down there right now, stepping past our little yellow love seat, making his way toward my mom's bedroom? Maybe he wields a machete or a chainsaw or has claws for hands, or something else all stereotypical serial killer, and he's heading straight for my mother's bedroom, ready to . . .

I whisper, "Mom?"

No answer. I try to think of a weapon capable of fighting off a demonic serial killer. My iPod Nano? Hardly. My pom-poms?

Pshaw. My lamp? That could work. I reach out and grasp the light stand. It's heavy enough.

Then comes her voice. It travels upstairs to my bedroom, loud and pinched. "You better not try it!"

You better not try it?

That is not the sort of thing Mom normally says. She's the kind of mom who acts like a church secretary. She mouses herself down, you know? No makeup. Baggy clothes. Quiet voice. It's like she's hiding from the world. Not that the world is even noticing or anything.

I try again. "Mom?"

No answer.

I let go of the lamp, pull the covers off, and haul myself out of bed. It is not easy. My mom says I'm a sound sleeper and a lazy waker. An oak tree once fell on our house during a blizzard; I slept right through.

Shuffling across the floor, I can't see anything. My leg bashes into the edge of my dresser. Pain shrieks up and down my shin. Great. That'll bruise and look lovely when I'm cheering. Fumbling for my doorknob, I find it and turn it, pulling the door open, and . . . *Light!* Horrible, awful light smashes into my eyes. My lids shut.

Moaning, I struggle to open them again, to adjust. Blink. Blink again. Okay. I stagger toward the stairs and pad down them. The runner on the steps bristles against my naked toes.

"I am serious!" Mom yells.

I make it to the bottom of the stairs and wait there a second. The front door window shows a world of blackness. Mom stands in the middle of the living room. Her narrow back quivers with emotion. She's not in her pajamas even. She is still wearing the same long, hippie skirt and sweater she had on earlier today . . . I mean, yesterday.

"Hey." I whisper-say the word, not sure if I should interrupt.

She whirls around, snapping the cell phone shut. Her hair is wild, glamorous in a celebrity red carpet way, and her eyes match.

"Mom?"

I can actually see her make her body relax. Her shoulders slump again and she smalls herself down. She seems more mom-like. "Honey? What are you doing up?"

"You were yelling."

Her eyes get big and innocent. "Yelling?"

"Into the phone," I add, leaning back against the wall and yawning. I am not the sort of person who does well when they randomly wake up in the middle of beauty rest time. Obviously.

She rushes over to me and wraps her arm around my waist. We're the same height now, which is wild really. It is so bizarre being eye to eye with your mom.

"You need to go back upstairs to bed right now, young lady."

"Do not go all official mother on me, because you are avoiding the issue," I say, but I snuggle into her and we trudge back up the stairs. My calves ache. I'm so tired from all the touchdowns at cheering practice. Each step is hell. "Who were you talking to on the phone?"

"Crank caller." Some pitch in her voice makes me feel like she's lying, but Mom never lies. Still, it doesn't make sense. She's not a person who gets mad that easily, and as we get to the top of the stairs, I still can't quite understand what just happened.

"Why did you keep talking to them then?" I ask.

She flicks on the light to my room and guides me in like I'm still five years old. She does a slight shrug. "I didn't want to let him just get away with it. It isn't okay to harass innocent people in their homes. If he does that to us, who else is he doing it to? I can just imagine poor little old ladies, grabbing their phones, disoriented in the middle of the night. Their first thought would be someone has died. It's cruel."

She says this all quietly but with force, and then she motions for me to get in my bed, which I do. She pulls my covers (penguin sheet, penguin blanket, second blanket, comforter, quilt) up to my chin, leans in, and kisses my forehead. Her small fingers smooth the hair away from my face. It feels nice. She gives me a tiny smile and says, "You have a good sleep, Mana."

"Okay."

"Don't worry about anything," she insists. "No being a little stress monkey."

"I am not a little stress monkey," I lie. My mom thinks I don't handle stress well enough; she wants me to start yoga or meditate. Like I have time for that. She says my stress comes out in nightmares—typical, boring nightmares about being defenseless and having little gray men abduct me, or being naked at school, that kind of stuff. And she goes on and on about how I need to keep my heart rate down and be mellow.

"You, my little sweetie, are getting all crinkly faced. That means you're worrying." She stares at me with mom-radar eyes and then tucks the quilt around me even more tightly before she adds, "I've got everything under control."

My mind can't wrap around what she's saying, because I'm too busy trying to remember my last nightmare, which involved voices in my head, I think telling me the wrong answers for a computer science test. "Huh? What do you mean?"

"Nothing."

She smiles at me. I smile back, and my eyes start to close, and I'm already thinking of Dakota and how his forearms look when he drums.

"I will always keep you safe," she says, which is what she has said to me every single night since I can remember the actual tucking-into-bed process. Mom tends to baby me a bit.

I lift up my arm and wiggle my hand, but I'm so sleepy it's barely a wiggle. She knows what I want though. She wraps her fingers in between and around my fingers.

"I love you, Princess Jelly Bean," she says, placing my stuffed penguin next to me. I have a thing for penguins. This is normal, despite how much I get teased about it. Penguins are adorable. They mate for life. They waddle. They have built-in tuxedos. "I love you the whole world."

I smile. "I love you, too."

She squeezes and lets go. I fall back asleep before she has even shut off the light. Poof. Just like that . . . I am off to Beddy Bye Land with the Kissy Penguins. At least, that's what she always used to call it when I was little. Back then, she would tell me a story before I went to bed. It would always be about a girl hero, conveniently named Mana, and how she would rescue the world from space monsters. I would snuggle up against Mom and listen to her soft voice and fall right asleep every single night. I was such a baby back then. Now all my good dreams are about Dakota and his forearms.

Mom and I head to a cross-country meet on Saturday, not because we are runners but because Lyle, one of my two best friends, is competing, and we like to support him whenever we can. Plus, to be truly honest about it, a cross-country meet is much quicker than winter and spring track meets with their multiple events that take all day. So we try to get all our supporting done in the fall. Next year Lyle will be up at Dartmouth. My heart kind of sinks when I think about him going off to college and me still having a whole other year of high school.

But Mom is obviously not thinking about these sorts of things, and is her usual happy, caffeinated, wiry self as she pulls the car into a parking space by the field. She taps me on the knee. "How are you feeling today? Everything working well?"

"All body parts in regular working order."

Lyle thinks it's amusing that she phrases things this way. "She makes you sound like a machine," he always says, and I always tease back, "I am a machine. A tumbling machine of awesome."

We are sarcastic goofs. We have been sarcastic goofs forever, friends since I moved into the neighborhood in lower grade school, back when he was super awkward and gangly and his head seemed too big for his shoulders. He is not like that now. I spot him in his warm-up pants and windbreaker, and his shoulders stretch out the fabric of the jacket; his thigh muscles even stretch out his warm-up pants. He has gotten so-o-o huge. It's kind of stunning. He waves and I go up on tippy toes, waving back.

Mom hooks her arm into mine. "That's an awfully big smile, young lady."

Lyle starts jogging over.

"Don't give me that scoffing face. You know what I mean," she teases.

"I have no idea," I answer. Actually I have *sort of* an idea, but this peculiar jumble of feelings I have for ancient friend Lyle is not what I want to diagnose or even poke at right now, especially since Lyle is already with us.

"Hey." He smiles. "You came."

"Of course!" I bounce on my toes again and reach up to get a twig out of his thick, brown hair. A tuft of it bumps up in the back. I resist the urge to smooth it down and instead give him the twig. "Are you playing Grim Dawn out in the woods instead of on your laptop?"

"I wish!" He turns to Mom and greets her, and she presents him with a tin of cupcakes, which pretty much makes him explode with happiness. "Seriously? You are the best! Mana, your mom is the best!"

"I know."

Lyle holds the tin delicately in his long-fingered hands. When we were little we used to call them wizard fingers, but his palms have caught up in size, so now I think they're just manly. I try to process this thought: Lyle is manly. Lyle is manly in a way that does not fit how a cheerleader is supposed to think of her best male friend. Lyle is manly in a way of defined quad muscles and big hands and—maybe more manly than Dakota Dunham—more than—

Lyle interrupts my thoughts. "I'm going to bring these back there."

"Don't eat until after the race!" Mom calls after his retreating back. "We don't want any cramps impacting your performance, young man!"

"No worries!" he yells to her, and then he shifts his focus to me as he strides forward, not watching where he's going. Other runners skitter out of his way and he calls to me, "See you after, okay? Scream for me!"

"Always! Like I've just witnessed a disembowelment!" I yell, and he turns, and I'm stuck watching his retreating back as he returns to the rest of the team. A couple other people wave and I wave back, like a normal person does. People give Mom thumbs-up signs indicating their love of her cupcakes. "You should just be a baker."

"I should! It would be much more fun. Not as many work trips." She laughs and pats her belly. "But you would have two times the mother you have now."

As the male runners disrobe and start trotting over to the starting line, I hip check my mother, who laughs and does it back. She waves to other parents if they wave first, but she stays with me, which is okay.

"I should make you those penguin cookies with the salted caramel," she announces. "I haven't made you those in a long time."

When we get near the starting line, Lyle gives me a little wave/salute thing and I arrange my features into an overexcited smiley face for him, just as his mom walks toward us. After she does the small talk with my mom, she offers me a sip of her Coke, but I don't even get a chance to decline.

"Mana is allergic," Mom says, which Lyle's mom knows. She has known me forever.

"I always forget!" she titters just as the bell goes off. "All the children with all their quirks. Caffeine allergies. Latex allergies. Peanut allergies. It's funny how we've managed to survive so long as a species."

Lyle instantly breaks away from the pack. I'm not sure how he does it, because I'm not much of a runner, but he makes running seem effortless—just all loping, quick legs and loose arms. He's not even trying.

"He's holding himself back," Mrs. Stephenson says as the runners head into the woods. "He always does."

"He's a good boy," Mom answers as the crowd starts to move to a better vantage point.

"He should do his best. College recruiters want to see what he can do."

He has already gotten in early to Dartmouth, so this is a ridiculous thing for her to say. I can't stand Lyle's mom sometimes, and I say, before I can help myself, "He PRs by seconds every race, and he will do his best at states. He always does."

Mom touches my arm. Then she nudges me into motion, calling good-bye to Lyle's parental unit as we head toward the railroad tracks. You can see runners at the mile and 2.7-mile points from there. We get there just before Lyle strides past, still in the lead, still not sweating. He gives me a cheesy finger point. I give him one back.

"I'm glad he's your friend," Mom says out of nowhere.

And it is such a silly thing to say, but such a *Mom* thing to say, that I can't help but smile even as I clap for some other students I know. "I'm glad you're my mom."

"Oh! Sentimentality alert!" She blushes. "I should record this and play it back to you the next time you're mad at me for hassling you about your homework, or leaving socks on the couch, or eating all the cookies for the boosters table at the basketball game before the game even starts, or failing to put the cap on the toothpaste."

I ignore this little litany.

"Mana is all lovey-dovey. Yes, I am." I announce this to her, and it gets the appropriate Mom smiling response. Happiness settles into my chest as we wait for Lyle to appear again, running fast and strong toward us and the finish line.

He crosses and smiles, entering the chute where they funnel the runners post–finish line. It keeps them all in order. The wife of the coach takes his number off Lyle's chest and people give him congratulatory back slaps, high fives, and fist bumps. He has a personal record. Again. He doesn't even seem winded. Again. He trots over to us and gives me a huge hug. I inhale. Not even smelly. My hands touch the muscles of his back. Not even sweaty.

"PR!" He swings me around and I laugh. My feet leave the ground. My mother rather conveniently disappears and starts picking up discarded water bottles. She's pretty environmental like that.

"You were amazing," I tell him as he sets me back down.

His head bobs up and down. "I was, wasn't I?"

"Amazing and humble," I tease.

We fist bump and make explosions.

"You know what I was thinking about when I was running?" he asks. "I was thinking about that time in sixth grade that you were in the *Les Mis* play for show choir."

"I hated show choir," I interrupt.

"I know. But do you remember, you played Whore Number 2, and we went to music class and Mr. B. could not remember your name, and he actually called you Whore Number 2?" Lyle starts laughing, remembering while I pretend to pout. "That was beautiful. And you? You just turned bright red and answered anyways. Brilliant!" He fist bumps me again. "I was remembering how awesome that was and I just forgot about running. I totally lost track of time. It was the best race ever."

"Cool," I say, but I kind of want to say, "Yay! You were thinking of me."

The rest of the day I am so ridiculously happy that I actually doodle penguins and hearts on my mom's grocery lists and on the to-do list, and try really hard to not think it means some sort of amazing thing. When it comes to liking your best friend, life can be kind of disappointing. You think things mean more than they do. You search for signs in the way his lips move, in how quickly he smiles, in the way his hip bumps into your side when you walk. And usually? The signs don't mean anything at all.

Anyway, if it turns out to be nothing? Well, there will always be Dakota Dunham.

Two mornings later and nothing has changed in my best-friends-with-Lyle status. I wake up and Mom is gone before I get up for school. She has pushed a note underneath the kitchen timer shaped like a chicken. It doesn't work, but she won't throw it away. Lyle got it for her at the animal refuge zoo place he interns at during the summers. She wrote on the note in big, green magic marker letters:

DEVELOPMENTS AT WORK. HAD TO GO IN EARLY. I'M SO SORRY. THERE'S A BAGEL IN THE FRIDGE. I MADE CHOCOLATE-DIPPED PRETZELS FOR YOUR FUNDRAISER. LOVE YOU!!! SEE YOU AT THE GAME.

XOXO
LOVE,
MOM

She drew a big heart on the side, too. Sometimes, she is just too sweet. Sometimes, like when she's yelling at me about how I tend to put the wet towels on top of the rest of the laundry, she is just annoying.

I open the fridge to pull out the bagel. My report card falls off the door. Yes, it is up there, stuck with a magnet of a Scottish Highland cow thing. Yes, that is geeky. That is my mother. I take the magnet and the report card and anchor it again. There.

When everything is back just the way it's supposed to be, I thrust the bagel in my mouth and chew. After I shuffle out of the kitchen and up the stairs into my room, I pretty much just stand there for an extra second and gawk at the piles of clothes that are strewn all around my floor. I have to get ready for school and I don't want to because it's going to be just another boring stressful day in the otherwise boring stressful life of me. The getting-ready process goes quickly and before I know it I'm back in the kitchen where I seize the Hello Kitty pretzel container. There is a cute penguin sticker on there now, amid all the happy kitties, which Mom must have put there. Lyle says she spoils me. September, my other best friend, says Mom babies me. I can't say that most of the time I mind. Shoving my bag over my shoulder, I head out.

September has parked her truck in the driveway and is waiting.

"Hurry," she yells. She is tall and long. She's one of my bases for cheering, and even though her arms are about as thick as those pretzel sticks, she is super strong, like a farm girl, which she is not. Her mom is a doctor. Her dad is a nurse. They own no mammals or poultry. They do have a fish, Mr. Awesome.

I pull in a big breath. The cold, gray winter sky bleaks me down despite Hello Kitty, chocolate-dipped pretzels, and the new penguin sticker. I'm tired again today. For a second I wonder if I could pretend to be sick, but it's game day, so I hike my bag higher on my shoulder and balance the pretzel container in my hand.

"Mana! Hurry!" September yells again. The sun glints off her skin. Kids use to call us Oreo when we were little because Seppie is so dark and I am so undark. I used to pray at night that I could resemble her instead of a ghost. That was before I understood about racism and how when some idiots gape at Seppie they don't see someone beautiful and funny and brilliant; they see "other." Idiots. Sometimes people think about me that way, too.

I rush down the cobblestone path to our driveway and haul myself up into her truck. Yes, she has a huge, gas-guzzling, black pickup truck. Do not ask me why.

"We're not that late," I say, slamming my bag down next to my feet. "You always get so stressed about being two minutes late. You don't always have to be the orderly and perfect student."

"Yes, yes I do." She shakes her head. Her pigtails flail about and then she reverses out of my driveway like Satan is after us.

She pulls into the Stephensons' driveway, which is barely worth driving over to since our houses are so close, and we wait. She honks. "Where is he?"

Lyle, all Gap clothes and smiles, comes barreling out of the house, slamming the door behind him. "Sorry! Sorry! I was engrossed in something."

"I am so going to kill you if you make me get a tardy. Three tardies equal detention. Detention equals poor academic record. Poor academic record means bad college. My fine self is not going to a bad college because you were climbing a tree." Seppie executes a perfect K-turn while Lyle buckles up. His face is all smooth, squeaky clean like he just scrubbed at it with a wet facecloth. He always appears that way, and he smells that way, too, like mint-scented soap, the same kind my dad uses.

When I was super little, my dad taught me to hunt and to wash my hands after hunting, after being in public places, after touching raw meat or going to the bathroom. He's that kind of guy—the kind that can kill a deer but still worry about germs. Lyle is not like that. I can't imagine him ever killing anything. And germs? He eats Skittles he finds on the sidewalk.

A gash from shaving mars Lyle's cheek just to the right of his nose. He has a new cut every morning, I swear. I want to put little Band-Aids on them.

"We aren't really going to be late, right?" His shaggy brown hair flops over his eyes. Lyle nods at Seppie, then lifts one eyebrow over his dark brown eyes and asks me, "She will kill me one day, won't she?"

"Probably."

"What if we just left without you?" Seppie asks. "Did you even think about that?"

Lyle doesn't answer. Just for the record, Seppie and I are both cheerleaders, which Lyle helps with, too, actually. He's an over-achiever. Running is his big thing, but he helps cheer at competitions and important games because we need him for the ridiculous stunts where a good amount of upper-body strength is involved. A lot of kids in my school do multiple sports. I do not, but I am an underachiever. Seppie and Lyle are all about getting into Ivy League colleges. It's one of our essential differences. They worry about college; I do not. They get amazing grades; I get by. They will have scholarships; I will have loans. Lyle has claimed the window side, so I'm smashed between the two of them in the truck cab.

"My feet are freezing," I say as Seppie swerves around a pothole. Her elbow knocks into me, so I smoosh closer to Lyle.

"You should wear socks," she says. Like she knows. "It's almost winter. It's getting cold."

"Seppie, have you ever worn a sock in your life?" Lyle asks, stretching out his long legs, which he can do because he's not stuck sitting in the middle. "You are the Sockless Wonder. That would be your superhero name: the Sockless Wonder, whose excessive foot odor thwarts all foes."

"Shut up. You'd be Geek Boy. Cheerleader by day; *Doctor Who* watcher by night. Unable to match a single outfit even if his mama picks them out for him the night before. Permanently attached to his little online game. What's the name of it? *Lounge Lizards Take on the—*"

"Unfair!"

They keep bickering. We drive through our subdivision and out onto Back River Road, with all its curves and supermarkets. I turn up the music. I close my eyes and try not to think about Lyle's leg pushing against mine, or the test I have today that I totally forgot about, or Lyle's minty smell, or why I am thinking about Lyle this way. Lyle of playing *Doctor Who* in the woods when we were seven, Lyle of the gaming fixation, Lyle of the newly developed chest muscles, Lyle of the—

Lyle's voice interrupts my thoughts. "And *then* I professed my undying love to her and Mana just stared at me and said, 'But I only love khaki-wearing koala bears who are into drumming and rolling up their sleeves to show off their forearms, Lyle. You would never do. You are far too manly-macho.'"

I open my eyes, blinking away all these random thoughts of Lyle and me growing up together, and sputter, "What?"

He starts laughing and punches me in the arm. We pass a school bus on the right—totally illegal, totally Seppie.

"She's really out of it." Seppie turns off Back River Road and onto the highway. "What is up with you today?"

I shrug. My shoulders bump against them. "I didn't sleep much last night."

"What, were you out late partying?" Lyle asks. "Partying on a Sunday night?"

"Funny." I punch him. He punches me back. "I'm just tired."

"Do you want some of my coffee?" He picks up his metal no-spill thermos.

Seppie snarks at him. "You know she can't have caffeine. It makes her wild. You're just tormenting her because you know she loves the smell."

"I don't actually remember ever having caffeine," I say, whiffing in the warm, nutty scent. "Is that hazelnut? Wow. That smells good. I mean, that smells really good. I grab it and take a micro sip. It's warm and sugary and nutty.

"Well, you're not starting now." Seppie reaches across me, takes the thermos, gulps, and says, "Yep. Hazelnut."

"And you call me cruel?" Lyle snatches back his thermos and turns his attention to me. I swallow hard, which is ridiculous. My pulse rate seems to be getting higher. I lick the coffee off my lips as Lyle asks, "Why didn't you sleep well? Are you getting sick?"

He puts his hand on my forehead. It feels nice, like all the tension is just oozing out of me and into his hands. We slow down, pull off the highway, and head toward the school parking lot.

"No fever," he announces, and then goes into nerdy speech. "I declare this specimen devoid of fever."

"No fevers. I just had more nightmares." I stretch up. Lyle moves his hand away and I want to snatch his wrist and pull it back to my forehead. I kind of miss it. Seppie turns into the school parking lot and pulls the visor down to check out her reflection in the mirror instead of actually trying to find a parking space or anything like that.

I rub at my forehead. All the tension is back. And I swear I feel sweaty, like I've just run a marathon. "I don't want to go to school."

"Does anyone?" Lyle asks.

Seppie clears her throat.

Lyle goes, in a too-high, fake Seppie voice, "School is a magical place to find potential mates, enjoy learning, and practice my social networking skills that don't involve the actual Internet."

We all start laughing. The truck hits a frost heave in the parking lot. Lyle bashes his head against the ceiling because of the bump. This makes us laugh more, for some reason. By the time we get to school, my bed feels a long way away.

Lyle helps me out of the truck. It's pretty high, and he and Seppie always take care of me because I'm shorter—and the whole flyer thing. "You seem better."

His hands linger on my waist for an extra second and I *so* do not know what to think. "I feel better, except I think the coffee made my pulse rate go up."

"The magical power of coffee. I don't think you're actually allergic. You're probably just hypersensitive to it or something," he says.

"Mm-hmm," I say. "Right."

"What? Do you want me to say it's the magical power of friends that makes you feel better?" He smiles and lets me go.

But the truth is, that is it. It *is* the magical power of friends. I stand there, full of energy, so much energy suddenly, and jump into the air, possibly performing my highest back tuck ever.

"Whoa . . . that was almost—unnatural," Seppie says, eyeing me.

"I feel so hyper!" I giggle, hugging her.

"And this," she says, "is why your mom probably never wants you to have coffee. You didn't drink any, did you? You were just pretending, right?"

"Right!" I shout a little too loudly.

She cocks her head and speed walks toward the school, yanking me along. "You are the worst liar ever."

"I don't think it even counted as a sip," I say. "Just a taste. And now I'm all hyper. Coffee is wonderful!"

We make it into the building just as the first bell rings, and Seppie bolts off, Lyle following after her. They have to go to first period in the language wing, which is pretty far away. I watch them go and try not to feel all alone. Hyper and lonely is an unusual combination. I close my eyes and try to will myself to calm down. I already want more coffee. Maybe the real reason my health food nut of a mom doesn't want me to have coffee is she knows that I'd be addicted after one tiny sip.

CHAPTER 2

need an entirely new body. This becomes obvious to me at cheerleading practice, when even doing a squat jump feels like a big deal to my sleep-deprived muscles. No wonder my mom doesn't want me to have coffee if this is what it feels like after you come crashing down from the caffeine high.

School was basically hellacious all day. I managed to get through Latin and SAT Prep class and Computer Science before practice this afternoon, but it has all made my stress levels so high. It's unfair to put my three hardest and most boring classes after lunch. Still, that's no excuse for how tired I feel after our tumbling drills. It's weird. It's like ever since my mom got that random crank call, my body has just not been able to catch up with sleep.

"Are you still tired?" Seppie asks. She stands there without breaking a sweat, which is because she's not much of a tumbler. Her drill is doing cartwheels across the mat. My drills are back tucks and back layouts, front layouts and twists. Doing one tumbling run is fine, but doing them over and over for an hour kills my shins and jars the tiny bones on the outsides of my ankles.

"More stressed."

"Maybe you shouldn't go up so high." She grasps my shoulders and does a tiny rub. "Loosen up! You're so tight! Did you fail your computer science test?"

"Yes. I mean—possibly. I got a D, but then he'll let me make it up at lunch, but I'll probably still fail." I sigh dramatically for effect. "I am a failure."

I make a giant F shape with my fingers and put it on my forehead for extra emphasis.

"You are not a failure; you just suck at computer science."

"And Latin."

Seppie wiggles her lip, which she always does when she is trying to decide if she should lie. "And maybe a little at Latin. But you're so good at other things . . ."

Mrs. Bray, our coach, eyes us. She's always worried everyone is gay. She's pretty homophobic, but she doesn't tell Seppie to stop rubbing the knots out of my shoulders. Instead, she says, "It's Mana's height that makes her runs exceptional, and those muscles. That's lift. It's Olympic caliber. We're so lucky you never went off into the gymnastics world."

"Mana doesn't like competitions," Seppie answers for me. I don't. I mean, obviously, I'm a cheerleader and I want my team to win, but I feel so badly for the other team when they lose. I hate making people lose. She drops her hands, and another cheerleader, Kristen Bean, does a series of back handsprings. It's almost my turn again.

"Lucky for us!" Mrs. Bray smiles at me. "Will Lyle be here for the game? I'd like to practice the stunts for regionals during halftime."

"He texted he would be here," I answer.

As soon as Mrs. Bray turns away, Seppie says, "She thinks you're a thing."

"A thing?"

"A couple. You and Lyle."

"Oh . . ."

"Do you want to be a couple?" She stares into my eyes. "Oh my God! You do . . . don't you?"

I try to answer. "D-Dakota? He has nice forearms."

"You're stuttering!" She starts laughing. "And I asked about Lyle. And you know it."

"Mana! Your turn!" Mrs. Bray yells, and I am saved from answering Seppie by having to do another tumbling pass full of back tucks and twists. I am actually grateful, and at the end, Mrs. Bray enthuses, "Solid landing! Solid! Girls, we should pay attention to how Mana lands. Beautiful, Mana! Tight!"

And then we move on to jump drills, which are so labor intensive and cardio heavy that nobody can talk. You use a basic eight count, where you set a high V, hold it, start jump, get the height of the jump, land, hold the land, stand, and then hold the final standing position. Girls are sweating by the time we have finished our jumps in sets of five, which include T jumps, tucks, right hurdlers, left hurdlers, pikes, toe touches, doubles, and then doing it all in reverse.

The away team arrives for the game and heckles us, which is normal. A couple girls manage to give them the finger when Mrs. Bray is not paying attention. It is pretty much an additional hour of hell before we're allowed to go shower and change for the game.

"Cheering is hard," I moan.

Seppie's hands go to her hips. "You love it."

"I do?"

"You know you do. You kick ass at it. You could totally be a professional if you wanted," she says as we walk into the locker room off the gymnasium. "Have you decided yet what you want to do when you must be gainfully employed?"

"Gainfully employed?"

"Well, I'm not going to say 'when you're a grown-up,' because that makes us sound five."

"True." I think for a second, press my hand into my heart, and say brilliantly, "Not be a cheerleader."

"No. Really." Seppie the Sarcastic yanks off her T-shirt and throws it in her locker.

The thing is, I have no idea. Seppie and Lyle have their whole lives planned out, days organized in lists on their phones, and I forget that I even have tests. "Save the world?" I kid.

"Lofty goal," she teases back, and leaves me for the shower.

"Fine! How about a penguin refuge? Like a shelter! I could save penguins for a living!"

"This," she calls after me, "is why you and Lyle are soul mates. Savior complexes. I have no clue why I love you two martyrs."

"But you do?"

"I do!"

The game itself is a no-brainer. First Seppie, Lyle (who arrives just in time and still wearing cross-country clothes—he hates cheer uniforms; says they're not manly enough), the rest of the squad, and I raise our pom-poms and hold banners as they announce the players. Dakota is drumming, looking like the male model he probably should be. He points a drumstick at me. I try not to swoon in a fangirl way. Then we cheer along the sidelines during the plays. We are a peppy kind of squad, so we cheer a lot. This is supposed to be a good thing, but some people always have a hate on for cheerleaders. Sometimes, they start young.

To prove my point, some arrogant little brat kid sitting in the bleachers yells, "Will you just shut up?" He has pretty massive cojones for someone who is like, oh, I don't know, in first grade. "I'm trying to watch the damn game."

"D-E-F—E-N-S-E. It spells *defense,*" we keep cheering, because if you stopped cheering every time someone heckled you, there would be no cheers. Although, to be fair, that is probably the hecklers' goal. "Defense. Let's play defense. Woo!"

To continue to be fair, this *is* a really dumb cheer. However, I am a pro here. I point my pom-pom at the kid and think about giving him a not-so-subtle salute with my middle finger. I am so not in the mood.

The kid stands up and glares at us. His little button-down dress shirt seems ridiculously out of place. Everybody else under ten has

T-shirts on. I almost feel bad for him, stuck here under the yellow gym lights, stuck between sweaty grown-ups in their maroon high school spirit sweatshirts smelling like cigarettes, body odor, and popcorn. Almost.

"D-E-F—E-N-S-E. It spells *defense*."

"Beyotches, I know you can spell. Just shut up," he yells. He brandishes his floppy blond-haired head at us.

I glance at Lyle. He raises his eyebrows, because no matter how secure in his manhood he is, he is not into being called a beyotch by some brat kid. Lyle's cheek twitches like he's about two seconds away from running up the old, wooden bleachers and pummeling the boy, which would not be good, obviously. Dakota just bangs his drum. I don't think he can hear anything over that.

I try to catch Seppie's eye, but she's oblivious, as is basically everyone else. The mom next to the yelling boy is fixing the bra strap beneath her ancient black Metallica T-shirt. She has no clue. Neither do the rest of the four hundred or so people crammed into the gym. They're watching the basketball game. They're watching each other. Nobody is watching this weenie kid.

Nobody except me and Lyle and the guy sitting diagonally behind the boy. That guy is wearing sunglasses inside, but you can still tell that half his attention is on the kid and not on the game, which is slamming on behind me and Lyle and the rest of the varsity squad. He also seems to be staring at Dakota a lot, which is kind of weird because Dakota is just sitting there, occasionally playing drums when the pep band crashes out another rah-rah support-our-team song. Then again, I'm pretty much constantly staring at Dakota too, so who am I to judge?

Someone in the bleachers yells, "Go, Thomas!"

Thomas is the point guard and crowd favorite. He is incredible. Judging from the cheers, he must have stolen the ball. Obviously, our cheer worked. Take that, kid.

Other people start jumping up and down. I turn to see it. A shot from way past the three-point line, almost at half court, right at the halftime buzzer. Swish. It is all net and all beautiful. The crowd screams. All the cheerleaders scream, except Lyle, obviously. He yells. I do a couple herkies to show my support. Everything reeks of popcorn.

We run to the net end of the court as the ballplayers head off to the locker room for a halftime talk. Lyle and Seppie roll out the long, blue tumbling mat. I wipe my hands together and try to pump myself up. I scan the crowd, trying to locate my mom. She's not here yet, I don't think, which is weird. Punctuality is her middle name. (Not really. It's Denise.) Dakota gives me a thumbs-up, which is nice, and a drumroll, which is even nicer. My stomach becomes a cliché of butterflies fluttering and all that stuff. Dakota will have to be my winner in the next-guy-to-like contest, because Lyle is unfortunately off-limits, thanks to his best-friend status. Speaking of . . . I sneak a peek at Lyle, who is outgrowing his shirt in a good chest-too-big way.

Do not stare.

The voice commanding my head is a guy's voice. My subconscious is a polite, commanding male? It makes me laugh because it is just so bizarre.

Bunkie Brady, the school's athletic director, yells some encouragement, and I bounce on my toes. I'm up. Lyle smiles at me and I power run ten steps. I double back handspring into a back layout and then a back twist. I land on my feet and raise my hands up, turning to face the home crowd. They go wild. They always do, which is really nice, and more than makes up for the D.

I hustle out of the way for Lyle to blast down the mat. He front tucks three times. It's his only tumbling talent but he has perfected it. Girls swoon. That's just how he is. People start screaming, all pumped up. He takes my hand and we start making them frenzied.

That's our job. That is the point of cheerleaders, and Lyle may love cross-country while hating cheering, but he completely adores the attention.

"We ARE West High!" we chant. "We ARE West High!"

They chant it back to us, clapping two beats at the appropriate time. The rest of the squad comes up behind us, screaming it, too. It is insane, all noise and feet-stomping, hands-clapping craziness.

"We ARE!"

Stomp.

Stomp.

"West High!"

Stomp.

Stomp.

Kind of another stupid cheer, honestly.

"We ARE!"

I'm midstomp when there's this flurry of action over by Dakota's drum set. The sunglasses guy has captured Dakota by the shoulder and is yanking him down the bleachers, past all the clappers and stompers, right toward the side door. Dakota is screaming too, but not our cheer.

"WEST HIGH!"

I snatch Lyle's elbow and point. I don't know if he sees. Poor Dakota is trying to jerk away from the sunglasses guy but he's not getting anywhere. The guy in the glasses smacks him across the face and hustles him out the door to the locker rooms. How can no one notice this? Crud.

There's nothing else to do. I book after them, race in front of the screaming basketball fans, and dart toward the locker-room doors. I am right at the doorway that leads out of the gym to the locker-room hallway when Lyle yanks me by the elbow.

"What's going on?" His eyes are round, worried. "Why'd you take off?"

"Dakota." I point down the hall. My hand trembles. "This guy with sunglasses took him and started beating on him. He yanked him back here."

Lyle sturdies his shoulders, calm as he always is, despite the craziness of the situation. "To the locker rooms?"

"Yes." I try to pull my elbow away. "I have to stop him."

"You think he's kidnapping him or something? Really?" Lyle's eyebrows shoot up like they're trying to escape his face.

"Yes. No. I don't know. He was hitting him, and Dakota was screaming." I start pulling away from him. I am all wild strength. He lets go. "Lyle! We have to do something."

He nods quickly, all in charge and sensible. "Let's go get the sheriff deputy guy."

"Okay." That will take so much time.

Lyle gives me one of his *everything will be fine* expressions, which he usually reserves for when I stress out about tests, and then runs off toward the doors where the sheriff's deputies always stand. I follow him, but he gets stuck behind masses of hungry high school basketball fans. And then people cut between us as he has to shove through all the tired moms buying cheesy nachos for their kids and the baseball hat dads clustered around the bake sale table. It'll take him too long, way too long to get the deputy. Anything could happen to Dakota and his forearms.

So I don't stay put like Lyle wants me to. Instead, I rush down the hallway. Sweat, old socks, unwashed T-shirts . . . the smells hit me as I run under the fluorescent lights. Right now, the home and away locker rooms will be filled with guys talking about strategy and zones. So the sunglasses guy wouldn't bring Dakota there unless he wanted an audience. That leaves the girls' locker rooms. I smash open the door to the room for the away cheerleaders. There are clothes and duffel bags everywhere. Hair products roll about on the floor. I slam around the room, searching, searching.

"Hey!" I yell. "You in here?"

I check under the toilet stalls, bash open some doors. Nothing. I slam out of there and rush into our own locker room. *God. God. God.* I can barely breathe, there's so much adrenaline running through me. My heart feels like it's exploding inside my chest.

"Hey!" I yell again as I step inside the locker room.

They stand there on one of the long wooden benches in the center of the room, in between the rows of freestanding lockers. Well, that's not true. The sunglasses guy stands. His dark hair ruffles like there's a fan on somewhere. But there aren't any fans in the locker room.

He has Dakota all tied up on the bench. He used duct tape to wrap his ankles and hands together, doubling Dakota back onto himself. Dakota's eyes meet mine, and you can tell he is so not into this S and M crap.

"Help!" Dakota says, in a kind of oddly calm way for someone being abducted. He looks strangely sexy.

"It'll be okay, Dakota." I storm in, and even now I'm blushing because it's Dakota. I stop a few feet away from them. I stare up at the sunglasses guy. Way, way up. "Let him go."

Sunglasses Guy jumps off the bench and strides over to me. "Don't be stupid."

"No. *You* don't be stupid," I say, angling toward Seppie's bag, because I know she stashes pepper spray in there. Super against the rules, but like I care. "The police are coming."

"I've been saved by the Asian cheerleader; how perfect," Dakota says. "Breaking the stereotypes. How droll."

Droll?

"Are you pulling the race card on me, Dakota? Seriously? What the hell? You just asked me to help you. Why are you being a dick?" I sputter. "You're never a dick. You're sexy and you point your drumstick at me, which could totally be misconstrued, obviously . . . but um . . ." I backtrack, because despite this situation, I'm pretty horrified that I just said all that out loud. "What's with the race card?"

"Of course . . ." Dakota smirks. "Race card."

Sunglasses Guy glowers back at him. "I should've duct taped your mouth."

"Probably," Dakota says.

I step a little closer to Seppie's bag. "Are you kidnapping him?"

"Nope."

"I saw you hitting him. You can't just hit someone and tie them up and expect nobody is going to try to stop you, even if they are acting racist instead of just being hot like they're supposed to." I pretty much put it all out there, because hopefully my crushing on Dakota will distract Sunglasses Guy.

Another step.

"I knew you liked me." Dakota actually winks. He's really taking all this well.

"It's what happens when I work solo," Sunglasses Guy says. "My partner has more finesse." He ignores my conversation with Dakota and steps in between me and the bag. I swear he smiles at me. I shudder.

"Partner? What? You're like some professional kidnapper?" Bad news.

His lips part and he sort of smirks. "I prefer abductor."

I lean toward the bag. I have to save Dakota, who is obviously not himself right now, unless he really is some sort of freak bigot, but whatever. Panic can do weird things to people. It just means I won't like him. I try to keep the guy talking. "Lovely. I will remember that. Abductor. How's it feel to be abducted, Dakota?"

"I'd rather it was you doing the abducting," he says.

"You're flirting with me now?" I ask, as I lean just a tiny bit more toward the bag. "I've liked you for weeks, and now you get kidnap—sorry, abducted—and poof! Now, you like me."

Sunglasses Guy loses his smile and interrupts me. "What's in that bag?"

"Nothing." Standing up straight, I try not to sigh from frustration.

He reaches forward, lifts it up, opens it.

"Hey! That is private prop—"

"Pepper spray?" He holds the can with distaste. "That's the best you can come up with?"

I jump over the bench to Dakota and start trying to get his hands untaped.

"Don't touch him!" the guy roars.

He shoves me away and I fall to the disgusting linoleum floor, smacking my shoulder into a row of lockers and Jordan Riley's heels. A heel flies up into the air from the momentum and lands stiletto down into a tube of baby powder. A white cloud of soft talc explodes into the air and all over me. I sneeze instantly, and the lockers wobble. I round off out of the way, instinctively, and somehow land halfway across the room. Dakota's eyes widen in a *how did you do that* sort of expression. If I can get us both out of this, I will tell him I have no idea how I just leaped a good twelve feet from the floor, but that I am going to try to do it again because—seriously?—how cool was that?

But the guy? He doesn't even notice, or try to help me up, just says in this dirt-hard voice, "You have no idea what he is."

"A flirty drummer," I say, standing up again, trembling and rolling my shoulder. "A flirty *racist* drummer, but that still doesn't make it okay to beat on him and tie him up and . . . do whatever sick thing it is you and your partner are thinking of doing to him. Sex trafficking? Is it sex trafficking?"

He snorts, in disgust I think, and turns his attention away from Dakota for a second to focus on me. Something inside me shivers.

He says, all quiet menace, "You have no idea."

Dakota shudders and his tongue lashes out. Only it's not a normal-size tongue. Is it even a tongue? It's where a tongue should be, but it's three times as long as a normal tongue (twice as long as a 1980s glam rocker's) and it is spraying some green liquid. Green! This wipes out any forearm sexiness.

"Watch out!" Sunglasses Guy leaps in front of me. His back starts to sizzle. "Crap!"

He whips around, like he's protecting me. There is a mark across his back that has seared right through his leather jacket and the shirt underneath, all the way down to his skin. A long burn. The scorched leather smells like burning hair, but sweeter somehow.

I press my back into the locker row that's still standing, just as Dakota rubs his duct taped hands into the leftover liquid on the floor. The tape snaps right off. So much for the power of duct tape.

"This is not good," Sunglasses Guy says. "Stay behind me."

"He's just Dakota," I insist, but even I can hear the doubt in my voice.

"I am not just Dakota," Dakota says, standing up. "Am I, China?"

The man—China?—doesn't answer. His back straightens, like he is trying to make himself even bigger.

"Okay, maybe you're not 'just' Dakota. You are a racist Dakota who somehow has a green acid-tongue thing going on, which you managed to hide all during English class, but . . . You're a good guy, right?" I babble.

"I told you, you should have taped my mouth," Dakota says to China. "Although I could have spat through that, too. You seem like you're too cheap to use the good tape."

China snarls at him. "I didn't know you were a spitter."

"You didn't do your homework, then, did you, hunter?"

Spitter? Hunter? A voice that sounds like Dakota's bounces around in my head: *Stupid human.*

"What is going on?" I whisper. I almost reach out and touch China's leather jacket, but I stop. Some instinct makes me stop.

"Are you going to shut the human up or am I?" Dakota asks.

"Although, with the way you catapult yourself around like that . . . Are you even human, Mana?"

What kind of question is that?

"You know, Dakota, you are definitely no longer on my potential-guys-to-date list."

He snickers. "Despite my tongue?"

"Especially because of your acid tongue."

Suddenly, the guy in front of me lunges forward, tackling Dakota. His massive hands circle Dakota's throat. Dakota's face turns white and blue and he chokes.

"You're killing him." I don't shout this like an action hero. I whisper it like a wimp, because I am suddenly not sure who *is* the good guy here and who is the bad guy.

"I wish it were that easy." China/Sunglasses Guy grunts as Dakota twists and slams his fist into China's gut. China staggers backwards against the row of lockers and then flops down on his butt.

Dakota captures me by the wrist like he is trying to take me somewhere, but I execute a cartwheel the moment he grabs me, and the momentum twists my hand free even as China snaps him on the rear with a towel in a signature locker-room move. It must take him by surprise, because Dakota squeals and leaps up straight. He pivots and opens his mouth, ready to spit again, I think, and I do the only thing I can. I front handspring right into him, smashing him with my feet. He windmills. Acid flies into the air, splatters into the ceiling, and makes a hole.

"You—" He says an unsayable word here and leaps for me, but I back tuck up and out of the way and somehow land on top of the lockers, standing there, trying to keep my balance as they sway. Dakota's eyes widen. "Well, that's not right."

And it's not. It's not right at all. I can't quite figure out how I got up here—I should not be able to back tuck so high. I'm flipping around the room like some sort of deranged kangaroo, but it's all instinct. I'm mid-handspring before I even have a chance to think about it. Somehow, though, it's *working*—but whatever. I jump from the top of one stand of lockers to another and land on the vending machine, but unfortunately, Dakota is not about getting *away* anymore. Now, he is all about getting *me,* and he comes rushing after me, knocking down the locker rows as he surges forward, like some kind of human bull—if a human bull had an acid tongue and was kind of hot in a bad-boy drummer way. I spring in the opposite direction, whip tucking once, then twice, and somehow clearing two rows of lockers and ending up near where the China guy had been. I back up into the remaining row of upright lockers. A jock-strap lies on the floor. Why would that be in here? This is a girls' locker room. And I thought everyone was wearing compression underwear now. But more importantly: where is the China guy?

Dakota smiles at me, and it is a wicked smile, not sexy at all, not cool. "You aren't all that normal, are you, Mana?"

"I do not know what you're talking about." Is he talking about the jockstrap? Because that is so not mine, not that I'm judging. Or is he talking about the leaping?

He makes a scoffing noise, half choke, half laugh, and with a tiny bit of acid gurgle. "Playing dumb? Really? All this time? I bet you aren't even stupid in school. That was all an act too, huh?"

I have no idea what he is talking about, so I eloquently say again, "I have no idea what you are talking about."

We could be on the same side.

That voice is in my head again.

"You can hear me." He laughs and claps his hands together.

"Lucky freaking me." I tuck down as he gets close, lift, and I am up in the air, executing a perfect freaking Arabian double front, the most impossible of girls' gymnastics moves. I land behind him. The moment I stick my feet, the locker doors fall over and smash on top of most of Dakota's body so that only his arm and hand stick out. I quad twist out of there, stunned.

"How did I . . . ? What did I . . . ?" I cannot even speak, I am so freaked out by how good I am at gymnastics. I have never even tried those moves before. And I went so high. Plus, Dakota is smooshed beneath the lockers, and that is totally freak-out worthy.

China stands there for just a second, examining Dakota's hand and the lockers. He must have been hiding behind them. Another second passes and then he's yanking Dakota out, twisting him face-down on the floor, face in the jockstrap, arms behind him. I cannot believe I was considering him as a potential boyfriend. I shudder.

China orders, "Give me that cell phone."

"What?"

"The cell phone. On the floor. Give it to me."

"Now isn't really a good time to check Facebook," I quip, but I shuffle over and grab it. Then I just sort of stand there holding it, because the guy now has both hands around Dakota-who-is-no-longer-a-love-interest's throat. I swallow hard. "This is too weird. This afternoon I was failing my computer science test and now it's all *Attack of Dakota the Acid-Tongued Douchebag.*"

He ignores my delightful commentary and just orders me to "Open it up. Press Star and throw it at me. Do not miss."

"Throw it at you?"

"Yes! Now!"

I open it up. I press the Star key, and throw. It smashes into his back, and then comes this noise, a horrible shrill noise like five thousand mosquitoes. Then—poof!—they are gone. Just gone.

Holy crap.

Holy . . .

Holy . . .

I think that I swear aloud, whipping my head around, searching, searching for them, trying to figure out what happened. A little green fluid rests on the floor. Staggering against the wall, I replay the last few minutes in my head. Seriously. How did I do that? Jump like that? Leap?

I have to try again. I attempt to think of a stunt harder than the

Arabian double front. And I come up with a piked double with a full twist. It's a men's Olympic gymnastics move. I should not attempt it.

I attempt it, launching up without even a lead-in tumbling run for power. My feet slam a hole in the ceiling because I go so high, but I do it, and land it. Perfectly.

I think I swear again, a really good swear this time, but I'm not sure, because right then Lyle and Sheriff's Deputy Troy Bagley rush in. Bagley looks as though he has maybe run down the hallway and it's not going well because he has had one too many donuts, because he's covered in sweat, all red-faced, and his hand is on his gun.

"Freeze," he yells. "Hands where I can see them!"

Which does he want me to do? I pick freeze and have second thoughts, so then I put my hands up. I freeze again.

Lyle makes big eyes, and judging from the way his hands have clenched into fists, gives the impression that he is super stressed or maybe angry or maybe both.

"Where are they?" Bagley demands. He waits a second. He holsters his gun. "What the hell happened in here?"

"I don't know," I say, which is totally true.

"We heard voices," Lyle says. "And you didn't follow me."

I shrug, but keep my hands in the air, which is pretty awkward. A little voice in my head says, *Crap. Crap. Crap. Crap.*

This voice, fortunately, is female, and my own.

Bagley waddles over to me. He is staring me up and down, not in a dirty way but in an annoyed, I-know-you're-lying cop way. My stomach folds in half somehow, or at least it feels that way, like it does a back tuck all by itself.

I gawk at Lyle, pleading for him to help me. He does not get it and says, "I mean, I really thought I heard yelling in here."

Bagley nods. "Me too."

"They're not in here," I say, and I drop my hands to my sides. For a second I want to tell them that Dakota Dunham had this freak lizard acid-tongue thing going on and that they Star Trekked out of the locker room and vanished, but Deputy Bagley is a pretty old-boy, I-eat-donuts kind of cop, and I do not want to go to the hospital for a psych evaluation. So I just add, "I swear. I would be all over them if they were."

Bagley eyes me as if I have no fighting skills at all, which I can understand, because I kind of don't. "Where else could they go?"

"The boys' locker rooms?"

He nods. "I'll check there. This guy, can you describe him?"

"Tall. Leather jacket. Sunglasses. Dark movie-star hair. White with a tan."

"And he was taking a student?"

I focus on Lyle. "Dakota Dunham. The drummer. For pep band."

"You're sure?" Bagley asks in a fast staccato way, already heading toward the door.

"Yes."

He yanks the door open and says, "You sure *you* didn't see Dakota in here? Maybe have a little altercation? Lovers' spat?"

I cross my arms in front of my uniform. "No. Why?"

He lifts an eyebrow. "There's pepper spray on the floor and your leg is bleeding. Every single row of lockers is knocked down."

I touch my leg. Blood comes back on my fingers. Lyle sucks in a breath and comes all the way into the locker room, yanking some paper towels out of the holder and pressing them on my leg as I stare at Deputy Bagley and Deputy Bagley stares at me.

"Well?" he says, putting his hand on his hip by his billy club.

"I thought they were hiding in here, and I pulled out Seppie's pepper spray from her bag and bashed into the bench," I lie. "It started a chain reaction with the lockers."

"And the hole in the ceiling?" he asks.

"I was clumsy."

He doesn't believe me. I can tell. His hand flexes and then latches into his belt. "You? Clumsy?"

"I was scared," I say.

"And the mess? The hole?"

"It was there when I got here," I say, trying to make my voice all cheerleader sweet and little-girl helpless, which totally works on guys like Deputy Bagley, usually, even if I am sort of changing my story. "Tell me if you find them, please. Okay? And hurry?"

He nods and says, "Obviously."

"And I am not a couple with Dakota!" I add, and try not to shudder at the thought, which would have been a fine thought before the whole racist, acid-tongue stuff.

"Mm-hmm. I'll be back to question you." Deputy Bagley raises his hands up in the air like he has heard it all before, and then he's out the door, leaving just Lyle and me in the locker room. Lyle bends down and wipes the blood from my leg with his hand. I resist the urge to sink my fingers into his hair and stroke his head like he's some kind of puppy dog. Wow, there *is* something wrong with me. Maybe I'm in shock?

"You want to tell me what happened?" he asks, calm again, normal Lyle.

"You would *not* believe it." I stagger away and sit on the bench.

"Try me."

I would tell him, but I think I actually *am* in shock. And how could he possibly believe me? I don't even know if *I* believe me. "There are blood spots on my shoe. There is a gash in the side of my calf. I don't even know how I got it. Oh, my God. I sound so pouty. Plus, I'm covered in baby powder!"

Lyle throws me his most intense facial expression, which I think he has modeled after one of the guys on *Game of Thrones*. "What happened to Dakota?"

I throw my hands up in the air. "I'm not sure."

"Mana . . ." He gives me this look, this absolute Lyle look that's a cross between a boy you lust after smiling at you and your grandfather telling you that in his day people didn't evade the truth. "Did he hurt you? I will kill him if he hurt you. You can tell me. We can go get Deputy Bagley right now."

"No! Why would you even think that?"

"You're bleeding, and there are obvious signs of a fight." His voice softens. He is so calm and stable, so forward moving. "Please tell me."

My voice comes out tiny and weak. "You won't believe me."

"Try me." He pushes the paper towels back on my leg, which is now starting to hurt. "I mean, something obviously happened. Lockers are everywhere, there's a hole in the ceiling, you're all cut up . . . Seppie's pepper spray is on the floor. And I swear I heard yelling."

"We should pick that up." I motion to the mess.

"You're changing the subject—"

"I know, but—"

"And you're shaking." He waits. He gently wipes at my leg. "You might need stitches."

"I do not need stitches." My voice softens. He is helping me. He does this to animals at the wildlife refuge, too, for his summer job, so I shouldn't think too much of this, right? It's just his nature to care. He probably feels the same way for me as he does for an injured moose.

"You're just afraid of hospitals."

"I am not afraid of hospitals." I quake though, even as I say it. Most of my nightmares involve hospital-type rooms with creepy, big-eyed doctors.

"Right. Like the time you broke your ankle when you missed the mat, learning your back tucks, and we had to pry your fingers off because you were hanging on to the edge of the car door, and then you still wouldn't go and we had to carry you into the emergency room and you kicked me."

I glare at the floor. Sometimes having best friends stinks because, well, they just know too much. "That was seventh grade. I cannot be responsible for events that occurred before puberty."

Lyle's hand with the paper towels eases the dirt away from my leg while his other hand maintains pressure. "Okay. No hospitals if you tell me what's going on."

My eyes meet his eyes. "Fine."

Outside, the basketball teams smash through the corridor back to the courts. I haul in a breath and say, "They disappeared. There was this fight. Before that, Dakota was tied up. Sunglasses Guy didn't want me to get the pepper spray. Then I let Dakota free, which was stupid, I now realize, because Dakota had this weird tongue thing and it sprayed acid. He pretty much knocked down all the lockers while I ran on top. And, oh, the most awesome thing of all of this was I was doing these ridiculous gymnastics moves. They were amazing and the sunglasses guy made me throw his cell phone at him, and when I did, they both just disappeared."

Lyle's mouth sharpens into a straight line. His hands stop moving. "Mana . . ."

"What?"

"Do you feel like you're going to throw up?"

"No. Why?"

"I think you have a concussion." He puts his face an inch away from mine and stares hard into my eyes.

"What are you doing?" I lean away.

He follows me and says, "Seeing if your pupils are the same size."

"I don't have a concussion!" I stand up and storm away. Pain scissors down my leg.

Lyle runs after me and wraps his arm around my waist, which feels much sexier than it should. "Yes, you do. That guy obviously whacked you in the head. You should sit down. You might pass out."

"I am not going to pass out."

"I think you are."

"Lyle, cut it out!"

He pulls me toward the bench. "Sit down, Mana."

"Dakota disappeared. I swear. It was like some sort of sci-fi movie. It was insane, but that's what happened, and I don't need to sit down!" I yell as he shoves me back down again.

"Watch." I make myself break out of his grip normally and calmly, standing up slowly and waving off his arms. "Watch what I can do."

No tumbling run again. Just a launch, and I'm up into a quad twist, a men's gymnastics move that is level ten or beyond, really, and *smack*—my feet punch another hole in the ceiling during the last rotation. Poor Deputy Bagley. That's going to be hard to explain in his report. Then I'm down, sticking the landing, staring into Lyle's astonished face.

"What the hell?" He grabs my hands in his. I like how his fingers feel.

"I know, right?"

"Holy . . . Wow, that's hot," he blurts.

"I know, right? Wait. Really? You think it's hot?" I blurt right back.

Just then, the locker-room door opens and Mrs. Bray, our cheering coach, barges inside. Her face is all twisted up with rage. Her pudgy hands go to her waist. "The game is back on. You should both be out there right now. And what in heaven's name are you doing in the girls' locker room, Lyle? Oh! The lockers! Oh, heavens! Are those holes in the ceiling?"

Lyle backs away from me and holds up his bloody hands, trying to calm Mrs. Bray down. "Mana got hurt."

Mrs. Bray gasps and turns white. She and blood do not get along.

One time I came down funky from a twist and knocked Seppie's nose with my shin, and it started bleeding all over the mat. Mrs. Bray passed out.

"Oh, don't pass out, Mrs. Bray," I say, rushing toward her.

But of course she doesn't listen. No way. Because that would be what would happen on a good day, and today is definitely not that.

CHAPTER 3

It takes almost an entire quarter to revive Mrs. Bray, find Deputy Bagley—who tells me we need to make an appointment to talk—and for things to straighten out again. The game continues on, with Thomas being his superstar-point-guard self and making Seppie swoon silently. We crush Central. All is good.

But it's not, because I keep remembering what I saw and what I did.

"It's time to start . . ."

How can someone spit acid?

"A new tradition . . ."

Or vanish?

"The Knights are back . . ."

I mean, Dakota and that guy vanished—just—poof!—gone. And I leaped around like I was in Cirque du Soleil.

"And we're on a mission."

Lyle peeks over at me, even though we are supposed to be staring straight ahead like good little cheerleaders.

"The time has come. What more can we say?"

I wink at him to show I am not concussed.

"West High. Falcons. We'll blow . . ."

We all blow a kiss. I blow mine at him. His face actually flushes.

". . . you away!"

Right at the buzzer, Thomas sinks a three-pointer from way

outside the curving red line. The moment we're all done yelling and applauding for the boys and their collective glory, we head to the locker rooms to change. Seppie jerks me aside, bringing me over by the rows of sinks, and gets all demanding. She yanks her braids out of the elastic that was holding them all into one thick ponytail and grunts at me. "What is going on?"

I shrug. I do not want to get into it with Seppie, because Seppie is the sort of person who never believed in Santa, not even when she was two. She's the sort of person who doesn't believe in true love. She believes in endorphin rushes and hormonal surges. She is not the type of person who is going to believe in disappearing men, or boys with acid-tongue spitting abilities.

So I answer her the only way I can. "Nothing."

"Okay, right." She starts anger-bopping her head at me. Her nails scratch lightly into my upper arm. "You *don't* have a big gash in your leg. You and Lyle *weren't* hanging out alone together in the locker room. And Mrs. Bray did *not* pass out."

"Random stuff." I pull my arm away and check out my reflection in the mirror. I'm pale, way too pale, and there are ugly splotches under my eyes.

"Don't you ignore me, Mana." She shoves her face right above mine. Her jaw rests on the top of my head, and when she talks, it moves against my hair. "You were off in the cheers, like, a beat behind, and so was Lyle."

"That has to be one of the seven deadly sins, right there. Pure evidence of brain trauma," I quip.

"Shut up. For a cheerleader it is. You're never off."

"Lyle thinks I have a concussion," I admit, because sometimes it's better to give a nugget of truth instead of just denying everything.

"Do you?"

It would be better to pretend I did, better than trying to explain, so I sigh and say, "Okay, maybe."

She steers me to the bench and sits me down.

"Do not change your clothes," she orders. "I'm getting Lyle and we're getting out of here."

My hand touches my too-fast heart. "Out of here sounds good."

She thumbs-ups at me, all in-charge doctor's daughter. She scoots past the fund-raising food table, where the leftover moms of freshmen who don't have cars are tidying up and waiting for their kids. Our chocolate-covered pretzels are still there; most of them sold, of course. Who can resist a chocolate-covered pretzel? Not my mom. Usually she eats any that don't sell. There are a few pretzels slanted and leaning against the rim of the container. They seem abandoned, unwanted, and yummy.

"Hey!" I yell after Seppie. "Did you see my mom anywhere?"

She thinks for a second and says, "No. Weird."

If she only knew the things I could tell her about weird.

*P*eople are always trying to protect me. I think it's because I am the flyer. I get thrown around, flipped in twisting tosses, held up in the air, grasped and cradled when I dismount. Seppie and Lyle are my bases, my foundation; they catch me, refuse to let me crash to the mat. They keep me safe when we stunt, and they sometimes get carried away and do it with our lives, which is usually annoying, but tonight . . . tonight I just let it happen.

Seppie feeds me Advil in the car. Lyle checks my leg gash and my pupils. He takes my pulse.

"It's a bit high, but I think she's good to go." He makes this funny motion with his hand. "Of course, I'm a cheerleader, Jim. Not a doctor."

"*Star Trek* references now . . . nice," I mutter. "Next, you'll just have a little plaque on your forehead with a constantly running red digital readout that says GEEK ALERT."

"Hey. I wouldn't talk," Lyle says, eyes flashing with happiness. "You *got* the reference."

I groan. "Too true, but only because you insisted on that marathon this summer before you would let me watch the movie versions with all the hot actors."

"*Star Trek: The Original Series,* or TOS, as we call it. Good times . . . good times . . ." Lyle adjusts his coat and yanks up one of the laces on his shoe. His fingers move so quickly. I blink to force myself not to stare. "Always better than the J. J. Abrams versions."

"So much less hot."

"Excuse me," he counters. "Nimoy versus Quinto. Old Spock wins and you know it."

"Yes, but Shatner versus Pine. Pine is so-o-o much hotter."

"Shatner was hot in his day." Lyle blinks hard.

"You are so wrong."

Seppie clears her throat. "You two are tangenting again."

"I prefer the word *digressing,* personally," Lyle says.

"Whatever." Seppie starts the engine. Heat blasts out of the vents, for which I am grateful, and we drive home. "Mana. No parties for you tonight."

"But it's party night! Teacher in-service day tomorrow. No school. Those are the best parties."

"She's whining. Mana, you're whining," Lyle says. He pulls me over so that I can lean on his shoulder. Car headlights flash into the cab of the truck, illuminating his face, which seems a little funny from my angle. I'm kind of beneath his chin, and it's so nice there that I might never move, at least not of my own free will.

"I am not whining," I mumble, but I am, and it's because I'm completely freaked and I don't want to be alone, thinking about what just happened. About Dakota and his tongue. The cranky man named China. How I could jump like that, like some sort of frog.

"Delayed response." Seppie turns on her high beams and zips down the road.

"Very delayed response, indicative of her head trauma," Lyle mocks.

"I have no head trauma," I say, and sit up straight, remembering.

"Seppie, you're supposed to be at Anna's tonight, because tonight is—"

"My fantastic hookup night with the fantastic Tyler Carter, and if not him, then the equally fantastic point guard, Thomas," she finishes. "Yes, I know."

A car approaches. She turns on the low beams. Lyle rubs at my arms, trying to warm me up, I guess. Seppie sighs hard.

"Seppie is still going," Lyle explains. "She's just dropping us off first."

"Us?"

"You and me," he says. "Damn, Seppie, your heater sucks."

"I know." She turns onto Hardy Road, which is almost to our subdivision.

I sit up straighter and put my hands in front of the heater vent. Then I say, pretty reluctantly, because I'm just trying to be polite, "You don't have to come home with me."

Lyle taps my thigh with his fingers. "No big. I live, what, three houses away?"

"But you probably want to go hook up, too."

Seppie snorts. "When does Lyle not want to hook up? The key word here is *want*; notice that the word *want* is not the same as *does*."

He reaches behind my back and punches her in the arm. She swerves. "Jerk. Way to win over the ladies, assaulting them."

"It works for all the neanderthals," he deadpans, and we both groan and hit him. Seppie calls him a sexist, even though we both know he doesn't mean it, and he pulls me back against him. "How is our little concussed one? Still seeing people disappear?"

"No," I say. "Why is there no music?"

"Loud music sucks for concussions." Seppie turns again. "You saw people disappear?"

I shrug. She's reacting like this is a big deal, and we haven't even told her about what I can do. What I did.

"We should probably take her to the hospital," Seppie says.

"I'll ask her mom. We'll need insurance cards and all that," Lyle says.

"Hey, I'm right here." I unbuckle my seat belt as Seppie swerves into our driveway. I stare up at the house. The lights aren't on. "She's not home?"

"Probably not back from the game yet," Seppie says.

Some hard thing nests inside my gut, a giant ball of dread. "My mom always zips out of there. She hates talking to the other moms."

"Maybe she met someone," Lyle says, shrugging off his seat belt and opening the door. We are no longer touching; this sucks.

"And they are having a romantic rendezvous at his place." Seppie singsongs it out like a soap opera character.

"Right. My mom . . ."

Lyle laughs. "Maybe Deputy Bagley."

"Do not make me puke. I really don't want to have to talk to him." I pull myself out of the truck. The impact of landing on the driveway sends little shock waves around the gash in my leg. Seppie argues and frets that she should stay with me and Lyle till Mom gets home, but we convince her that leaving me does not equal being a bad friend.

I finally order her, "Go be a total flirt, okay, Seppie?"

"Obviously." She laughs.

I slam the door shut and she backs out of the driveway, honking as she goes.

"Poor Tyler," Lyle says. "He stands no chance."

"It'll be good for him."

Above us, the night sky stretches and stretches across everything, black and deep and full of unknowns.

Lyle sneaks his arm around my waist and carries both our bags over one arm. "Just to make sure you don't fall down."

"Lyle, you are being super sweet and awesome, but you did see me do a quadruple twist, right? You did see me when I cheered a whole quarter. I am not concussed. I am okay," I say, but I don't move away. I know I'm hyperfixated on all this touching, which is not how you are supposed to be when someone is just your best friend, but for some reason Lyle's arm makes me feel better, like it always does when I'm coming out of a stunt and plummeting toward the ground. I know he will catch me. I know the moment I feel his arm that I will be safe.

He mocks Mrs. Bray's voice. "Yes, you were a good little cheer-leader, all sticking in there for the squad."

"Better than Mrs. Bray."

"A hell of a lot better," he says as we walk across the porch. "I can't believe she went home in an ambulance."

"She is pretty melodramatic. I mean for a—"

"Cheerleading coach?"

"No, for an old person."

"They did a good job stitching your leg up, though," he says as I search for my keys. He pulls them out of the front pocket of my bag. "You always put them there."

"Thanks." I smile at him.

"We should probably talk about how you did the twist. That was beyond amazing. I had no idea you could do that." He smiles back down at me and it feels funny, different between us, all of a sudden. It feels like the air vibrates or pulses. Maybe I really did hit my head. I glance away first and move to put my key in the doorknob, but the moment I do, the entire door swings open. It's already unlocked! I jump back. Lyle's fingers tighten their hold on my arm.

"What is it?"

"It's *always* locked." I pull away from him, flick on the lights, and yell, "Mom?"

The lights blind me for a second, but just a second. Then I see it. The entire living room is demolished. The couch is upside down. The cushions are spilled across the floor, ripped apart. Mr. Penguinman, my ancient stuffed animal that I named when

I was three, who should be in my bedroom, sits all the way up in the ceiling fan. Television wires and cables lie tangled on the floor, and the sliding glass door to the porch is . . .

"Holy . . ." Lyle mutters, but he doesn't move.

"Lyle!" I scream. "Get down!"

And just as I scream, something smashes toward us, flashes fast above my right shoulder, and crashes through the double windows. Glass shatters. I race after it, bashing past the still-frozen Lyle and onto the porch. Dakota freaking Dunham flies down the driveway and then gains altitude, zipping up above the trees.

I start chasing after him, but I am not Lyle, and a flying Dakota is a too-fast Dakota. It's pointless, totally pointless, so I stand there in the freezing cold, in the middle of my driveway, staring up at the dark sky. Pain shoots up my leg. Lyle appears next to me.

"Mana?"

I whirl to the side. "Still think I have a concussion?"

His mouth works hard at forming my name again. His broad shoulders tense up. "Mana?"

I start running back toward the house to see what's gone, what has happened inside. Why would Dakota rob my house? It makes about as much sense as him being able to fly.

Lyle yanks me back toward him.

"Mana. Was that . . ."

He can't say it. He can't believe it. But somehow, somehow I can.

"Yes," I say. "That was him."

"Dakota?"

I blow warm air into my hands and try to quiet my heartbeats. "Dakota. He must have gotten away somehow."

Lyle staggers backwards and bangs his head on our stupid HOME SWEET HOME sign. "Holy crap."

The plaque falls to the floor behind his sneakers and he jumps. I fast walk into the house and pick up one of the slashed yellow cushions from our love seat.

"We should call the police," Lyle says.

I whirl around, clutching the pillow. "And tell them what? After I reported him assaulted and potentially kidnapped, Dakota Dunham came here, trashed my house, and then flew out the window?"

Lyle starts trying to put the love seat back on all four legs. I help him. It resembles a great, cushionless oasis in a sea of mess.

Then he says, "I think I'm in shock."

"Yep."

"You, too?"

"Me, too."

"I've never been in shock. I always know what to do. I'm really just not the kind of person who goes into shock." He sits on the love seat and reaches out his hand. I take it. I have held that hand a million times in cheering, but this time it feels different, charged, like we are trying to meld our palms together, give each other strength and take it at the same time, you know?

"It's okay," I tell him. "Weird stuff is happening. Everyone has to be in shock sometimes. You should have seen me in the locker room."

His hand is so much bigger than mine, but he doesn't squeeze too hard when he says, "Your mom is going to freak when she gets here."

I nod. She is so orderly, so neat. "She loves the love seat."

Normally Lyle would mock me for saying "loves the love," but instead he just says, "Maybe we could sew up the cushions."

We sit there another minute.

"I should check out the rest of the house," I say. "And get my stuffed animal off the fan. And clean up and stuff."

"Sure . . ."

We do not move.

"I'm glad she wasn't here when it happened," I add, staring at a shattered, framed picture of me and my mom on the back of the Cross Sound Ferry, on our way to Long Island, when I was eight or so. She has her arms all wrapped around me and we are both laughing, our hair whipping each other's faces, thanks to the wind.

"Mana?"

I snap out of it. "What?"

"What if she was?"

"Was what?"

"Was here."

As soon as he says it, Lyle jumps up and runs across the living room. He leaps over cushions and books and pictures so ridiculously fast. I follow him into the kitchen. Shattered glass crunches beneath my cheer shoes. Lyle yanks open the door to the garage.

"Crap," he says, and turns to gape at me with terrified eyes.

I stare past him and see it: Mom's car.

om!" I yell for her without really thinking about it. My mom's car is here and that means . . . that means . . .

Rushing into the garage, I yank open the door of our dark blue Subaru station wagon, the perfect mommobile. Her purse still sits on the passenger's seat. The keys dangle from the ignition, but there is no mousy woman there, no small, smiling Mom.

Whirling around, I bash into Lyle. "She was here."

"Mana, it's—" Lyle catches me by the shoulders, but I push him away and rush back into the kitchen. "You're jumping to conclusions. Slow down."

I zigzag around the splattered orange juice puddle soaking into the floorboards and slam the refrigerator door shut. "She might have been here when it happened. She might still be here."

I step on a broken teacup; its scattered blue pattern is like sea glass that has been battered by rocks and sea.

"Look at that," I say to poor Lyle, who is still open-mouthed, standing right where I pushed him. I have never pushed anyone before in my life. "Look! This whole place is a mess. And Dakota flew. Did you see him fly? You saw that, right? Still think I'm hallucinating from my concussed brain?"

"Okay. Hold on. Let's be rational." He puts his hands out in front of him like a politician. Lyle is not a politician, and I know he's only acting this way to try to calm me down. It has the opposite effect.

I point at Lyle's face. "I will kill him for doing this to our house. I do not even care about his acid-tongue issue."

For a second there is silence. Then a wind picks up outside. Lyle hauls in a breath so deep that his whole body moves with it, and then he says, "You're . . . you're kind of angry."

"Lyle." I stop ranting and really stare at him. He is trying so hard to be his composed, normal self. His hands are still up in the air, waiting for me to take them. I do. I force my voice to be calmer, more steady, and ask, "Where is my mother?"

One of his shoulders moves up just a tiny bit. He tightens his hold on my hands, his face concerned. He gropes for an answer and offers, "Maybe she's at a neighbor's?"

"If she was at a neighbor's, she would have contacted me. This is the woman who expects updates hourly if I'm not at home or at a game or at school." I let go of him and yell for her again. *"Mom!"*

Nothing answers. Nothing except the thuds of Lyle's feet following me into the kitchen and . . . another noise?

I motion for him to be still. His foot squishes into a pile of super-spicy hummus. He stops.

"Do you hear that?" I whisper.

He doesn't answer, just moves in front of me. His voice is a quiet command. "Stay back."

Right.

I step beside him.

"You never listen," he mutters. "If we were in *World of Warcraft*, you would be in the prison at Render's Valley for insubordination."

He glares at me in a way that I would normally classify as geek cute, but that's not why my stomach crashes into itself and the hairs on my arms stand up. It's the noise, a heavy banging from my mom's bedroom . . . a banging that is coming closer. Terror shuts my throat. Lyle's muscles tense.

"What is it?" I whisper as I stare across the living room at my mom's bedroom door. Nothing. But whenever we watch scary movies, Lyle always shouts at the actors to look up, so I do. Something moves on the ceiling, creeping out of Mom's bedroom and into view. I yank his shirt. "Lyle . . . Lyle . . . Look up."

His voice is like a machine—a dead, robot machine. "See it."

"What is it?"

He doesn't answer for a second, a big, horrible second, and then he whispers, "Unearthly? Maybe undead? Maybe cyborg? Um . . ."

This thing . . . I can't look away. It's like a man, but not a man. It's gaunt, almost emaciated. The skin is pulled tight over bone and muscle. It's the color of death, ashy gray, and it smells like death, too, like decay and garbage and dead mice in the basement, like mold on books.

"Holy crap. It's got webs for feet," Lyle whispers.

I nod in the tiniest way I can, but it's not the feet I'm worried about. It's the mouth, which is open and full of razor teeth, scissor sharp and wild. It's the mouth that terrifies my heart into trying to beat its frantic way out of my chest. And its eyes . . . its eyes are black, all black, and they stare at us.

"Exterminate," it says.

Crap.

"That's a *Doctor Who* line," Lyle says, looking at me all excited for some reason.

"God, Lyle."

"It is. It's from *Doctor Who*. Only it's the Daleks who say—"

"Lyle!"

The thing does not care about never-ending British television series. It leaps toward us, makes it halfway into the living room with one bound. Muscles move over bone. Web feet connect with hard wood. It leaps again, right at us.

I dive for a butcher knife on the floor while Lyle flies sideways into the kitchen counter, awkward, not sure where to go, and slipping on orange juice. The creature lands three feet in front of us, on all fours. Claws on its hands carve grooves into the wooden floor. I swear it smiles.

"Run!" Lyle yells and scrambles. He rips a silverware drawer out of the counter. Forks and spoons clank onto the floor. He whales it in front of him, holding it like a shield, just as the thing's claws rips four long gashes down its length. Lyle throws the drawer at the beast, clobbering it in the head.

The thing pushes it off, pretty much casually. Great.

I grapple for Lyle's hand and yank him. We run into the garage, slipping on hummus and orange juice and the remains of a jar of pickles. Lyle slams the door closed, but we can't lock it from this side.

Lyle clenches the doorknob and pulls, trying to hold it shut with his weight. With a high kick, I smash my foot into the garage door opener. The door starts to rumble up.

"I can't keep it shut." Lyle's face twists with effort.

The little blue door to the house vibrates. Four giant slash marks go through two inches of metal. Lyle gulps.

"Get in the car," I order him. I hold my knife out, but I'm thinking it's not going to be too effective against this web-footed, claw-handed thing.

"Mana . . ." Lyle's big hands flail out against the door.

"Do it!" I yell, ripping the fire extinguisher off the wall. I pull the pin out of it and point it at Lyle's back, which is still stupidly in front of the door.

"Mana . . ."

"Do it now, Lyle. Get in the car and start it, now. Fast. You're the fast one."

"Okay, I'll count to three."

The door rattles and almost gives.

"Count to two!"

"One . . . two . . ." he yells, and dives out of the way, flipping over the car hood and launching himself inside via the open window, in the way only a really good athlete can.

The moment Lyle's body weight leaves its place against the door to the house, there is nothing stopping the creature. The door crashes open. The thing definitely smiles at me, showing off its teeth.

"Exterminate," it croaks, reaching forward. Its muscles tense. It readies itself to jump.

I squeeze the lever on the fire extinguisher. White foam rockets out as the creature leaps toward me, hurtling itself into my space. It smashes into me. My lungs lose air. I can't breathe with the weight of it against my chest. My ribs feel like they're being crushed, and the teeth . . . so many . . . dozens of teeth, covered in fire extinguisher spray but still ready to chomp or rip or tear. Its breath smells like mildewed books and blood, all mixed together.

"Get off me!" I gag.

"Exterminate."

"Shut up!"

With my free arm, I smash the fire extinguisher into the side of its head. It does not seem to care. Letting go of the extinguisher, I take the knife and jab it up and in. It hits part of the thing's body. Bone? Its weight shifts and I am free. I roll away, scrambling across the cement floor for the car and Lyle.

It seizes my ankle. Claws slice open my skin. My knife dangles out of its chest.

"Lyle!"

I'm not sure if I'm yelling because I want help or because I just want him to save himself, get out of here, get away.

"Come on!" He revs the engine. Elevator music blares out of the car. My mom has the worst taste in music.

The thing hauls me back toward it. I slide along the floor like a sack of nothing, not even potatoes. My fingers search for something to hold on to. There is nothing, just cement floor. I bend double, twisting until I can reach around, yank my knife back out of its flesh, and then slice it across the thing's wrist. It lets go of my foot, howling. I somersault backwards into the car, diving into the back-seat as Lyle reverses out of the garage. Instead of buckling up like a good girl, I clench the headrest.

"Holy crap. Holy crap. Holy crap," Lyle mutters. We're almost all the way out to the road when the thing stands up again and leaps—once, twice, three times—and lands on the hood. Its spindly arm smashes through the windshield. The glass spiderwebs out from the point of impact.

We scream.

Lyle slams the car into gear. The creature falls off. Seconds later, the car thuds over it. There's a sick lurch as the tire drives on top of it, and the sound of bones crunching, which is sort of beautiful when the bones belong to a hideous thing that thinks *exterminate* is the SAT practice word of the day.

"Crap. Crap. Crap," Lyle chants.

I slip myself into the front seat. Lyle reverses and we thud over it again. The last thing I ate, a chocolate-covered pretzel, returns to my mouth. This time, Lyle reverses all the way out to the road and stops the car.

"Is it dead?" I whisper, trying to see around the cracks in the front window to the body in the middle of my driveway.

"Maybe? I hit it." Lyle's still clutching the steering wheel.

"I know you *hit* it. But did you *kill* it? Like, kill it dead?"

He bites the corner of his lip. "I'm not sure. In movies, these things never die."

"These things?"

"These undead alien monster from hell things."

"Lyle!"

"What?"

"You are supposed to be the expert. *You.*"

"Okay. Um . . . I would say, yes? Yes. It's dead." His voice gets all fake low and overly confident, which I appreciate, but I know him too well to be fooled. If calm Lyle is faking it, then all hell has broken loose.

"Turn your headlights on," I demand.

"You sure?"

"We have to see."

"Why? Why do we have to see? Why can't we be all 'Yep, nothing's happened. Let's go get some pizza, have a little teenage sex, drink a beer?'"

"You want to do that?"

He nods. I wonder if he means it, especially the teenage sex part, but that's only for a second. Reality slams back into me.

"My mom might still be inside," I say.

"I know." He turns his headlights on. An unmoving lump waits on the driveway. He holds my arm in his hands. "Whatever you do, do *not* get out of the car to check it out."

"I am not an idiot."

"I didn't say you were."

We stare at the lump. It still doesn't move.

"Do you know what it is?" I ask Lyle, shutting off the radio.

The silence is big. I almost miss the elevator music.

Lyle breaks it. "Why would I know?"

"You watch all those old sci-fi movies."

"Vintage TV shows. And some are quite modern, honestly."

"Whatever. And all those gaming thingies you do."

"Gaming thingies? Are you trying to emasculate me? Gaming thingies? They are battles of skill and persistence and intellect, Mana."

"Once again . . . whatever, Lyle. I am not trying to emascul . . . de-man you. I am just saying you would have a better idea about this stuff than I would."

He picks at the edge of the steering wheel. "It kind of reminds me of a Windigo."

"What is that?"

"There's this old Algonquin story about how if you eat the flesh of a person, you turn into a Windigo, and you're always starving, craving human flesh." He thinks for a second. "But they don't have webbed feet."

"Maybe it mated with Donald Duck or a platypus or a penguin! No, not a penguin. It would be so much cuter if it was part penguin."

"Funny." He pauses. "It still isn't moving."

"Good."

"It could be the only one of its kind, and we killed it." He looks traumatized, and he actually seems a little sorry.

"Lyle!"

"What?"

My words pound out like each is its own sentence. "It was trying to kill us. It wrecked my house. It was evil."

He nods. "I know. I know, but still . . ."

Sometimes I cannot believe him. Now is so not the time to discuss the moral ramifications of killing in self-defense or the possible extermination of a species that *is* most likely rare, albeit predatory.

I lean forward in the seat, staring through windshield cracks at my house, my formerly safe, cozy house. "Do you think my mom is in there?"

"In the house? Or in its stomach?"

I gasp. "Lyle!"

"I definitely don't think it ate her."

"Lyle!"

"Sorry, sorry."

"We should check in the house," I say. "It might have . . ."

I don't finish my sentence, but the thought dangles there, broken and horrible.

"She's okay, Mana."

"How do you know?" I sound like a baby, pleading.

He touches my shoulder. "I just know."

I nod. I have to choose to believe it. "Do you have your cell phone? Mine is in my bag."

He reaches into his pocket and hands it to me. I flip it open, call Mom's cell. It rings. It's on the floor of the car. "Great."

My insides start to shudder. I check to make sure the lump hasn't moved, then open the door just a bit so Lyle can't lock me in.

"What are you doing?"

"I have to see if she's in there."

"No! What if that . . . that . . . *exterminate* thing isn't dead?"

"You will stay in the car and run it over if it moves." I say this like it's the most rational request in the world, like I ask Lyle to run over things every day after cheering practice.

"Look . . ." He runs his hand through his hair. "You can't do this. There could be other things in the—"

"My mom could be in the house," I interrupt. I pull one of Mom's scarves off the backseat, wrap it around my ankle so I don't bleed everywhere. It doesn't even hurt much, I am so full of adrenaline. My pulse must be up around three hundred beats a minute, which would actually make me dead, but whatever.

Lyle watches me and then sighs. "We should call the police."

"And tell them what? We just killed a monster? Or maimed it? That a boy flew through my house? They are not going to believe that. That's why I couldn't tell the truth to Deputy Bagley before."

"You can just say that your mom is missing."

"You can call," I say, "but I'm not waiting. She could be hurt in there. She could be dying."

"Be careful . . ."

I open the door and bound out of the car. Even with the adrenaline and fear, the movement makes my ankle hurt. My leg hurts, too. Blood drips through the scarf and onto my ankle sock, turning it red instead of white. Everything inside of me tenses as I stare at that thing on the driveway, waiting for the slightest twitch, any sign it is still alive.

I lean into the car again and whisper to a pale-faced Lyle, "Promise me you'll kill that thing if it moves. No worrying about killing one-of-a-kind species and making animal rights activists hate you or anything like that."

"I'm more worried about crazed cryptozoologists." His eyes are big, huge, terrified.

"Lyle."

"Mana, I promise."

"Swear."

"I swear." Lyle flips his phone open again, punches in 9-1-1, and says, "Mana, come right back out, okay?"

I nod.

That will be easier said than done, if there are any more of those freak Windigo things in there. But if there are, they sure as hell better not have hurt my mom or they are going to have to deal with one angry cheerleader.

CHAPTER 5

I tiptoe-run around the Windigo thing's lumpy form, giving myself a lot of room. I am aware that it's not moving, but I don't want to take any chances that it might *start* moving, you know? My adrenaline pumps so hard as I scoot across the grass and onto the porch that I can barely feel where it scratched my ankle, but I know the pain will be back soon.

The front door still hangs wide open. Lyle never shut it. The window next to it is smashed and there is glass all over the porch. It doesn't even resemble my house inside; everything is so messed up, dumped over, broken apart. But my mom . . . she could be in there. And if she is in there, she could be hurt. I can't wait for the police to come. In health class we learned that in emergency medical situations, response time is critical to the potential saving of a person's life. Yes, I think they were mostly talking about heart attacks and not monster attacks, but whatever.

Wait. I keep forgetting.

There could be other monsters in there.

I listen but don't hear anything. The lump in the driveway doesn't move. Lyle stares at me from behind the shattered windshield of my mom's car. I give Lyle a cocky thumbs-up sign so he won't worry too much, and then I haul in a big breath and step into the porch light. I scan the room for evil exterminating creatures. Nothing. Then I remember to check the roof. Clear.

I walk farther inside, scurry past the ruined love seat, and head into Mom's bedroom. Pausing at the doorway, I survey the room again. Everything is a mess. The covers are off her bed. Her books and jewelry slop all over the floor. The closet door is flung open and all her long skirts, in all their boring neutral colors, clump in piles on the floor. A few still hang off-kilter on their hangers.

What had it been searching for? Was it even searching at all? Maybe it just likes destroying things? But why here?

And what exactly *was* it?

I lean against the wall for a second, just a second, and try to put it all together. Dakota at the game *and* here, China (Sunglasses Guy), the house, the weird gray monster . . . I can't. I can't put it together. It makes no sense. The world sways a little. I stand up straight, blink hard, and continue my search. Swallowing, I try to just focus and be thorough and push all my worst fears down low into a place where they won't bother me, telling myself good hopes, like, *Everything is fine. Mom is fine. There are no more monsters.*

I search through all the rooms on the main floor and upstairs but don't find her. That leaves nowhere except the basement.

The basement. You are never, *ever* supposed to go into the basement in scary movies. That and the attic are always off-limits . . . and the greenhouse, and outside, and, well . . . pretty much everywhere.

Still, I pause outside the basement door, frozen. I am really, really scared of going down there with all the boxes and the Ping-Pong table and the treadmill. My legs wobble.

I don't get a chance to make the decision before steps pound across the front porch. I clutch the TV remote because it's the closest weapon-like thing I can find.

Lyle bursts into the living room. His hair is wild, sticking up everywhere. He holds my bag.

"I thought you died," he says.

I unclench the remote. "What?"

"I thought you died; you were taking so long."

He runs over the cushions.

I hold out my hands to stop him.

"Lyle . . . what about that Windigo thing?"

"I put the tire right on top of it." Lyle cringes. "It can't move."

"You're sure? One hundred percent sure?"

"The entire car is on top of it, Mana. It's not going anywhere."

Mr. Penguinman falls from the fan in the living room. I snatch him up off the floor and clutch him to my chest. "Did you call the police?"

"They said they'll be here as soon as they can. One cop is at a DUI stop and the other is at a domestic."

I groan. "Our town only has two cops? That is so ridiculous. That is beyond ridiculous."

He doesn't answer, just takes the TV remote out of my hand and lifts an eyebrow at it. "Anything good on?"

"I thought you were some evil exterminating thing." I realize this is a bad explanation, even if it is the truth.

"And you were going to bludgeon me to death with this? A remote?" His eyes actually twinkle despite the circumstances.

"Shut up." I open the basement door. "I've searched everywhere upstairs. There's no sign of her."

My voice breaks. I close my eyes and take my weight off my ankle.

"We should wait until the police come," Lyle says, leaning next to me. He drapes an arm across my shoulders.

"I am not waiting." I open my eyes to look at his face. It's so anxious and scared that it frightens me a little. "I'm going down to try to find her. I cannot leave her if she's down there."

"Do you really think she is?"

"No."

I turn on the light and brace myself for something horrific. I don't even know what. I take a couple steps down the wooden stairs. My mom made a pantry along the sides of the walls years ago. She stores the Campbell's soup and extra sugar and things like that there.

"Everything's in the right place," I whisper to Lyle, moving forward so his arm drops from my shoulders. I miss it.

He touches a can of golden raisins. "Weird."

"I know." Although maybe they didn't have time to search down here yet, because we interrupted them. Who knows? Or maybe they're not trying to find anything, just destroying . . . I don't know. I don't know *anything*.

Lyle clutches my hand. "Maybe you should stay upstairs and guard."

"No way."

"Lyle . . ."

"Listen, I was out-of-control worried in the car. There is no way in hell that I'm going to just let you come down here by yourself."

He stares at me. He means it, and I'm glad. I nod and trek down the rest of the stairs, into the cold basement. The cement floor is well swept. The treadmill is right side up. The holiday decorations are still in the proper plastic bins.

"Mom?" I whisper.

Lyle comes and puts his arm around my waist, holding me up.

I try a little louder. "Mom?"

No answer. Of course there's no answer; there's no one here.

I slump against him. Tears wait behind my eyelids. I will not let them out. I refuse. I refuse.

"Let's go back out to the car and wait for the cops, okay?" Lyle says.

He steers me back up the stairs and out of the house. I limp a little bit, still clutching Mr. Penguinman. The monster remains under the tire of the car. It's getting pretty flat, like a deflated balloon. It gives off a skunk smell.

"That is disgusting," I manage to say.

"Do you want me to move it?"

I shake my head. "Too big a chance."

We get in the car.

"What are the police going to think?"

"Good question," Lyle says.

He blasts the heat, takes my hands in his, and blows into them, trying to warm me up.

"Where is my mom, Lyle?" I sound all pathetic and weak.

Lyle kisses the tips of my thumbs and repeats, "Another good question."

I groan and sink back into the seat. "I should call my dad."

"Is he in town?"

"I think so."

My parents are divorced. They have been divorced since I was five. I don't even remember them married. My dad is an independent contractor for places like NASA. He does things like make the tiles on satellites and stuff like that.

Lyle hands me his phone. I call. It rings. The car starts to get warmer.

I get my dad's answering machine and leave a message. "Hey, Dad. It's me. Weird stuff is happening. Mom is missing. The house is trashed. Can you call me on Lyle's cell?"

I leave the number and hand the phone back to Lyle.

"You didn't tell him about the Windigo."

I consider giving him our patented Lyle–Mana one-eyebrow raise, but I am too tired, too scared. "He would think I was kidding."

Lyle thinks about this a second. "Probably."

He takes my hand in his and it feels really normal and good for some reason, like we always hold hands, which we do not. "Everything will be okay, Mana."

"You don't know that."

"It will." He gives a little squeeze.

I expect him to let go. He doesn't. So I hold on, too.

"Seppie would give us hell if she knew we were holding hands," I say, trying to pretend like everything is all light and normal. "Also, you kissed my thumbs before."

"I don't care what Seppie thinks. Do you?"

"Nah," I say, even though I'm not sure if that's the real answer. "We'll tell her it's a side effect of my concussion."

"Obviously, because you'd only hold my hand if you're brain damaged."

"Nice."

We don't let go.

He shifts a little closer to me. "I can't believe I let you go back in the house alone."

"I told you to."

"It was an idiot move. I'd have to kill myself if anything happened to you while I was just sitting in the freaking car like a wimp."

Watching all the emotions crossing Lyle's super-expressive face is too much for me to handle right now, so I turn and stare down the road. There are headlights coming our way.

Lyle asks, "The cops?"

"I hope so," I say, letting go of his hand so I can jump out of the car. I run/limp down the road toward the headlights. I want to make sure they know where to go. The street numbers might not be easy for them to read, and Lyle might not have even given them an actual street number, and—

"Mana!" Lyle yells, running after me and catching me ridiculously quickly. "Don't!"

He tackles me into the ditch on the side of the road. We roll and tumble. Our bodies bash together. I try to smash him away. His face is just inches from mine.

"What are you doing?" I grunt.

"What if it isn't?" He whispers the words, but even in the whisper there is the really obvious sound of Worried Lyle.

I am totally confused. "Isn't what?"

"The cops. I've watched enough stuff to know that it's not always the cops that show up. Listen, there are no sirens. Cops would have sirens or at least blue lights."

As I pause to listen, the car flashes by and stops at the end of a driveway—my driveway. We both stay down, but angle ourselves so that we can see everything. Two men in black suits get out of the car, which is black, too, and has no flashing blue cop-car lights anywhere.

Lyle makes big eyes at me. The whites of them flash in the moonlight. The wind blows some dead leaves against his face. He sputters and swats them away with his free hand. His other hand is currently pretty close to my bum, which I will not think about.

"See?" he whispers.

I hedge. "Maybe they're undercover."

"Okay, right," Lyle scoffs. "Undercover in suits. Only bankers in Manchester wear suits."

"They aren't bankers," says a voice above us, "and they aren't undercover."

We both jump upright. I clutch the edge of Lyle's jacket. His hands are fists, ready to strike. A man steps out from behind the Johnsons' oak tree.

"You two getting a little romantic in the gutter? That's sad," he says. "When I was in high school, we at least did it in a car."

I point my finger at him as I stand up fully. "You . . ."

Lyle steps in front of me like he's a superhero instead of a cross-country-running cheerleader and gets all cop-show voice. "Don't even think about it, buddy."

China, aka Sunglasses Guy, snorts. "Buddy?"

I push my way in front of Lyle and angry-whisper at China, "Knock it off. I am so not in the mood. My mom is missing. Dakota was here—"

"Well, if you'd just let me kill him when I wanted to," he says.

"I thought you were *kidnapping* him," I say, crossing my arms in front of my chest. It is freezing out here.

"I was." China steps forward. The night sky leans in on us, deepening things, including my rage.

"You obviously failed," Lyle says.

"He speaks!" China snarks at him. "The boy toy speaks. I thought they only did that when you push a button on their stomach, or pull a string."

"Shut up. You make no sense. He talked like two seconds ago." I step forward one more time and smash my hands into China's big chest, trying to push him backwards. Nobody treats Lyle that way. My hands push against the leather jacket, but he doesn't move. The man is a tree. A slightly sexy and very sarcastic tree. It's so aggravating, but I sputter, "There was this monster thing . . ."

"That's why I'm here," he says, nodding.

"To exterminate us?" Lyle interrupts. He has straightened up, trying to appear bigger than he is.

"No." China shakes his head, obviously disgusted by our stupidity. "To get you out of here."

As appealing as getting away from freaking monsters and creepy men in suits sounds, I am not cool with that idea. "I'm not going anywhere without my mom."

There is a siren in the distance. I wonder if the police are actually going to show up or if they are responding to something else—another drunk driver or some family fight. The night is dark and full of menace and danger. I never realized before just how terrifyingly bizarre the world really is. I never realized that my mom, my sweet, dependable, pretzel-dipping mom, could just disappear. The horror of it makes my throat close. Lyle comes up and touches my hand, steady and calm. His touch slows my heart rate into a beat that is more normal. I don't know how he knows I need him. He just does.

I address China, though, because unlike Lyle and me, he seems to have a vague idea of what is going on—at least he did with Dakota. "Do you know what happened to my mom?"

Before he can answer, another set of headlights comes down the road. China motions for us to get behind a tree with him. We do. Another dark car pulls up outside my house. More men in suits hustle toward my porch door. One stands by the front tire of Mom's car, obviously checking out the squashed Windigo.

"You two need to leave the scene, and you need to leave it now," China says, all business. He captures both of our arms in his hands. Lyle yanks his arm free.

I stare at the guy, amazed that he thinks it's okay to be rough handling us. His jaw is set, the lines straight and strong. It's the kind of jaw you want to trust, but how can I? I steel myself. "Why?"

"Because they're coming."

"*Who* are coming?" I ask.

"More Windigos."

Lyle claps his hands together. The sound echoes. "I knew they were Windigos."

"Lyle, this is so not the time." I feel a little guilty for saying this, because he is so psyched about being right.

"You've got it," China says. "We do not have the time. You have to leave now."

"Why?"

His face shifts. "I just told you. The Windigos are coming."

"No. *Why? Why* are they coming?" It takes a lot of nerve to get the words out. The wind picks up again, and cold slashes into my teeth, but I keep going on, keep asking questions, because it's not like I'm just going to trust him because he says so. "And who are those men in the suits? And where the hell is my mother? Did you hurt my mother?"

I am right up next to him, and yes, he towers over me, but I don't care. Not at all. He grasps my shoulders in his hands, not too roughly but not gently, either, and he says, "Mana . . ."

"How do you know her name?" Lyle pushes his way in between us, jostling to protect me and distance me from Mr. No Answer Man.

China ignores him. "Mana, I would never hurt your mother. I am extremely worried about her, but right now my priority is you. You have got to get out of here now."

"And go where?" I ask.

He is about to answer when his attention shifts away from us. Wincing at whatever he sees, he pushes at me, shoving me toward the woods. He shoves Lyle as well. His voice is an order and a whisper and it is full of fear. "You two go in the woods. Find somewhere safe. Hide."

"Why?" Lyle asks, clasping my hands.

"They're leaving the house, coming to search for you. I'll hold them off, but you need to hide. You need to hide *now*."

I'm not sure what to think, but there is a quality to his voice that makes us believe.

We run.

CHAPTER 6

My mom and I first moved here when I was little—six or so. I was terrified, because the neighborhood was pretty white (and by "white" I mean descended-from-Puritans, we-came over-on-the-*Mayflower* white). My mom is white, too, but my dad is obviously not. His people are from Hawaii. Everyone calls me Asian, or sometimes Latina. Once someone called me a derogatory term for a Native American. I don't know. Mom said I'm beautiful and an individual and all those perfect mom things that are in the mom handbook for situations like that.

Anyway, Lyle was the first kid I met in the neighborhood. I remember him standing at the end of my driveway wearing this filthy Thor T-shirt that he hadn't taken off for two weeks. He was holding two sonic screwdrivers with sword attachments. Mom pushed me out the door to say hi. After he told me I would be much cooler if I was a boy, and I punched him, he took me to these same woods behind the houses and we found some dead tree branches, bundled them up like people, and played war. Then he accidentally slashed a tree branch with the screwdriver. The branch fell off and cut my arm. I bled all over the place. (I'm a big bleeder. There aren't enough clotting agents in my blood or some such weirdness. It's not life threatening; it just means that when other people would bleed for one minute, I bleed for ten.) Anyway, he fixed me up with five hundred million Angry Bird Band-Aids. The next time we played, we were on the same side, fighting this huge, imaginary time-traveling dragon who breathed fire. But even though the dragon was imaginary, Lyle always had to be three feet in front of me, facing it first, making sure I didn't get hurt again, even if there was nothing that could actually hurt me, even if no threats were remotely real.

That's how it is now. He's one step ahead of me, obviously keeping his pace just slow enough for me to stay close. Tree branches stab at our bodies as we run through the little wood that hides behind the houses on our street. We stumble on the uneven ground, holding hands. Our feet don't know where to step. The cold air slashes at our lungs. We're running blind, and running without a purpose other than to get away.

"This is ridiculous." I stop.

Lyle tugs on my hand. He could run forever. Not me. I do *not* like running. "C'mon."

I don't move. A bright flash lights the air behind us. It looks like it comes from where we were standing before, by the road. There's no exploding sound, just a light.

My fingers dig into Lyle's. I can't see his face because it's so dark beneath the trees, but I can imagine it: strong, scared.

"What the hell is going on?" he whispers.

I don't answer. I wait for a clue, a sign, some sort of signal that will tell me what to do next.

"Mana?"

"I don't know, Lyle. How would I know?"

One of our hands is sweaty, even though it's cold. I can't tell whose hand it is. I don't care. This is so unimportant compared to everything else, but here I am thinking, *One of our hands is sweaty.*

I repeat myself. "How should I know what's going on?"

"It's . . . Well, it's happening at your house. You saw that guy, and . . . he knew your name." Lyle's voice meets the air, quiet and hurried. It's his exasperated voice, the one he uses when our English teacher fails to know the proper use of a semicolon. Lyle has a big love for semicolons.

I try to focus for both of us. "What's important right now is finding my mom, getting safe."

"I'll get you safe." Lyle squeezes my hand. "But I think we have a better chance of finding your mom if we know what's going on."

Another light flashes, huge and bright. It should make me feel okay. Isn't that what light is supposed to do? Make us feel safe in the darkness? It has the opposite effect. The air vibrates with danger. An owl hoots warnings. My breath comes rapid quick, and I'm not sure why but there's this scared shaking inside of me that is threatening to burst out, take control of me. Fear. It's pure fear, and I cannot give in to it because if I do I don't think I'll ever stop screaming and shaking until another one of those Windigo monster things finds me.

You would think I would feel protected, hiding in the trees, in the dark, but I don't. Not even close. I tug on Lyle's hand again. The tree branches hide the sky. The sky hides the world. And in the world there are things I never imagined were possible . . . things with sharp teeth, things that appeared to be normal high school drummer boys but weren't.

"We should go somewhere," I say.

Lyle inhales. "My house."

"Are you sure?"

"I'll sneak you in."

A twig snaps in the distance. Bile moves up my esophagus. "Okay. Fine. We should hurry."

L yle's parents have strict no-girls-in-the-house rules, which are antiquated and old and beyond stupid. They say it's not that they don't trust me and Seppie; they just don't trust hormones. Whatever. It's not like people only fornicate in houses. Not that Lyle roasts the broomstick with anyone, but . . . Still, if he actually had a current girlfriend, I'm sure they would find places to thump thighs. Or he would just sneak them in the house the way he always sneaks me in.

The Stephensons live in a big rectangular house that is supposed to look like an old-time New England colonial, but it's new. A mudroom with a low roof attaches the house to the garage. Lyle's room is right above the mudroom roof. So all you do is go to the back, step up onto the edges of the monstrous ceramic planter, grab onto the roof edge or Lyle's hands, and he hauls you up onto the roof. Then you both go back into his room via the window. As neighbors, we have done this about ten million times, and this is what we do tonight, but tonight it feels dangerous. Tonight it feels life-or-death.

Just as we both get onto the roof, and I look back toward my house, the men in suits get into one of the black cars. It drives by the two houses between mine and Lyle's. Headlights flash into Lyle's yard just as we flatten ourselves onto the roof shingles.

"Should we be hiding from them?" I ask.

"Maybe."

"In all those shows you watched, were the Men in Black good or bad?"

"Both. In those old movies with Will Smith, they were good. Most conspiracy theorists think they're bad."

"Conspiracy theorists?"

"The people who think the government is covering up the whole UFO thing. I talk about it all the time. Don't you listen?"

"Not really," I admit.

He lets out a big breath. I've disappointed him, which makes my stomach back twist again.

"I'll listen better next time," I whisper-promise.

He studies me for a second too long. "I can't believe you sometimes."

"It's not like you listen to *me* when I talk about lip plumpers, and *I* don't get all pissy about it."

After contemplating this for a second (I am assuming here), he says, "Point taken."

He hustles in the window and gives me a hand into his room. I stand there and stare at all his *Doctor Who* posters as he plops the window screen back on and shuts it. No real lights illuminate the area, just a night-light, which is kind of cute, if you think about it. It would be cuter, however, if it wasn't a White Walker from *Game of Thrones*. After the Windigo, all pseudo humanoids creep me out.

"The other black car is leaving," he whispers, all urgently.

I go to stare out the window with him. "Weird."

"Ultraweird."

"Super ultraweird."

He crunches up his face at me. For a second everything seems normal. But it fades, because normal is not true. Normal is *never* true; I know that now.

I walk around the game controllers and running crap scattered all over the floor. I grab the sword he made back in seventh grade, when he was into those fantasy reenactment games. Then I hop over his trail runners. Lyle is one of the best cross-country runners in the county, which is why he's heading to Dartmouth on a scholarship. That's not until next September, though. And I have another whole year before I get to go, leave this place. That is, if we don't get eaten by monsters first.

"I wish we could run away from this," I say.

"We don't even know what we'd be running from." Lyle yanks his hand through his hair. "You're bleeding again."

I peel away the scarf. My ankle has gashes along it that are still bleeding. "It's not that bad."

"It's awful." He takes a new sock out of his drawer and wraps it around my ankle. He tosses the bloodstained scarf into his little metal trash can. I wonder if his mom will notice it. She's the type of mom who would go through her son's trash. He comes back and squats in front of me. The top of his head is full of ruffled, light-brown hair, thick and soft-looking. "It's really awful, Mana."

"Fine. I'm a total mess like normal; a stupid, horrible mess."

"What are you talking about?"

I want to shout about how I'm not as smart as him or Seppie, not as good a runner, about my D, how I will never get into Dart-mouth . . . but he meets my eyes and all my words get stuck some-where behind my heart. He asks, "Did the Windigo thing do this?"

I shudder but don't answer.

He grits his teeth. "That's so wrong. I should've killed it."

"I think you did."

"I should have killed it before it hurt you." He lifts my foot up gently and peeks beneath the sock again. "We should probably clean it out. I don't want it to get infected."

I suck in a breath. "Does it feel weird?"

"Your foot?"

"No . . ." I don't want to actually say what I want to ask.

He guesses anyway. "Killing an unspecified life form?"

"Exactly."

Shadows make homes beneath his eyes. "Kind of. I mean, it was going to kill you."

"Kill us."

"Right. It's just . . . I don't want to be the guy who kills off the one piece of proof we have that there's this bizarre species no one knew about."

"I don't think you did."

"Huh?"

"That guy, China, said that the Windigos were coming. That's why we had to hide. Windigos, plural." I shudder again, maybe because I'm so creeped out or because I'm in shock. Maybe I'm cold. The body shudders when it needs to get warmer, right?

Lyle's face goes soft. He places my foot back on the floor, super gently. "Mana. It'll be okay. Your mom will be okay."

"How do you know?"

"She's really capable, you know, as far as moms go, and *we* managed to get away from it."

"She would have called me if she was okay," I mumble.

"She doesn't have her cell."

"She would find a cell. It's my mom. She's practical. Like Seppie."

Blue lights flash in through the window. Lyle leans away from me to peer outside. "The police are here. At my house."

"Wait. What? Why?"

"I gave them my name when I called. I'll have to go talk to them, explain stuff to the parents."

"Should I come?"

"No."

"Why not?"

He scratches at his ear, nervous. "I just have a feeling. Trust me on this, Mana, okay?"

"Okay."

The truth is that I don't want to have to try to explain everything to Deputy Bagley or some other cop. I've already lied about what happened in the locker room. The truth is that I'm not a good liar. The truth is that I'm more than happy to just hang out in Lyle's room, hug my knees to my chest, and rock back and forth for a little while. Some would call it my impersonation of a cheerleader having a nervous breakdown. I would say, *What impersonation?*

He's gone for about ten minutes when a noise scuttles alongside the roof of the house. I bury myself under the covers, hiding, clutching the edges over my head like it's going to protect me somehow.

The scuttling pauses, then starts again, and gets closer. It sounds like it's walking along the side of the house now. Another pause.

Every single beat of my heart pounds against my ribs, making them ache. I flatten myself down, but turn my head the smallest of bits so that I can lift up the covers enough for my eye to peek out.

The window is dark.

Then the scuttling happens again, much louder. I hold my breath, will myself not to move, not to scream. A face full of teeth appears at the window. The eyes track around the room, searching, searching for me.

Locate. Exterminate.

I cannot even swallow. Any scream I would want to make is trapped somewhere down by my pancreas and is not coming out. One second passes. The Windigo peers into and around the room again and scurries on, moving to another window.

Locate. Exterminate.

I don't move until Lyle comes back, and even then I'm not sure if I will ever be able to move again.

So, the police interview Lyle in front of his panicked parents. He tells them all that I was scared and ran off into the woods after we realized my house was broken into and that my mom's car was still there. We thought we heard a noise inside, he lies. I freaked and ran off. They only half believe him, he thinks. He tells them I'm worried frantic about my mother. They believe that, he says.

He does not tell them that while they are interviewing him, I am upstairs cowering in his bed like a baby. When he comes back, he helps me out from under the covers and tells me all about it.

"I am so freaked out," I say, when I finally can speak again. He opens his arms. I step into them and I feel a little better. "You are the best friend ever."

He tenses up, holds on another second, and then lets go. I tell him about the Windigo at the window.

"It was trying to find you? You, specifically?"

"I think so."

He lets that settle in his brain, I guess, because there's a big pause before he says, "The parents are going to bed. They're beyond upset."

"Me, too."

He pauses again, thinking, the way Lyle does. I can tell because, whenever he tries to think of what to say, his eyes gaze toward the sky or the ceiling or whatever. Up. They focus upward. "We'll find your mom."

I would like to believe that. I need to believe that, but—

"Come sleep on the bed with me," he says.

I lift an eyebrow. It's a calculated lift, the kind the actresses execute in movies and the main characters do in books.

He says, "I won't feel like we're safe unless you're right next to me."

This is true, but still. I feel sort of . . . um . . . awkward? Awkward about this, but kind of excited about it, too. I hide my awkwardness the way I always do: I tease him. "I think you're just doing some patented guy move, which I will call Offer to Share my Bed with Traumatized Girl in the Hopes of Polishing the Porpoise."

"Polishing the porpoise?"

"Riding the baloney pony?" I offer up.

He laughs quietly. His dimples show when he laughs. I love his dimples. "Can you blame me?"

Lyle isn't really a total geek boy. It's just fun to torment him. Like everyone, he's a bunch of things all tangled up and beyond labels. His muscles are too big for a total geek boy. His hair is too nice. He runs like a jock. He works summers at the animal refuge like a hipster. He's charming, too. He has had a million girlfriends. They never last long. He always says he gets bored. Would he get bored of me? I wonder. Not that he would ever like me that way . . . but if he did . . .

He yanks a big T-shirt off a pile on the floor and pulls open a drawer. He holds up flannel boxers. "You can sleep in these."

"They're kind of big."

"You could sleep naked." He gives a fake wink.

"Nice try."

"Just seeing if I could convince you to do the naked horizontal dance of lust." He tosses the clothes to me.

I catch them and change the topic. "Maybe we should call Seppie."

"She's partying. She won't even hear her phone."

"I know."

Lyle cocks his head. He rips off his shirt. I refuse to stare at his muscles.

I stare at his muscles. What is wrong with me that I even notice his muscles? My mom is missing. My life has turned into a horror movie, and I'm staring at his abs, basically drooling. I hum under my breath to distract myself.

"I don't think we should involve her. I think this is kind of dangerous stuff."

I swallow. Guilt burrows into my chest, making it hard to breathe. "I involved you."

Nothing can happen to Lyle. Nothing.

"I involved myself." He says this quietly, just like the rest of our conversation. We don't want his parents to wake up and figure out I'm here. Still, he says it in such a strong tone that I don't argue with him. He's being so brave, which is what he always is, always.

"You, Lyle Stephenson, are the best friend ever." I go into the closet and shut the door. Lyle's clothes flutter around my head. Metal clothes hangers bang against each other. I pull on his stuff and step out. He's already under the covers.

His gaze goes up and down me. He starts twitching with laughter. "You look like you're three."

The T-shirt goes down to my knees.

"You're bigger than me." I state the obvious.

He lifts the covers so I can climb in. We both pull the covers back up and I turn on my side so we're facing each other. Our bent knees touch, skin on skin. He must have taken his jeans off. His knees aren't too hairy, but they're not girl smooth either. They feel foreign, but nice against mine.

"You *are* wearing *some* clothes, right?" I ask.

"Want to feel and find out?"

"Nice try."

"A boy can dream."

He's fake jolly. All show, trying to get me less scared, and it is so nice of him, but . . .

"My mom—"

"Will be okay."

He takes me by the hands and pulls me in for a hug. I lean toward him, nestling into the comfort. He's wearing boxers or shorts, too.

"How do you know?" I ask him. "How do you know she'll be okay?"

"She just has to be. That's all. She has to be okay. So, she is." His hand cups the back of my head. "The police will take care of it, you know that, right? It will all end up okay. Your mom will be home soon, making cupcakes and straightening the house and nagging you about studying."

I pull in a breath. It brings the smell of warmth, and boy deodorant, and goodness. It brings the smell of Lyle.

"You are the best friend in the world," I say again, even though I said it earlier. I want him to believe it.

He laughs. I feel his stomach wiggle against me when he does. He kisses the top of my head. "Don't forget it."

"Like I ever could."

Eventually, Lyle falls asleep. He makes tiny snore noises, which are kind of nice because it makes me know he is there, he is breathing, and I am not alone.

My eyes stay open.

Darkness fills the room. He unplugged the night-light. Clouds have covered the moon and the sky and all the limitless possibilities that poets and scientists always blab on about. I keep imagining that Windigo thing, creeping up the stairs, slashing through the door, finding us.

"It's dead," I tell myself.

But there are others. Obviously. One was creeping along the side of the house just a little while ago.

I ease myself out of Lyle's bed and check his cell to see if my dad has called back. He has not. This figures. He's the kind of dad who's never there when you need him, always busy, always working, always in another place, another city. I shuffle over to the laptop and flip it open. The blue screen casts light on the room, and I use it to check everything out. No monsters. Lyle's mouth is open a little bit.

The wireless is connected already, so I Google "Windigo." The first link that shows up is from a pseudo-cryptozoology site. It says, "Deep in the world of woods and forest, in the dark abyss of no-man's-land, there are accounts of malevolence and horror that cause even the pluckiest of men to crumble in fear. These are the stories of things inhuman, things usually unseen, and when they are seen, it is too late."

Oh, that is beautiful. That's going to help with the whole falling asleep issue. I check the windows. The shades are down. I still get that wiggly, awful feeling, like someone is watching. I am totally psyching myself out.

The website goes on to say that Windigos are humans who have turned cannibal, that they are large and hairy. It sounds nothing like what we saw.

I check out other sites. It's just more of the same, only with less over-the-top language. I even Google "exterminate monster," but I just get a lot of hits for role-playing games and Daleks.

Totally frustrated, I pick up Lyle's phone and try my dad again.

Nothing. No answer. How can he not answer? I try Seppie. The whole time it rings, I pray, "Please pick up. Please, please, please pick up."

She doesn't pick up. And I scroll through Lyle's contacts because I am honestly that bored and that desperate, thinking that there must be someone to call for help. I get to my number and there's a picture of me sarcastically pointing a finger at him. He has my name as Mana Banana. I change it to Mana the Awesome.

When we were little, Lyle used to obsess about my name, because Mana is what a lot of gamers call the amount of magic spell energy you have. Mana. He called me Magic Girl after that, until he actually researched my name for real and found out that a lot of people think that it means "thunder," or "wind of a storm," or some sort of natural force created by a supernatural entity.

I can still remember us sitting together under a tree, jamming out to tunes on my phone, slamming down the snickerdoodle brownies my mom had made, and him announcing, "You have the coolest name ever."

"Your name is cool," I told him. We were, like, twelve then.

"Lyle the Crocodile is not a cool name," he said, citing my favorite picture book when I was little. I think I pounced on him then, screaming "Crocodile!" and doing a tickle torture until he started chanting "Mana Banana." Good times.

I close the laptop, shut the cell phone, and tiptoe over to the window, staring out at the darkness and nothingness. I feel so alone, even though Lyle snores on the bed. I hope that obnoxious China guy is okay out there. I hope the Windigos didn't get him.

China is the name of a country. It shouldn't be the name of a guy who isn't even Asian.

I go over to my bag and haul out the pretzel container, twist off the cap, and eat one. It's crunchy and sweet. I touch the new penguin sticker with my fingertips.

Lyle makes a little snorting groan noise on the bed. I put things away and slip back over there, slide in, and sigh. Eventually, sleep will come, right? And maybe I'll be able to think of some intelligent course of action for the morning. And maybe I don't think my shirtless best friend is ridiculously hot.

I am so good at telling myself lies.

CHAPTER 7

I t's morning, and I'm kind of in the half-slumber zone. During the small part of the night when I was actually asleep, Lyle somehow spooned up against my back, with his arms wrapped around the bottom part of my rib cage. It feels good, and safe, and warm, like we're some old couple who sleeps together every night and still manages to love each other even though we both snore and emit stuff like the occasional sleep fart. I snuggle in a little bit closer and breathe deeply.

The half-sleep happiness where I don't really remember the situation that got me here doesn't last, though, because the door to his room flies open and there is his mom, Mrs. Stephenson.

There's no time to hide.

She starts to say, "Lylie, you've been sleep—"

I jump away. It does no good.

She shrieks.

Lyle's mom is tall and has church-woman hips, wide and strong. She gives the impression that she could battle monsters on a prairie and win, that kind of woman. And that's how she appears now. Her face turns white, then red. If humans were capable of having steam come out of their ears, she would have steam coming out of her ears. She quivers with emotion and I try to figure out what to do. Right now, I'm sort of huddled backwards against the wall, my legs tangled in sheets and draped over Lyle's midsection. I try to pull the comforter over my head, but it's tucked under us somehow.

"What is going on? What are you doing? Oh!" she yells.

"Mom, it's not how it seems," Lyle mumbles, starting to sit up. He's all groggy.

"It is indeed how it seems. There is a girl in your bed . . . a *half-naked* girl in your bed."

"It's just Mana," he says.

Just Mana? Do I not count as a girl? Nice. He puts his hand on my shoulder and then takes it away, like my ungirlness is burning him.

"I know who it is," Mrs. Stephenson says, and focuses all her mother force on me. She starts pointing. "The police are trying to find you, young lady!"

"I . . . Um . . . I—"

"And you, mister, having a young . . . young . . . female . . . human being . . . in your bed. *In your bed!* Under my roof." She backs up against the *Doctor Who* poster. Her hand covers her mouth. "Oh my word. Oh my word. *Oh my word!* And of all people? Mana? How could you do this to me, Lyle?"

"Mom . . . I didn't do anything. We didn't do anything."

Right. Who would do anything with "just Mana"?

"Ha!" His mother spits out the laugh.

I wonder for a second what my mom would do. She would be mad, but she would probably be a cold, calm kind of angry, which is much worse. My mom . . . My stomach folds into itself again. I press my hand against it.

Lyle's boxers are a wee bit revealing. I make bug eyes at him so that he can fix himself. The tops of his ears turn bright red. He pulls the covers back up and over him.

While he does, I try to give him some backup. "We really didn't do anything, Mrs. Stephenson."

She whirls on me. "Don't you pretend to be all polite with me, young lady. Get out."

I stammer, think, cannot get my brain around what she just said. "What? I have no place to go."

"Mom . . ." Lyle protests, sitting up and putting a pillow over his lap.

She points at me with a finger full of *leave*.

Hopping off the bed, I rush to the door and stumble down the hall, past Lyle's dad, who is standing there with shaving cream covering half his face and a razor in his hand. I throw open the door and run into the cold, wearing nothing except Lyle's T-shirt and boxers. The frozen ground stings my feet and pricks my lungs as I inhale. I think I make some sort of screaming noise from the pain of it. Lyle's voice echoes out from the open door.

"Mana! Jesus, Mom, she doesn't even have any shoes," he yells. "Mana! Wait!"

She yells over him. "Don't you take the Lord's name in vain, young man. You're in enough trouble as it is."

I keep on running because I can't think of what else to do. I run on my toes because it's all that my skin can stand, and in less than three minutes I'm at my house, staring at yellow tape. There's no sign of the Windigo except for a wet-looking smudge on the driveway. I quell the urge to vomit, and bolt onto the porch to try the front door. It's locked. The police locked it? Why?

Okay. Okay. That's probably standard police procedure and not a random fact I should be stressing about at the moment. The sky above me is gray and dull and seems like it's going to leak snow any second.

I need to get inside.

Hopping up and down, shivering, I try to figure out what to do. I rip the sock from around my ankle and shove it on one foot, even though it's bloody and stiff.

The broken window is boarded up. Then I remember the spare key. It's under a rock that I painted a daisy on, back when I was at YMCA day camp. I find it and go in, closing the door behind me.

The place is still a mess, but it's home. One of my duffel bags is on the floor by the door. I yank out an old dirty sweatshirt and jeans, plus some socks, hauling them on as quickly as I can. My cell is in there, too. I pull it out, flip it open. One message received, it says. It was sent at 7:08. Maybe it's from my mom. My heart leaps with hope—A.M.? 7:08 A.M.? No, no, it's P.M. Yesterday. Just after the game started.

I retrieve it.

It says, "Do not come home. Will tell more later. Do not come home. Stay at seppie's. Wait 4 my call. I love you. Mom."

How did I miss this? Did I just totally fail to check? Or did it come through late? Gulping, I make sure that there aren't any missed calls. None. She texted me. She never texts me. I didn't know she knew how. It makes no sense that she wouldn't call and leave a voice mail. And it makes no sense that she didn't want me to come home.

Why?

I lock the door. It clicks into place. The thermostat is right near the door and I crank it all the way up. The furnace shudders on, making me jump. The baseboards start thumping. It reminds me of last night and the creature, and for a second I think maybe that's why she didn't want me to come home. But she couldn't have known about the Windigo. Not Mom. My mom doesn't believe in craziness. Once, when Seppie and I were in seventh grade, we had this séance, and we swore that we saw a sparkly lady in white walk across the living room and disappear into the bathroom. Mom? She scoffed. Really. *Scoffed* is a stupid word, but that is totally what she did.

I was so mad at her. I was all, "Why don't you believe me?"

And she straightened the hem of her slip and said, "I only believe the things I see."

I thought that was so boring, almost as boring as actually wearing those beige slips under her skirts, but maybe it wasn't boring at all, because I sure am seeing a lot of things that I never, ever would have believed if someone had just randomly told me.

I dial her cell phone. Nothing. It goes directly to voice mail, like it does when it has lost its charge.

Wait. It was in the car anyway. Ugh. I am losing it, just operating on automatic and not even thinking about what I'm doing anymore. Slumping over to the love seat, I end up sitting on the one cushion that has been put back in place, and pull my knees up to my chest. I know it's stupid to be here. Especially if Mom warned me not to come home. But right now I have nowhere else to go. Right now, if a Windigo thing appears, then, well . . . let it freaking exterminate me. I don't care.

How can any of this be real?

"This makes no sense," I announce to the room, to the house, to the possible hiding Windigos.

"Sure it does."

I startle and see China standing in the kitchen. "God! What is up with you? Do you have to keep creeping up like that?"

He shrugs. His shoulders are massive under the leather jacket. His eyes don't shift, totally unreadable.

All the weird stuff? This all started with him and the gym.

I stand up and stomp over to him. I make my voice strong, bossy. "I mean it. What are you doing in my house?"

He doesn't back down. His voice is mellow, with just a tinge of anger. "A better question is, what are *you* doing here?"

"It's *my* house."

"It's dangerous." His eyes scan the mess, the Windigo footprints on the ceiling.

"Obviously."

He moves a step forward. He brings his eyes back to me. They're dark eyes, deep. They match his voice. "I thought you and your little boyfriend went to his house."

"He is not little and he is not my boyfriend."

"He'd like to be."

"Whatever. Wait. Really?"

He starts laughing. "Nice comeback."

"Nice comeback?" I stare at him. I force my mouth shut, my hands to unclench. "Is that what we're doing? Trading comebacks?"

He spreads out his hands, then drops them again to his sides. "It seems that way."

"That is so stupid. My mom is missing and you think it's fun to banter."

"You have to have a little fun. Even your mom had fun sometimes."

"Like you would know." My fists clench up again, because he just shrugs, and this time I don't unclench them. Instead, I ask, "How did you know I went to Lyle's house?"

He leans against the wall. "I put a tracking device on your clothes. Obviously, you are no longer wearing the same clothes, because according to my tracker you're still upstairs at the boy's house."

"Lyle. At Lyle's house. Not 'the boy.' He is not a boy." As soon as I say this, I realize it sounds pervy somehow, like "He is not a boy. He is a man . . . all man."

"What happened? Did you have a lovers' spat?" He smiles like this is possibly the funniest idea in the known universe, which makes me want to kick him.

"Spat? You are so stupid. I just told you . . ." I give up, whirl around, pick up a pillow from the couch, pivot back. "Never mind. Why did you put a tracker on me?"

"So I'd know where you were."

"Obviously. *And* . . ."

"And what?"

"And *why* do you want to know where I am?"

"Because you're in danger."

I put the pillow in place. "Right. And you care that I am in danger because why? Let me guess. You're magically in love with me, instantly, devotedly, after our wonderful interaction in the locker room? That would be a lovely cliché, wouldn't it?"

"Stop smirking and being so sarcastic. You know you are."

"I am not in love with you!"

"Not in love with me." He laughs. He actually laughs. "In danger. You know you are in danger."

"And *why* am I in danger?" I swear, it's like trying to get information out of a three-year-old.

He kneels down and picks up a copy of *The Naked Gun,* my mother's favorite movie. It's old, and one of those comedies that are really stupid on purpose. He smiles, a real smile, softer. It makes his face glow. How can his face glow when everything is so crappy? I snatch the dvd case out of his hand.

"Are you always so grumpy?" he asks. His smile vanishes.

"Yes." I hesitate and wobble my head around like an idiot. "No."

It's like all the air inside of me suddenly *whooshes* out. I flop back down on the love seat and say, "You just bring it out of me. I mean, I thought you were a kidnapper, and you keep surprising me, and . . . and . . . everything is so inexplicable, you know? It's hopeless, and all the weirdness seemed to start when I saw you at the game."

China lifts a slashed cushion off the floor and plops it onto the love seat. Then he sits next to me. I lean forward and rest my head in my hands.

"I'm not always grumpy," I say. "Only when my mother goes missing, I fail tests, and find out aliens are real."

His voice comes out soft and almost nice. "Just most of the time, then?"

I half punch him. I cannot believe I do that. It's like he's Lyle or Seppie or one of my friends. He almost smiles. He's not really that old, I guess, and he has crinkles around his eyes, which are nice, now that they aren't hidden behind sunglasses. The crinkles are like he's been squinting in the sun, not like he's ancient. His hair is dark and cut close to his head, like he's been in the army or the marines, but not anymore.

"Checking me out?" he asks, leaning back. "Evaluating whether or not to trust me?"

"No."

"Liar."

"Are you going to tell me why I'm in danger?" I ask.

"How about you go take a shower and get some clean clothes first?"

I raise my eyebrows.

"It's safe," he says. "I've checked out the house. You're shuddering."

Technically, I'm shivering, but I let it go.

"What if the Windigo thing comes back?" I ask.

"They're nocturnal."

"That's convenient."

"Yes, it is. It's one of the few things in our favor."

Our? We're on the same team? I guess we are, since he saved us in the woods, but still . . .

I stare him down. "And how do I know I can trust you while I take the shower?"

"You can lock the door."

"I bet you can pick it."

He laughs a choking sort of laugh. "True."

"Will you tell me what's going on, after?" I ask, standing up, because the truth is I am bloody and gross and I need a shower—like, really, really need a shower.

He holds up his right hand. "I swear."

"And nothing bad will happen while I'm in there?"

"I'll keep you safe."

His eyes gaze at my eyes. My eyes decide to focus on the ceiling.

"This is all too weird," I finally say.

I start walking to the stairs. He follows me up. He watches as I find some clothes in my demolished bedroom. I pull some clean jeans down from the ceiling fan. I find two matching socks. A pair of clean underwear is inside my copy of Brian Kell's *Crud*. I take a new shirt that is wrapped around Sherman Alexie's *Diary of a Part-Time Indian*.

He scoops the book off the floor. "You read?"

"Yes."

He gives me this expression and I have no clue what it means.

"What?" I say, stomping away from him toward the bathroom. "Why does that shock you? Everyone thinks stupid people don't read. It is so bigoted."

I turn to watch his face. An emotion flickers past it.

"I wasn't saying that you're stupid. It's just that your mother's not much of a reader," he finally says, flipping through the book, not making direct eye contact, not reading any words on any pages, just flipping the pages fast.

I stop. "You really know my mother?"

"Yes."

I wait for more. He does not give me more.

Pulling my clean clothes closer to my chest, I ask the obvious question. "How do you know my mother?"

This time, emotion catches on his face. His lips move in and out again. It would be sexy and endearing if he wasn't such a jerk. He stops riffling through the book. Instead, he holds it still in one big hand.

"She's my partner, Mana. Your mother is my partner."

"Whoa. Whoa. Whoa." I back up against the wall. My head knocks into one of the paper lanterns on this electrical chain that is normally hanging nicely on the ceiling. Now, it's dangling down, kind of like my tongue. Not really, but it might as well be.

I swallow, try to calm down, try to tell myself that this is not ridiculous, that mothers have secrets, that they do not have to tell their kids everything, and that, yes, just like all the old-women magazines say, women can get it on after thirty, even with hot men who are younger than they are.

"So," I finally say, "how long have you and my mom been doing it?"

His shoulders jerk back. "What?"

"How long have you been together?"

"You said 'doing it.'"

"If you heard me, why did you ask me to repeat it?"

"Because I couldn't believe you said it." He pulls his hand over his buzzed-off hair and starts smiling, really smiling. "You're difficult, aren't you?"

"Better than being easy." Which, apparently, my mother is. I lift Teddy, my oldest stuffed animal, off the floor. He's missing an arm. I haven't actually slept with Teddy for a decade, but rage still fills me. "Those bastards hurt Teddy. At least Mr. Penguinman is in one piece still, but really? Hurting a teddy bear?"

China doesn't respond. I stare out the window and hug poor Teddy and think about how life was so much simpler when I got him, innocent and simpler. Now, like Teddy, that innocence is all ripped apart. I outgrew Teddy and innocence long ago, but that doesn't mean that I want to throw it away or have it ruined. I'm not taking this well, and I try to focus on the immediate world. It snows now, tiny little flakes fluttering down. Soon everything alive will be covered in white.

"Is she okay?" I ask, pivoting to face China. My toe touches a disembodied teddy bear arm. I try to stick it on. It won't go in right, just dangles. "Is she?"

"I have no idea. I wish I did. Believe me."

I turn around again, stare out the window, watch the snow touch the ground. More comes, falling, falling, falling. China takes a step toward me and rests his hand on my shoulder. It's not a bad feeling, so I don't move away.

"You're scared?" he asks, but he's not really asking. All of his questions are more statements.

I nod.

"The tough thing was just an act, huh?" He waits for me to answer, and when I don't, he keeps going. "That's okay. The act keeps you moving. Almost all of us have an act."

"Do you?"

"Yes. I call it the Rambo–Terminator–Death Squad, He-Without-Emotions act."

"You're pretty self-aware for an old, mean guy in a leather jacket."

"So are you . . . for a cheerleader."

"That was low," I say, "but funny."

"I couldn't resist. Plus, you called me old."

"Everyone over eighteen is old."

The snow keeps coming, giving a visual to the cold, obscuring the old grass, the driveway, the walkway, all the things that I should be able to see. God, everything is so messed up.

"Go take a shower, quickly." He steers me away from the window and gives me a tiny push across the room. "I'll stand guard. Then we'll go search for your mom. Deal?"

He stands there, calm, far too handsome for Mom, whose last man was Dad, and let's face it . . . my dad? He's kind of bald and not much of a looker. This guy is so different—younger, obviously. China's feet are planted. He has a wariness about him, a stability thing. And I don't know if I can trust him, I just know that I have to. But, if Mom trusted him, if she dated him, she would have told me about him, right? Maybe all this is his fault.

I stand on the threshold of the bathroom but keep my eyes on him before I go on in.

"Were you guys dating long?"

He groans. "We weren't that kind of partners, Mana. That's why I laughed."

"What? Like dating my mom would be bad?"

"No. Not at all. We're not exactly each other's type."

The bathroom door frame feels a bit loose beneath my hand. I press my clothes into the frame. It wiggles as I study China.

"You're a little too leather for her. You probably have ink. She hates ink."

The corners of his mouth creep up. "I do have one. Want to see?"

"No. With my luck, it's on your butt." I smile back at him, because I know he knows that I know he's teasing. I shake my head, confused anyway, and throw my clothes into the bathroom. They land in a heap on the floor, right on top of the yellow ducky rug. I toss Teddy and his broken leg in the trash can. There's no fixing him. "So, what kind of partners *were* you?"

He walks across my bedroom and stands in the hallway, right by the bathroom door. He moves me in, flicks on the light switch. There are no windows in here.

"We worked together keeping people safe by capturing aliens. Now take a shower. We need to get moving."

He nudges me into the bathroom and shuts the door before I have a chance to close my mouth, or say the obvious thing here, which would be, *"What?"*

CHAPTER 8

I decide that he's full of crap, and that he just wants me to slam open the bathroom door and get into it with him right there. So I rebel instead and take my shower. The water warms my skin. It lulls me into believing things could be all right. I have someone who is going to help me find my mom. I am clean. I am warm.

Then I start thinking about what the guy just said.

Mom never really explained exactly what she did for work. She always made it sound stupid and dull.

Mom was actually really brilliant—*is* really brilliant. She always knows all the answers on game shows like *Jeopardy!* or *Who Wants to Be a Millionaire?* I would tease her about going on and she would be all, "It's too high profile for me, Mana. I want to be under the radar."

I pick up the soap that's on the floor. It's cracked in half, like someone threw it down hard.

Mom always wears skirts. You can't be an alien hunter if you wear flowing cotton skirts with beige slips. She makes chocolate-dipped pretzels. Alien hunters would make guns or bombs or sonic screwdrivers or something.

There's a dent in the soap, too.

China's obviously teasing me. Right? Right.

But if he isn't . . .

That means that the monster/alien things at the game were here because of her, for some reason. That means this is not random, and that she is in some serious danger. I can't just hope that the police do their best and find her, because this is bigger than the police.

And what about me? What about that weird leaping stuff that happened in the locker room? How does that fit into it?

I step out, dry off, and put my clothes on, trying to hurry. My hair drips because I haven't wrung it out well enough, but I don't care.

I step out of the bathroom. "China?"

No answer.

He's gone.

"What a complete asshole," I announce to the empty hallway. "He said he would guard the door."

When I was little, I saw this snippet of the movie *Psycho*. It totally freaked me out because it had this scene where a woman was in the shower and this crazed guy kills her. There's a lot of scary music, and slashing, and blood. Lots and lots of blood.

For a whole year I wouldn't take a shower without Mom standing outside the door. The thing is, she never complained about it. She was always straight out of the *Good Mother Handbook*, saying, "There are times in our lives when it's okay to be scared, Mana. I'm just glad I get to be here for you during one of those times."

"This is one of those times, Mom," I say. The empty stairs wait below me. She should be running up them. She should be throwing open her arms and getting ready for a hug, about to explain everything away—a big practical joke, a mass hallucination caused by some sort of chemical released from the locker room . . . anything.

"What's one of those times?" comes a voice.

China appears at the bottom of the stairs.

"Those times when you're supposed to be standing guard outside the bathroom like you promised," I say.

"I was just cleaning up downstairs." He smiles like he's being a good doggy and has finally mastered the Sit command.

I do not throw him a bone. "Whatever."

"Don't 'whatever' me."

"Whatever." I turn away as he bounds up the stairs in, like, three steps.

He touches my shoulder. "How are your scratches?"

"Healing."

I turn around and face him, crossing my arms over my chest.

"Your hair's all wet," he says.

"So?"

"So, your mother will kill me if you catch cold," he says.

I blink hard. I try to focus on the promise of his words. "Do you think we'll really find her?"

"Yes. I do. We have to."

Water drips down my spine. I really did not dry off well. "And are you going to tell me what's going on?"

"How about I tell you in the car?"

I eye him. "You have a car?"

"Of course I have a car. Actually, it's a truck."

I think about it for a second. "Where are we going?"

"Regional headquarters."

"Regional headquarters. So official," I say. "Can I bring Lyle?"

He straightens up, all rigid-backed. "He's already too involved, Mana. I don't want to be responsible for him, too. You're already too much."

I bristle. *Too much?* "You're not responsible for me."

"Of course I am."

"Right," I say, totally resisting the urge to argue. My mother raised me well. Mom . . . "Okay. Let's go."

We book it down the stairs and he *has* straightened up the living room a little bit. You can actually walk across the floor without stepping on coasters and cushions and books now.

"Thanks," I say, gesturing at the floor.

"Your mom's a neat freak. Seeing that mess would drive her

crazy," he says, opening the front door. "I didn't finish cleaning the kitchen, though."

"I will later."

"Sure." His eyes cloud over and he motions for me to hurry up and follow him. "Get a jacket."

I pick up an old one, navy blue, minimally warm, but it has a cute light-blue cable-knit hat and mittens stuffed into the pockets. I eye him, standing on the porch, waiting, eyes scouting up and down the street, all wary-confident like a soldier or a cop.

"You know," I say, pulling the coat on, "I'm probably not being very smart—trusting you like this."

He turns to gaze at me. The early morning sunlight makes a glowing halo around his dark hair. "You trust me?"

"Well, not really."

He straightens my hat over my ears. "Good. Trust no one, Mana. Not anymore. Okay?"

"Not even you?"

"Not even me."

I follow him down the porch and pick up my duffel bag, because it has my cell and Mr. Penguinman, and my makeup bag and stuff. "Nice. That's a super-nice way to live."

He stops walking and turns around, cringing. "I'm sorry for that. For the way you have to live now."

I'm not sure what he means, but I know that I'm sorry, too.

He leads me down the driveway and around the corner, where there is a large, black pickup truck parked at the side of the road, right outside the Johnsons'.

"Yours?" I ask as he unlocks it with his key fob.

"Obviously," he says as the truck beeps.

I climb in on my side. He jumps in and turns it on. It smells new. We start driving down the road past Lyle's house. I check to make sure my cell phone is in my duffel and transfer it to my coat pocket.

I'd try to call Lyle but, knowing Mrs. Stephenson, he would get grounded just for talking to me now.

"So, are you going to ask me where we're going?" China says, turning out of the subdivision.

"You already said 'regional headquarters,' in that nice, cryptic way of yours."

He turns to face me. His eyes flash. "You think I'm cryptic?"

"No offense, but I'm more interested in what's going on with my mom than figuring out how you should fill out that question on matchmeup.com, okay? Or are you more of a lovemecupid.org kind of guy, or maybe hornyhotsingles.com?"

He sinks his teeth into his lip, and for a second I think that he really is pretty hot, but then he talks again and spoils it. "Fine. I told you that we hunted aliens."

"Right."

"With what you've seen, you're actually doubting me?" The one hand he's been casually draping across the steering wheel suddenly clenches. The knuckles whiten. He's got a temper, this guy.

I cross my legs and open the heat vent wider, hoping to inspire it to bust out some more warmth, and try to explain. "No. I believe there are aliens or . . . something. It's just hard to imagine my mom hunting them."

"She's really good at it," he says. "She's pretty much the best there is."

I have this sudden vision of Mom all decked out in black leather with these monster-alien-killing guns holstered to her waist. It is too ludicrous. I push the image away. "Okay. Let's just pretend that I totally accept this idea and you can continue on with your little story."

"Bitter."

"I am having a tough twenty-four hours. And I love my mom, but I'm mad at her for keeping all this from me."

He runs his nondriving hand through his hair. "Okay. Have you ever heard any alien conspiracy theories?"

"No." This is kind of a lie, because Lyle talks about this stuff when we're alone, but lately I zone out and stare at his hands or quads or lips instead. It's a lot more interesting.

China lets out a big breath, disappointed. "Great. Okay, I'll start at the recent beginning. There are a lot of beginnings. In the 1930s, the United States government realized that there were aliens monitoring the earth. Some of these aliens seemed indifferent. Some seemed kind of nice. Some seemed evil."

"Like Dakota the racist with the acid-tongue issue from last night?" I say.

"Right. So the government struck a deal with some of these aliens. They wanted to abduct a handful of humans every so often. The government agreed."

"What?"

"I know. The government agreed, in return for technology, alien technology. The aliens promised there would be very few human abductions and only for the purpose of trying to keep humans healthy and viable. But they lied. The abductions were many, many more than the government expected. And then there were the mutilations . . . and experimentations . . ."

Like in my nightmares.

Even though there's nothing in my stomach, I feel like I am going to throw up. I must cough or gag, because China's hand lands on my arm. "Mana? You with me?"

I try not to sigh, but instead I just sort of whine, which is really no better. "I wish Lyle were here."

"What? Why?"

"He would understand what you're talking about."

"The boy would understand? Okay, well, the Windigos . . . the gray men . . . they're cyborgish, and they're really underlings, doing others' bidding. That's the best way I can explain it. They abduct humans. Some they return. Some they exterminate. Some they mutilate. They take eyes, genitals, and bore tiny perfect holes in people's shoulders and arms, extracting muscles."

"Why?"

"We don't know." He takes his hand off my shoulder and it feels to me like he does know but isn't telling.

"You don't know a lot, no offense," I bait him, as he turns onto the highway.

"True."

We're heading south on the highway, like we're going to Boston.

"So, since the 1930s, special portions of the government have dealt with the alien issue. We've tried to expand on the technology, which has been farmed out to multiple independent contractors. At the same time, we've tried to keep the public from finding out about the alien threat. And believe me, there's a threat. There are at least eighteen different species monitoring the earth."

"And all of them are bad."

"No. Not all of them."

"So, why can't we just ask the good ones for help?"

"We have."

I let this sink in, and I feel like there's more there that I should be asking, but I want to get to the real issue. "What does this have to do with my mom disappearing?"

He clears his throat. "For all this time, the government has kept this information from the president and his cabinet."

"What? That makes no sense. The president is supposed to be the one protecting the country and making all these decisions."

"The theory was that the presidents change too often. Some of them might panic and tell the public. You can never tell how level-headed or how intelligent a president elected by the American public will be. It isn't like there's an IQ test or a stress test or any kind of freaking test that would make it easier. Anyway, Ronald Reagan came really close, back in the 1980s. He was always talking about alien threats. Nobody figured out what he meant, and he didn't even have one-tenth of the story. It could have been catastrophic if he really knew what was going on."

"Wow. So, you and my mom . . ."

"We used to work for the government, but we defected, basically. Your mom did a couple years after you were born. She took up a new identity and began work for a rogue branch, the TTT, that's determined to gather enough evidence to tell the president what's really going on."

"Uh-huh."

"And we had all the evidence in a chip, finally," he says. His eye twitches.

"Seriously? A chip? You couldn't come up with anything more original? Wow. So let me guess, my mother had the chip, so they took her," I say. "Did you guys ever think of maybe making a backup?"

He accelerates and clears his throat again. "Of course we did."

We start passing a convoy of National Guard trucks, all dark gray, covered in the back with some sort of rubbery tarps, full of men on missions. I wonder what they would think of our conversation, what they would think about the gray men and the boy with the acid tongue.

I wait for China to continue. He doesn't.

I prompt him, "You made a backup, and . . ."

"And the agent who had it was taken. Just like your mother."

"Oh, for God's sake," I start. "You make a *lot* of backups; everybody knows that. Even I know that. I cannot believe my mother wouldn't have made a thousand backup chips. This is the kind of woman who alphabetizes her to-do lists."

"It's not that easy, Mana. It's encrypted stuff, high-level codes, massive programs. There are lists of every person who's ever been abducted, every person who has been infiltrated, all the companies that have alien technology—a massive trail. It's decades and decades of work." His cheek twitches again.

"Still, it seems pretty stupid to just have two copies." And it doesn't add up. Something doesn't seem right to me.

"We were going to make more. But it all happened so fast. We didn't have time." His voice is higher now, agitated.

"Right," I say.

China starts to say a word that begins with the *sh* sound, but a loud pounding noise behind both our heads cuts off his sentence. We both turn to look. I gasp. It's Lyle—Lyle knocking on the rear window of the cab. Okay? I can't figure out what he thinks he's doing. The wind blows his hair in random directions and he pounds at the window with something dark and metal. My heart speeds up, all happy to see him, even though he's in the back of the freaking truck. "Lyle? What are you doing?"

"Let me in!" he yells. "I'm freezing. Let me in!"

He pounds harder and I start to pull open the window. China switches his driving hand to his left. He stops me, swats my arm away from the window, keeping me from opening it, and does it all in a super-macho, secret-agent-in-charge way.

"He has a gun," China mutters. "I can't believe he has a gun. I'm getting complacent."

"Pull over!" I yell.

He doesn't listen. Instead he yanks out his own gun. He points it at Lyle. He's still driving.

Lyle's mouth drops open. He ducks.

"Jesus!" I yell, and grasp China's arm. The truck swerves only the tiniest of bits.

He snarls at me, "You'll kill us. Never touch the driver unless you are prepared to roll the motor vehicle over. I wish your mother had taught you a couple of—"

"You cannot shoot Lyle!" I interrupt.

"He's in the back of my truck with a gun, Mana. Of course I can shoot him."

"Pull over!" I yank his gun arm. "Pull over, now!"

He sighs. "Fine. But the little bugger better have a good explanation for why he's in my truck with a gun."

"I'm sure he does," I say as we pull over to the side of the highway. I let go of his arm. He called Lyle a bugger? Seriously? A bugger? What kind of word even is that?

China doesn't put his gun away. "Right."

Cars flash by us. The sky lets loose with some snowflakes. Big naked trees fill the land outside the highway.

China eyes me and gets his bossy voice on as he unbuckles and opens the door. "Wait in the truck."

"Sure," I say, jumping out of my side of the truck. "Absolutely."

CHAPTER 9

Put the gun down." China fast-walks around the truck. His arm is outstretched like a cop in one of those reality law enforcement shows. He's all authority and decision and strength, and it's basically kind of scary. His finger is on the trigger of his own gun. His own gun points at Lyle.

The wind blows me off balance as I hop out of my side of the truck. I slip, hold the side of the tailgate, and start praying that Lyle isn't about to die.

But Lyle isn't wimping out here. He stands in the back of the truck like a perfect target, not even hiding behind the side or anything, which is what he should be doing. Lyle's slightly shaking arm points at China's big bulkiness.

"No," he says, in a voice that is pretty calm and serious. "*You* put the gun down."

Cars whiz by. An ugly gray sedan slides in the slush a little bit but makes it back to its lane.

"Drop it," China orders.

"No, you."

Wow. It's like they're both five.

"Both of you put your stupid guns down!" I yell, pushing my way in front of China. "This is so ridiculous."

Neither of them put anything down.

The bag I left at Lyle's house slips on his shoulder as he says, "Get out of the way, Mana. I'm not going to let him kidnap you."

"He is not kidnapping me, and if he was, you let him drive forever before trying to stop it . . . although I appreciate that you tried and everything." I turn enough so I can sneak a peek at China, and then refocus on Lyle. "Wait. Why *did* you wait so long?"

"I was trying to figure out what to do. I wanted a plan." He actually blushes. "When someone is kidnapping your best friend you want to make sure you do the right thing and not make the situation worse."

"He's not kidnapping me. He's going to help me find my mom."

Lyle snorts. "Right."

A Dead River Oil truck barrels past us. Sand and grit spray up into our faces. It stings.

"Crud," I mutter, wiping at my eyes.

The oil truck stops about two hundred yards ahead of us. He must have realized what he was seeing. Two men with guns. One girl in between them. A massive lumbering guy, yelling into his cell phone, hauls himself out of the cab and starts crouch-walking toward us, trying to be a smart hero, trying not to be a target.

"Great," China mutters. "More complications."

I turn back to Lyle, reach up, and grip his belt loop with my fingers. "We have to go. Get in the truck with us. I will tell you everything."

China bristles. "This kid is on a hero mission, and he's a liability. I don't want him coming with us."

"Well, he is," I say as Lyle jumps off the truck bed. "Put your gun away, Lyle."

"He has to, first."

"No way." A muscle in China's temple pulses.

The trucker decides to yell from where he is rather than risk coming any closer, which is a highly intelligent self-preservation instinct. "Hey! I've called the police! You best be putting those guns down before they come. You okay, lady?"

"That is the question of the day," I mutter, and resist the urge to yell, *Define 'okay'!*

Lyle gives me big eyes, but I can't tell what he wants me to do. So I make it up.

"Yep!" I yell. "Just a little lovers' spat! Nothing big! Everything is A-OK."

He straightens up. He's got on a giant red parka. He seems like he's somebody's dad. "I've called the police."

"That is so nice of you," I say as China gets back in the truck cab and Lyle and I slip around to the front of the truck toward the passenger's side door. "But it's not necessary. We'll just be leaving now."

The trucker pulls out a gun of his own. "Oh, I don't think you should do that. You best stay right here until the authorities come to handle this."

"Shit," China says. "Get in. Now!"

We dive inside the cab. Lyle slams in behind me, not even shutting the door, just as the trucker clicks the safety off his gun.

Lyle pretty much lands on top of me. We are just a pile of limbs, and he is shouting, "What the f—"

But his shouts lose to the sound of a gunshot. The oil truck driver is actually shooting at us. I think I swear.

"Ha!" China says, stepping on the gas. "What a lousy shot. Shut the door, idiot."

Reaching over me, Lyle shuts the door just as we speed by the Dead River Oil man, who is cursing at us and pointing his gun again. He shoots.

"That one hit the side," China says, grinning massively. "So he's getting better."

"How can you smile at this?" I say, trying to disentangle my legs from Lyle's and actually sit upright. When we're finally in proper sitting position, I grab Lyle's gun and put it on the floor between my feet. The safety is still on.

"Because it's fun," China answers.

"Fun!" I turn to Lyle for help. "There is something wrong with him."

"That's why I was trying to rescue you," Lyle says, handing me the seat belt.

I click it in. "I do not need to be rescued."

"Right."

"Lyle! Just shut up!"

"I will if you stop yelling," he says in a perfectly calm voice.

"I am not yelling!"

China grunts, and the truck engine revs under the pressure of trying to go so fast so quick. "Yes, you are."

I ignore that, watching behind us. "He's getting into the oil truck."

"Is he following us?" China asks.

"Yep." I turn around and stare straight ahead of us. "I cannot believe he shot at us. I cannot believe you two have guns, and pointed them at each other."

Whirling around, I stare at Lyle, who has his hand curled up like the gun is still there. "Do you know how dangerous that is? Have you ever actually even touched a gun before in your life?"

He squints his eyes at me. "Yes."

"Right. When?"

"Mana, let's not interrogate the boy yet. We have priorities at the moment. Can you tell me if you can still see the oil truck behind us?" China says.

"Is that not what your rearview mirror is for?" I say, turning around.

"I'm focusing on driving," he says, as the truck lurches around a Subaru station wagon like my mom's, only red.

I look behind us. The truck is cresting a hill on a straightaway. "Okay, he's still following us. But we're losing him. That's what you say in your line of work, right? Losing him?"

"Any cops in sight?" China asks, veering around a sand truck.

Lyle answers for me. "No."

The dark grit spills out of the sand truck and onto the road, trying to make us all safer as we drive in the snow. I wonder if the government really understands the threats we're living under. I wonder if it would waste so many tax dollars on highway maintenance if it did.

"Is that oil truck guy actually one of the bad guys?" I whimper.

China grunts.

"What?" My hands clench each other.

"Appears that way. At least he is now," he says. "God, what a day."

"Mana?" Lyle touches my shoulder, gently, which is nice for a change, since in the past twenty-four hours everything has seemed terribly ungentle. "You okay?"

I make myself nod.

"You're just sort of staring blankly. And your hands . . ." Lyle unclenches my grip.

"I think she's just realized everything that's going on," China says. "And it can be a little much to process when you first figure everything out."

Lyle pulls me against him. His gun is still down on the floor between my feet. I let his arm wrap around my shoulders, and lean into his puffy jacket.

"Figure what out?" Lyle asks.

China glances at me for permission, I guess. I give a thumbs-up sign. And then China starts to tell Lyle what he told me. All of it.

"I thought we weren't supposed to trust anybody?" I say, after a mile of this.

Lyle removes his arm from my shoulders, which is fine, but a little immature, I think. I give him a raised eyebrow. He flops his arm around. "Fell asleep."

Judging by the laugh lines near his eyes, China appears amused, and then he says to me, "People are always trying to protect you, aren't they?"

"It's because I'm short," I say. "You're not answering the question."

"The kid showed some spunk. He had a gun. He stowed away in the truck. I've decided he may be a liability, but he may also be useful," he explains, as we turn onto the exit for Maine, "if he can remember to take the safety off a gun."

Lyle cringes.

"Are we going to Maine?" I interrupt as we cross onto Interstate 95, the one real highway into the state. We pass a New Hampshire liquor store with a zillion cars in the parking lot.

"Yep. And I only had two choices," China continues, driving as calm as can be, apparently not worried at all about police possibly searching for us, or the fact that his truck has been shot by the oil truck guy. "I could trust your little friend here—"

"I'm not a little friend," Lyle scoffs.

China keeps talking. "Or I could shoot him."

My stomach lurches. China smiles at me. "I figured you didn't want me to shoot him. You'd probably run off or fight me, and that would make things more difficult, too."

Lyle's leg starts jiggling like it always does when he's mad or nervous. The whole damn truck vibrates. I decide to change the topic. "Why don't you tell him the rest, then?"

China talks. Lyle listens. I listen, too. I just heard it all, but how many times can you hear that your mom is an alien hunter, that the government has secret agencies dealing with aliens, that even the president doesn't understand the magnitude or nature of the threat?

One time is too many times.

But I listen again anyway.

I listen because it might bring me closer to Mom. Even so, it all kind of hits me in the stomach, punching it in with such great force that the only thing I can compare it to is the time I came out of a double tuck front twist and landed on Seppie's elbow.

"So, Mana's mother is my partner. We hunt aliens, mostly, and we try to collect proof of their plans so that we can present them to the president," China says, all matter-of-fact casual. He seems awfully young to be working with my mother, to be driving in a truck with a gun, explaining this to us. He's probably in his twenties, but he's so different than we are, so calm and confident and in charge. It's almost like *he* is the alien.

"That's why they've taken her," China continues. A hand lifts from the steering wheel to rub at his eyes. "They thought she had the proof on her."

"Whoa, whoa, whoa," Lyle says. He closes his eyes, like he is trying to figure it all out. "What did you just say?"

The edge of China's lip creeps up, like he's trying not to smile. "Mana's mom works with me. We hunt aliens."

Lyle sputters and then is silent, obviously stunned or astonished or whatever word you want to use to describe it.

And then we're all quiet.

W e drive across the big green metal bridge that spans the brown river of ugly marking the line between New Hampshire and Maine. Cars zip along with us. The people in those sedans and SUVs and trucks are probably talking about normal things, like Thanksgiving and grocery lists, probably thinking the biggest thing to fear is fear itself and all that crap.

Ha.

Lyle finally remembers how to talk. "Holy crap."

"That's a brilliant response." China laughs. "Sanctifying feces."

"Be nice to him." I pull closer to Lyle. "It's a lot to process."

China raises his eyebrows.

"You . . . you . . . you believe him?" Lyle gapes at me, stunned. "You just believe him, Mana? He could be insane, criminally insane. He could be kidnapping us right now."

"Why would I want to kidnap you?" China says, amused. "Mana, maybe. But you?"

"No clue." Lyle's exasperation shows in his head movements. His hair flops into his face and he shoves it out of the way. "It makes more sense than Mana's mom being an alien hunter."

"Lyle, think about it," I say. "Think about what we saw in my house last night, about what I told you happened in the locker room."

Air leaves Lyle's mouth in a slow hiss, and then he says, "I know . . . I know . . . But . . . Ah, God. Your mom is so *mom* though. I mean, she's not some kick-ass, Joss Whedon—or J. J. Abrams-style toughie, you know?"

I pat his arm. His pop culture references are kind of beyond me. "It's okay."

"Kid, you need to man up," China says.

I smack his leather coat sleeve. "Will you stop?"

He laughs and smiles. "You're pretty protective. Your mom is the same way."

I know. Or I think I know. I'm not sure how well I know my mom anymore, actually. "You don't need to put others down to feel better about yourself. Lyle is manning up just fine, thank you very much. He's not even hysterical. Most people would be hysterical, given these circumstances."

China turns off the Maine interstate. He points a finger at me. "Wow."

"What?"

"You sound just like your mother."

I'm not sure whether that's an insult or not.

As we drive down the bumpy streets, wind blows new snow across our path, twisting it into white fingers that always seem to be reaching out to capture us. Lyle slowly stops jittering, losing some of the anxiety that has propelled him forward, I guess. He slumps against the window as we drive past a big store advertising, in big block letters, GUNS, BAIT, WEDDING DRESSES, BEER.

"Love that sign," China says, nodding at it.

Dark brown wood the color of a UPS truck covers the store's exterior. The paint peels, to make it even more inviting. The OPEN sign is all lit up.

"Pretty white trash." Lyle snickers in a way that makes him sound like such a rich boy. It's ridiculous. He's only upper middle class. It's like Dartmouth's pretentiousness has already invaded him.

I hit him in the leg. "Shut up."

Lyle rubs his thigh. "What?"

I scowl at him. He still doesn't get it.

"What?"

"It's a mean thing to say."

China kind of chuckles, like a normal person, as he turns the truck into the empty parking lot and drives toward the back of the building. He pulls the truck next to a large green Dumpster and parks.

"This is it?" I say, but it obviously is, because China is already unclicking his seat belt and jumping out of the car.

"Stay here while I make sure it's clear," he says, leaning into the truck and staring at us super seriously. Snowflakes quickly conceal his dark hair. One lands on his eyelash. "I'll leave the key in case you get cold."

"And why are we here again?" I ask.

"Supplies and intel. Plus, I have to check in—in person—every week while working the field."

The door slams shut. We watch him amble-hustle, which you wouldn't think would be possible, across the parking lot. He leaves footprints in the snow and opens a marked-up door in the back of the building. The door was white once, I guess, but now it's just dingy. A giant black dirt mark shaped like a crescent moon marks the center of the door.

Lyle unclicks his seat belt and stretches out, groaning. His long, thick-muscled legs don't have quite enough room to stretch.

"God," he says. "What the hell are we doing here?"

I shiver. The truck is already getting cold. I repeat what China just told us. "Intel. Supplies. Check in?"

I unclick my seat belt and edge away from Lyle so we aren't smooshed together anymore. It feels good to move my body, but not good to be a few more inches away from him. This, I realize, is sort of pathetic.

"You believe this guy?" Lyle asks, picking up his gun from the rubber mat on the floor.

"China? Yes. Sort of. I'm not sure. Why wouldn't they back up names? How long does it actually take to get enough evidence to convince a president? His story doesn't seem right, really, you know?"

"I know." Lyle opens the glove compartment and starts pulling out papers. "I think he's only giving us half the truth. A chip is so cliché, you know? Like a bad movie plot from uninspired writers. It's got to be more than that. There must be some kind of detail that connects more directly to your mom."

I wrap my hand around his wrist. "What are you doing?"

"Trying to find some evidence. Factual, indisputable evidence. I believe him partially, but I don't know if I trust him." Lyle reads the registration for the truck. He sucks in his breath. "This truck belongs to your mom."

I snatch the yellow paper away. "What?"

"It's right there."

I read it.

Mom's name.

"I didn't know she had a truck," I whisper.

"Seems like you kind of didn't know a lot about your mom."

I let this brilliant statement settle in, and my head starts aching, right in the center, like thoughts about my mother are just pain-inducing right now. So I say, "How pissed is your mom?"

"Beyond pissed." Lyle sighs. "I'm grounded for eternity and never allowed to see you again."

"That's going to make cheering a little hard." I unzip my bag, pull out the pretzel container and get us two to munch on, then shove the container back in. I hug the bag to my chest and munch. It makes me think of my mom, eating these pretzels. For a second, I worry that they will be the last things she ever makes me.

No. I will not think that way. I am going to get her back.

"Thanks," Lyle says. He bites the pretzel and thinks for a second. "She also wants you to put the baby up for adoption."

I choke. "What?"

"She wants you to put our baby up for adoption."

"Lyle. We do not have a baby."

"I know." He wiggles his eyebrows pretty lasciviously.

"We haven't had sex," I insist.

"Believe me, I know that, too."

Fear overwhelms me. "Wait. Do I seem pregnant?"

"A little bulky right now . . ." He eyes all my clothes.

I hit him. "Shut up. It's cold."

His pretzel stick dangles out of his mouth. "I know you're not pregnant, Mana. It's my mom we're talking about here. I'm sorry she's so . . . so . . ."

"Nonsensical? Lyle." I point my pretzel stick at him. "Your mom thinks I am pregnant, and we haven't even kissed, let alone made the funky vertical monkey."

"Believe me. I know. I'd remember that." He makes this awkward laugh noise and starts shuffling around, fidgeting, checking everything out. He pulls an M&M's wrapper out of the glove compartment. "Your mom likes M&M's?"

I touch the dangling metal key that could turn the heat back on. "No. It must be China."

"He's weird."

"You just don't like him because he's cute for an old guy with bossiness issues."

"Right, if you think men who grunt are attractive."

"He does not grunt."

"Sure, he does. 'Ugh. Ugh. We go here. You stay in truck. Me no kill you,'" Lyle mocks.

I start cracking up. Lyle keeps doing it and I double over, laughing hard. I snort.

Lyle points. "You snorted."

This makes him lose it. We're both doubled over, hee-hawing and snorting, until he holds my hand and goes, "It's not that funny."

The laughter makes the words difficult. "I know."

We keep laughing. And it isn't. It's not that funny. But it is, you know, because it is funny-bizarre-weird that all of this is happening. It's funny-bizarre-weird that yesterday morning I thought my world and *the* world were all safe and sane and understandable, and now . . . now? Now, it is so far from that. Now, it's a mess of wonder and fear and heartbeats accelerating into overdrive. Now, it's some bad sci-fi movie/TV show that doesn't have commercial breaks or a script.

So I laugh.

I laugh and I laugh, leaning away from Lyle, leaning into myself, doubled up, because that is the only way that I can deal with this right now.

I laugh.

And while I'm laughing, the truck door flies open and horrible reaches in.

ands lunge into the cab of the truck, yanking at us, and suddenly we're not hyena laughing or pig snorting anymore. In less than a second, my elbow scrapes by the steering wheel. Someone is physically dragging me out into the cold air.

"Mana!" Lyle reaches for me. But this monster-large bald man with a goatee and a lot of metal in his lip hauls Lyle out backwards. Lyle's legs scrabble to find footing.

My legs must do the same, but I'm lighter, so the man who has me just keeps me smooshed back against his smelly leather jacket. It's all dead cow and body odor.

"Let me go," I order him.

"You're a little wildcat, aren't you?"

"Wildcat?" For God's sake, really? "How freaking sexist are you? Women are not cats. Or dogs. Or animals of any kind. But thank you for at least making me not domesticated."

My feet kick backwards. They connect with leg. My captor drops me and I land on the balls of my feet, just like after a stunt dismount, then whirl around to face a big—really big—okay, monster-sized man. A mullet haircut only adds to his air of disgusting evil. A giant dragon has been inked around his neck. His eyes narrow.

"Uh-oh," I mutter. "Hiss? Meow?"

He reaches out to seize me again. I dive away, pivoting, and bomb back into the truck. Throwing the door shut, I flick it locked just as he lunges.

"Lyle!"

I turn the damn truck back on. The engine roars to life.

Beefy-faced mullet man smashes his fist against the window. "What are you doing here?"

His voice is high like a sparrow's. Yes, now *I* just compared *him* to an animal. It almost makes me laugh. Almost.

Lyle is still trying to twist away from Baldy, but the guy has him in a stranglehold. The guy's arm wraps around Lyle's neck as Lyle flails. I swear, the arm is the same circumference as a freaking tree trunk.

Lyle starts choking.

The other guy keeps pounding on my window. I lunge across the seat and point the gun at Baldy.

"Do not tell me I have to save you," I say to Lyle.

He gasps for breath. His eyes bug out.

I hold the gun up and yell, "Step away from the boy!"

Baldy loosens up his grip, just a little, but doesn't let go. Lyle glares at me. His mouth tightens into a mean, angry line, and it takes me a second to figure out why.

"The man. Step away from the man." I mouth "Sorry" to Lyle.

Baldy nods toward my gun. He actually laughs. "You wouldn't."

Beefy Face starts quick-walking around to the front of the truck. I have no time.

"Fine," I say.

I point the gun down at the feet of the big idiot who is holding Lyle. I hope the safety is off. My fingers squeeze the trigger. The noise is massive, fireworks in my ear. Pain from the reverb shoots up my arm and into my shoulder. My whole body bounces backwards from the force. I don't see where the bullet goes, but Lyle is hurtling into the truck next to me, yanking the passenger's side door shut behind him.

"Go, Mana!" he yells right into my ear, but I can barely hear him. "Go!"

I am basically standing on the accelerator trying to speed away. We lurch forward, finally gaining traction on the snow-covered ground. The truck zooms across the parking lot. Flakes smash against the windshield. Then I realize it: these guys might know something about Mom. I yank the wheel all the way to the right and hold it there.

Lyle braces himself against the dashboard as the truck turns a mighty doughnut in the snow. It squeals and fishtails, just a bit. Nothing huge. I swear.

Poor Lyle is screaming at me as I aim the truck straight for the guys. "What are you doing?"

"They're our only link," I grunt, trying to keep the big truck under control.

"Link?"

"To my mom."

He disagrees. "China's our link."

He doesn't get it. China is just one guy, hopefully on our side, but kind of in the dark about where my mother actually is. These guys are the enemy. The enemy is usually much more knowledgeable about the actual location of kidnapped mothers. It would take too long to explain.

"Whatever. The more links the better." I slam my foot on the brake. The truck pitches. "I'm going to make them tell me where my mother is."

I jam the stick into Park, take Lyle's gun, and hop out. The two guys stand. They stare. One guy is balanced on one leg, holding his foot. I must have actually got him. I cannot believe I shot someone. My stomach lurches. I ignore it. I'll be tough.

"You jerks going to tell me where my mom is, or am I going to shoot you?" I ask. Then I wink at the man doing an impersonation of a flamingo, only not so feathered or pink. "Again."

Beefy Face glares at me and crosses his arms over his chest. "I think you're bluffing."

"You think wrong," I say.

Lyle touches my elbow, probably remembering my pacifist tendencies. And yes, my hand trembles, but whatever. "Mana . . ."

"You want me to prove I'm not bluffing?" I ask, pointing the gun at Baldy and then at Beefy Face, slowly, deliberately. "Because I will prove it. Which one of you guys wants to be the proof?"

I feel like a bad rip-off of some old western, but it works, I think. Nobody moves. The wind blows the snow sideways now. It flashes between us, swirls in the air past our faces, seeming so clean.

Beefy Face says, "Your hand is shaking."

I point the gun at him. "I'm thinking *you*, because, one, you're criticizing a woman with a gun; two, all your toes are still there; and three, it wouldn't be that fair to shoot Baldy again. A shot to the foot can do a lot of damage. There are bones in there. Or there were, until I blew them out."

Baldy cringes.

"I'm sorry," I babble. "I know 'Baldy' is offensive, but I don't know your names."

"Pronouns are so impersonal," Lyle agrees. His body tenses up, and he's pretty focused, like he gets right before a tough stunt or a killer tumbling run.

Baldy and Beefy Face glance at each other.

Baldy says, "I'm Brian."

Beefy Face says, "Aaron."

"Their names rhyme," I mutter.

Lyle lets out a disgruntled sigh. "Figures. Villains are like that."

"We aren't the bad guys," Baldy Brian says. A muscle near his eye twitches. "You two are the bad guys."

Lyle and I glance at each other and burst out laughing.

"*We* are not the aliens," I say. "*We* don't drag people out of trucks. *We* don't kidnap people."

Beefy Face Aaron snorts and takes a step closer. "What? We're the aliens? Is that what you're trying to say?"

"Not necessarily—" Lyle starts.

"Yes," I interrupt.

"But you could be in cahoots with the aliens," Lyle finishes.

Baldy Brian bounces on his good foot, trying to stay balanced. "Cahoots?"

He lunges as he says it—dives, really, right for me. I twist away, trying to escape, but he tackles me despite my efforts. His shoulder smacks my side, and just like that, I'm down. My knees and hands hit the freezing concrete first. The gun skitters out of my hand and slides across the parking lot. Beefy Face Aaron snatches it up.

"Mana!" Lyle's trying to yank Baldy Brian off of me.

"Enough!" Beefy Face yells. "Everybody up."

We all haul ourselves back into standing positions. Two wet circles darken the knees of my jeans. Scrapes redden my hands and there's a little blood in the snow. Shaking from fear and pain and adrenaline, I am completely and totally annoyed at myself.

"I cannot believe I dropped the gun." I cross my arms in front of my stomach, which threatens to explode.

"It's okay," Lyle says. He puts an arm around my shoulder. "I would've dropped it, too."

"Really? Are you just saying that to make me feel—"

"Enough," Baldy Brian says again. He points at Lyle, which is kind of insulting, if you think about it, because I'm the one who had the gun before. You'd think there would be some reciprocal gun pointing going on. Why is Lyle considered more worthy of the gun point? Probably because he's a guy. I hate that.

"Let's bring them in," Beefy Face Aaron says, pushing me forward toward the back of the store. Old mattresses lean up against the back wall. A couple of ratty tires are propped up next to them. Broken glass litters the parking lot, half hidden beneath the new layer of snow. I bet rodents love it here.

I stumble a little bit and grunt out, "Is that where you put my mom? In that dive?"

Beefy Face yanks me by the shoulder, whirls me around. "What are you talking about, kid?"

"My mom . . ." I stare at his meaty lips. "You took her here, too, right?"

He cocks his head. Snow falls down. It melts in his hair. "Who is your mom?"

"Melissa Trent."

Baldy gives a little whistle.

"Melissa Trent." Beefy Face turns me around, but not before I catch a tiny smile playing at the corners of his lips. "I should've known. You fight just like her."

"You know my mom?" I can't even breathe. Everything inside me clutches up.

Beefy Face doesn't answer.

I spit out the threat before I think about it. "I will kill you if you hurt her. You got that? I will kill you."

Lyle whispers, "Mana."

"What?"

"They're the ones who have the guns."

CHAPTER 11

Every year, for my birthday, my mom would make me a homemade peanut butter cake with salted caramel frosting (also homemade, thank you very much) and this toffee crunch stuff between the layers. It was a big deal because she never baked a cake from scratch the whole rest of the year. Even last year, when you'd think I would be more excited about the whole sweet sixteen birthday party thing, I was so psyched about this cake that I actually stood there leaning against the counter and watched her whisk the eggs, peanut butter, and butter (yes, real butter, not the Smart Balance Light spread stuff) all together.

"Does your wrist get tired, doing that?" I had asked, poking my finger in the bowl.

She bumped me away with her hip. "Absolutely. But you're worth it."

I licked my finger and laughed. "Oh, right . . ."

And she stopped right then, propped the whisk up in the gooey goodness, put both of her hands on either side of my face, and kissed my forehead. She said in this super-serious mom way, "You are."

It was so normal, so Mom normal, and now, remembering it, I'm like, *How could she have done all that normal mom stuff and been tracking down aliens at the same time?* How could she have not shrieked and screamed and given up, gone ballistic on the street corner by Hoyt's Cinemas, and yelled to the world about the aliens coming? Sorry. Scratch that. How could she have not shrieked and screamed and given up, gone ballistic on the street corner by Hoyt's Cinemas, and yelled to the world about aliens *being here*?

But she didn't. She held it together. She worked against how overwhelming it all was. So that's what I will do, too. I won't start hysterically crying as Baldy and Beefy Face, also known as Brian and Aaron, push Lyle and me into the building. I will not gasp from the stench. I will not wet myself when they force us down these rickety steps into the basement, where they will probably murder us. I will brave myself up.

Right?

Right.

Lightbulbs swing over our heads, dangling by wires that seem like they will snap and burst into flames any second. Concrete walls bar our way out of the hallway that just seems to lead one hundred feet toward the center of the building.

I try to pause at the door. Beefy Face doesn't let me.

"Get going."

He pushes me in behind Lyle and Baldy.

"Don't push her," Lyle says. His hair flops over his eyes. I want to lift it out of the way, see him under there, figure out what he's thinking. His mouth just presses itself into a line, coding his thoughts. I reach out and clutch his hand, cringing, expecting Baldy or Beefy Face to object. For some reason they do not.

"Go down the hall," Beefy Face says.

"Or what?" I say.

Baldy laughs. "We'll shoot you."

He turns around and winks at me over his shoulder. I try to be all brave and to smile sassily back at his abductor self, but I don't quite make it.

The hallway ends in stairs. We start down them. They're concrete, too, hard, hard surfaces, ready to break bones if you step wrong or some giant thug guy decides to bash your head into the steps.

"Where are you taking us?" I ask Baldy Brian, who is kind of hopping sideways down the stairs, grunting. His foot must kill him.

"Down the stairs," he says. Brilliant. The hand holding the railing shifts and moves as he hops down another step.

Some resolve in me softens. "You want to lean on me?"

His head snaps toward me. We make eye contact, real eye contact. "What?"

"Well, it's hard to walk when your foot is hurt," I try to explain.

He makes big eyes. "You're the one who shot me."

"I know . . ." I can't really explain. "I'm feeling kind of bad about that."

Baldy smiles. His teeth are nice and white and even, like moviestar teeth. He ignores me and says to Beefy Face, "She's just like Melissa. Tough, then sweet."

Beefy Face doesn't say anything. Lyle squeezes my hand. He must be able to tell I'm about to haul out some badass cheerleader attitude on this guy for even talking about my mother. I take the hint: try not to incense the big, ugly men with the big, ugly guns.

Baldy throws open the metal door at the bottom of the stairs. "After you."

Lyle looks at me. I look at Lyle.

Lyle goes in first. He doesn't let go of my hand, and his muscles tense beneath my fingers. He lets out a soft, low whistle. I've never heard him whistle before, and I'm about to elbow him, but then I see what's in front of us.

Computers and desks and monitors, about as high tech as they come, fill a massive room. Gleaming white walls reflect the overhead lights, and there are monitors all along two of those walls. What appear to be real-time images of space, spaceships, city buildings, and the White House flicker on the screens. One screen monitors the Weather Channel, for some reason, and two more are dedicated to world news outlets. Computer stations made of sleek black plastic hold shiny laptops and a couple regular old computers. The room buzzes with electricity.

"It's like what you imagine at NASA, at the Johnson Space Center," Lyle whispers.

"Where is that? In Texas or Florida or some big state with a lot of sky?" I ask.

"Yes. Only we're in Maine, beneath a crappy general store," Lyle says, still amazed.

Brian starts chuckling. "Move on in."

We don't move. We just stand there, staring at the two figures in the center of the room. One is familiar: China, my mother's partner. He's hunkered over a computer. His forehead is creased. He doesn't even glance up when we open the door. But the other figure does. She stares at us. We stare at her.

It's hard not to.

She is humanoid, but not human. Her skin is pale, ridiculously pale, and shimmering, like there are tiny crystals or fireflies embedded in her skin and eyes. Her hair is black. Her eyes flash from silver to black to an unsettling blue, like they're trying on colors to see which one scares us the least. Tears come to the edges of my own eyes because she is so beautiful. She makes me think of fairies.

"Come in, Mana . . . Lyle," she says.

China doesn't look up.

Lyle doesn't move.

"Lyle." I tug him into the room with me.

"What?" He follows my lead, hopefully snapping out of his shock or awe or whatever. "Yes, okay. Sorry."

Baldy and Beefy Face let us wind our way through the computer monitors, following us right up to where China and the woman are working. But when we're five feet away, strong, muscular hands land on our shoulders, holding us back.

"They're fine," China grumps.

The hands do not move.

Then the woman says, eyes shifting back to black, "Brian. Aaron. Let them be."

The hands drop, but Brian says in a somewhat whiny tone, "She shot me in the foot."

China finally pays attention enough to move his head and make actual eye contact. His lips purse together and squelch over to the side, like he's trying not to laugh.

The woman focuses on me. I shift my weight.

"Why did you do that?"

"I thought they were kidnapping us," I say. "They just yanked us out of the truck and yelled at us."

"We thought they were hostiles." Beefy Face shrugs. "The sensors went off."

The woman straightens up, all business in a very stereotypically bitchy, fashion magazine editor sort of way. "They've been near hostiles, that's why."

Aaron continues, "She said she's Melissa's kid."

China doesn't even move or twitch or anything, just says, "She is."

"She doesn't resemble her," Aaron says brilliantly, in an *excuse me for making a mistake* voice. Truth is, my mom and I have similar lips and body structure, so I know he's saying this because my mom is white and I'm not.

A computer hard drive starts whirling somewhere, fast and overactive. It almost sounds angry. It's the same noise my computer makes when it's downloading a CD or DVD, but I know instinctively that's not exactly what is going on here. I can't imagine them downloading *Vampires Suck*. Maybe *World of Warcraft* or the Twenty-fifth Anniversary Collector's Edition of *Street Fighter*.

The woman stares at the men, one at a time. She inspects me again, then addresses Brian. "Take care of your foot and stand guard. There is such a thing as diplomacy, you know."

They scuttle away, Aaron to stand at the door and Brian to retrieve medical supplies from a cabinet along the wall. The entire room seems to vibrate with their actions and with the noise of the computers, just an underlying hum to everything, the sounds of drives whirling, activating, pausing. It's like the computers have a life of their own.

"I am Pierce." The woman beckons us forward with an elegant flick of her right hand. "You are Mana and Lyle. China's told me about you."

"I'm sure he has," Lyle says. He sways a little, like he's lost his center of gravity, and shoots China a killer glare. China just smiles. "It's nice to meet you and everything," Lyle says, voice cracking, "and I don't want to be rude, but what are you?"

She gazes at each of us for a second, holds our eyes with hers. The air calms, somehow, even though I know—I really, really know— that we should be screaming scared and running out of here. "I am fae. It's an alien race. We've been here on the earth, forgotten by our people, for centuries."

"That's horrible," Lyle says. I bump him with my elbow. He is so obviously in like. It's disgusting. He'll start drooling soon.

"Horrible or not, it's a fact." She lifts her shoulders in a shrug and then waves the thought away. "We don't have the time to go into it. Suffice it to say that some of us are now working with humans like China, like your mother, Mana, to stop the devastation that's going on."

I gaze at her, really study her. She's beautiful and shimmery. "But not all of you?"

"Some of us cling to the old ways."

China's forehead crinkles up. "We don't have to go into that right now."

"Why not?" I ask.

"Mana . . ." Lyle puts his hand on my arm, holding me back like I'm being rude, which I'm not.

"Because it's not important," China says, finally meeting my eyes. "I just came here to check in, get some supplies, figure out where the chip and your mom are, and get them, not to have you interrogate Pierce."

"What? You know, China, you keep sighing like I'm such a pain in the ass, which I intend to be if we don't start doing things, like taking action. You're just sitting there at your computer checking your e-mail or something when you should be finding my mom!" I storm over toward them, crossing my arms in front of my chest.

"We *are* doing something, Mana," Pierce says.

"Oh, really? What?"

She points to the monitor in front of her. "We are attempting to locate this."

On the monitor is a picture of a tiny object that resembles a cross between an old iPod Nano and a circle that encompasses all these intricately designed other circles. It's all the size of a fingernail, which I know because there is an actual fingernail on the screen for comparison. I try not to be impressed.

"I don't see you actually searching," I say.

Lyle stands behind me. "Mana, stop being so spazzy."

I whirl on him. "My mom is missing. We were yanked out of a truck by thugs. We're meeting an alien who, granted, is beautiful and cool and everything, but she's only giving us partial answers, and you want me to stop being spazzy?"

"Yes." He actually sort of guffaws, because it's so ridiculous. "Deep breaths?"

That does make me smile. Seppie is always saying that, too, like deep breaths make everything okay.

"What is this, Anger Management 101?" China snarks, ruining it.

Pierce glares at him. "It's a lot to understand, China. You weren't much better when you first started."

"Sure I was," he says, turning away and typing a little too enthusiastically on his keyboard. "Just tell them what they need to know, please. I'm not good at this flying solo. Melissa was always the communicator. You know that."

Pierce ignores him and focuses on us. My skin feels like it's trying to shimmer like hers. It's like goose bumps and happiness combined. Pierce gestures at the monitor. "Have you seen this anywhere at your house?"

I shake my head.

She turns to Lyle. "You?"

"No." His shoulders slump.

She nods. "That's what we thought. Your mother would never be so careless."

"That's for sure. She alphabetizes her magazines on the coffee table," I say. "She puts everything away. And she didn't ever tell me, her own daughter, about all this alien stuff, so I don't think she would have left a piece of intelligence that is so important just hanging out on the kitchen counter. She shreds her grocery store receipts; she is not someone who misplaces things."

Pierce stands up, right next to me. She is so much taller than I am, and when she puts her hands on my shoulders it makes me feel so small. "We need you to think like your mom, Mana."

"So that's why we're here?" I ask.

"We need you to find this for us."

In my brain I somehow hear Pierce's voice say, *Please let her not be an idiot.*

I blink and wobble my head, trying to get the voice out.

"I am not an idiot," I stutter.

Pierce cocks her head like a dog trying to understand. "What?"

"I am not an idiot," I repeat.

"Nobody said you were," China mumbles, crossing his arms over his chest and leaning back.

Lyle shakes his head at me, the way he does whenever I disappoint him, but Pierce just keeps staring. Her thin fingers fiddle with the collar of her flowing shirt. Her eyes meet mine.

You can hear me?

I shrug.

Crap.

I like her more when she swears, and I snort. China figures something is up, I guess, because suddenly he's right next to us, putting his hand on my arm and turning me to face him. "What's going on?"

"Nothing," Pierce says.

Do not let them know you can hear my thoughts.

Why not? I think the words back but don't say them.

China's hand tightens on my arm. "Nothing?"

I try to concentrate as they all stare at me. Lyle's mouth hangs a little open.

"Nothing at all," I say. "I'm just thinking how pretty Pierce is, and worrying, and . . ." My voice cracks. I am the worst liar in the universe.

Just trust me.

"You just need a little space." She turns to China. "Give her some space while you collect your things. It's a lot to deal with." Pierce pulls me over to a console and sits me down in a swivel chair that is a good distance away from everyone. China stares after us for a second, then starts showing Lyle around. The computers buzz so loudly that I can't hear what they say.

I sway a little in the chair and Pierce whispers, "Mana, have you ever heard thoughts? Has this ever happened before?"

I shrug.

"With the Windigo?" she prods.

I'm not sure. Did I hear it say "Exterminate" before it actually said it? It's a good question. And what about that bizarre male voice I heard during the game? At the time, I thought it was stress, but what if it wasn't?

"The Windigos don't have minds to read, not really," Pierce says. She starts pacing back and forth, her long limbs taking her gracefully between workstations, chairs, and tables. Her skin flushes and sparkles even more radically. There is no mistaking her for human. She goes all the way across the room and stops by Beefy Face and Baldy, who are still working on Baldy's shot-up foot. *Can you hear me now?*

I smile and think, *You sound like a cell phone commercial.*

She grins back and almost laughs. She takes Beefy Face's and Baldy's arms. They all stand by the door. Beefy Face's and Baldy's faces blank out, all focus. From what I can hear, she's talking to them, aloud, about security, even as her brain is talking to me. *Has this manifested before recently? Before the events of yesterday?*

I think about it. *No. Why would it start now?*

Sometimes these sorts of talents are latent. Sometimes they're activated on purpose. It doesn't matter why, at this point. Just . . . This is amazing! It's like a yell in my brain. *A few humans have been known to be able to read aliens' brains. If you can read all species, not just fae—*

But why can't we tell them? I nod toward China and Lyle.

It's like you are a secret weapon. We want to keep it a secret.

From them?

From everyone. They will use you. Your life will not be your own. Believe me, I know. But the difference is that I have signed on for this. You? You've been thrust into it without a choice.

Lyle rubs his hand through his hair. He walks toward me. "This is so confusing. All this technology, and alien artifacts. It's amazing, but so confusing."

"I feel your pain," I say, all fake somber, but in truth I sort of feel like spinning around in my chair, because this means . . . this means . . .

We can use your gift to find the chip, Pierce thinks.

And my mother. And the people who took her. I stare at her to get my point across. A grin sweeps across her chiseled features. She has dimples—long, feminine dimples nestled in her perfect skin.

Across the room, Pierce nods. *And your mother.*

CHAPTER 12

We spend the next hour rehashing things in the control room, which, as I've said before, looks exactly like a control room out of a computer geek's dream. Lyle keeps randomly touching the computers, which are everywhere, whirling into overdrive. Screens show little dots of light on black maps of the United States.

I lean over China. "What are these?"

"On my screen? These are the last sightings of the Men in Black."

"Like the guys at my house?"

He clicks a few times and zooms in. All the streets of my neighborhood are listed against tiny lines. Bright dots line most of the streets. "That's the cluster here."

I stare at the map for a second and scrutinize the dots all over the country. "They're all over the place."

He nods, clicks the mouse, and zooms back out. "I know."

"Is this where they've been sighted this year?"

He zooms in on another section of the country. DC, I think. There are tons of dots.

"Is it the last ten years?" I ask.

"It's the last month, Mana," he grumps.

"You are kidding me." I smack him without thinking. He doesn't seem to notice the assault, which is kind of ego deflating, honestly.

"I wish. I'm looking for activity patterns that might lead us to Melissa or the chip. Hopefully both." He glances over at Lyle, who is peppering Pierce with a hundred million questions. She sighs and crosses her arms over her chest. Her thoughts barge into my head: *I am so bored of this.*

I blink her thought out and sway a little bit. China leaps up and sits me down in a chair, pressing his hands onto my shoulders.

"You going soft on me there?" he asks, and it's a cranky thing to say, but his voice is kind.

"No," I answer, pressing my fingers against my eyelids. "I'm good."

His hands stay on my shoulders and he squats down so that we're eye to eye. "We'll find her, Mana."

Something inside me quivers. A light on the ceiling flickers. When my words come out, they sound like little-kid words. "You swear?"

"I swear."

It's right now, right this second, that I trust him. Really trust him. He's got these big shoulders and dark eyes that just seem safe, despite the whole leather jacket, badass attitude. He nods at me, gets up, and motions for me to follow him to another computer terminal far across the room. I want to tell him I can hear Pierce's thoughts, but I don't, because she's right in the room and she . . . I just don't know. I think I trust her, sort of. But . . . I don't want to get her angry. I sure hope she isn't listening to my thoughts right now.

I imagine all the things I might hear aliens think, and ask China, "Do aliens have sex?"

Wow. That's what my brain picked to ask?

It doesn't seem to bother him at all. "Well, they all reproduce in some way. A good majority of them, from what we know, have sex in the human sort of sense. Fae like Pierce do."

"Do they think about having sex?"

"Doesn't everybody?"

"Oh God."

"Why?" He asks.

"No reason," I lie. "It's just creepy."

"All species procreate, at least that we know of." He lifts an eyebrow like he's onto me. "Why are you asking about this?"

"I was . . . I was just wishing I could magically know where my mom was and then I was thinking that it would be creepy to have telepathy with your mom in case she liked someone or could hear me lusting after someone. And then? My brain just kind of skipped to aliens." This, I think, is completely believable and exactly how my brain works.

He stares at me. I can't believe I just did that. I try to retrace our conversation. "I was talking about humans being telepathic. My friend, Seppie, has this wicked ESP thing going on. I swear, she knows whenever anyone has chocolate . . ." I babble this, but I'm thinking about what Pierce said. She said some humans can hear thoughts. But wait . . .

Everything seems to stop in the room. A few images flash in my head. My back tuck, post coffee sip. The amazing gymnastics moves in the locker room.

Pierce stares over at me. I meet her eyes. Her eyes are so . . . so . . . opaque and brilliant all at once. So . . . alien. That's just it. Alien. Otherworldly. Beautiful.

Some humans can read minds. It's rare. More aliens can do it than humans, but not all aliens are capable, just the fae and one other species. But there are not many of us left. You are not fae. And not all alien species' thoughts can be read.

Okay. I think this word. I do not actually feel this word.

Do not worry. You are human. Your mother would have told me if you weren't.

I think about this for a second and I'm not so sure. I don't really even have total proof that my mother was working with them at all. And Pierce doesn't want China to know I read minds. So, obviously, not all the truth is right out there for everyone to see, is it? I want to know why that is. It feels like every tiny bit of information I don't possess could be keeping me from finding my mother. Now I feel like every tiny bit of information also could be keeping me from the truth about myself.

Do you not trust China? I ask.

Of course I do.

Then why am I not supposed to tell him?

It's not about trust. I can feel her thoughts blocking me out. Everyone is blocking me out. Half-truths.

What I need you to do is to focus on the chip and your mother. See if you can hear thoughts that give you hints about where they might be, she says.

Why can't you do that? You're telepathic, too.

Everyone's mind works differently. Our thought patterns resonate on different levels, and when thoughts are hidden, they are especially hard to pick out and discern. It's a bit like sound waves. Some frequencies are easier to hear. Some voices are louder. Only it isn't sound waves; it is thought waves—or energy waves might be a better way of thinking of it.

I touch the computer screen. It's cold, flat. The opposite of my heart. Every single thing about this conversation is rubbing me the wrong way. Pierce has me totally confused about China, so I pace away from him. Heat fills my skin. I stare at the little dots, the little Men in Black sightings all over DC.

"How did you fix your jacket?" I ask.

"What?"

"Your jacket. Alien Dakota put a big hole in the back last night."

He grimaces. "I remember."

"So?"

"It's a spare."

"You have a spare jacket?"

"I like to be prepared." China settles back at his station like nothing's happened.

"He has about twenty-five of them. He's the same way with his pants and shirts and socks," Pierce calls over. "Part of why we love him."

Scoffing, China opens up a computer file just for me. I quickly realize it's a dossier of aliens on Earth—known species and their skills. Dakota of the acid tongue is from a species once likened to leprechauns, greedy miners who crashed on Earth multiple times while trying to exploit the minerals. The acid-spitting ability is theorized to have evolved on their own world as a defense mechanism, much as ants spit formic acid on their predators. Also like ants, they have a hive mentality with a rich hierarchy. Windigos are their workers, basically, doing their bidding.

The file goes on for a while about projectile use by living systems, but I move on to another species: shape-shifting aliens with telepathy skills, a subdivision of the fae, that take on the DNA of a human of their choice. No ideas about how that evolved. I guess it's a bit too much for our little human brains. I'd rather be that kind of alien than the acid boy–Dakota Dunham kind.

Even as my mind tries and fails to find thoughts about the chip or my mom, I keep skimming the files. The next alien is a blob that resembles a sea anemone, which appears pretty harmless. I know I can't be that, so I flip to the next file, but not before first wondering if there are any alien species that resemble penguins. I would be cool with that one.

The truth is, though, I have no idea what I am trying to find in these files, and my mind keeps drifting and wondering what it would mean if Pierce is wrong and I'm not human.

The leaping stuff was cool, but what if I can spit acid? That is disgusting. What if I accidentally spit acid during states and kill the judges? Or incinerate a pom-pom? Or what if I actually get to kiss Lyle someday and acid comes out instead?

I try to make spitting motions discreetly, just to see. China raises an eyebrow.

"Hair in my mouth," I lie.

You are human, I promise, Pierce says into my brain, but can I believe her? *Try to use your thoughts to find the chip and your mother.*

I settle into a tense silence, but Lyle asks everyone about five hundred questions, over and over again, and I just keep getting more and more impatient. We were supposed to be just gathering supplies and having China check in. We've been here forever, and Lyle is still shell-shocked.

"I can't believe this is real," he says a million times. "I can't believe all those freaked-out conspiracy people weren't nuts."

"*You* are one of those freaked-out conspiracy people," I finally say.

"I know." Lyle cracks his knuckles, smiling, and twirls around in his chair. "I can't believe I was right."

"Unfortunately, you are," I snark. "Unfortunately, you are right and my mom is kidnapped or dead somewhere. Yep, I am really, really glad you're right, Lyle."

"Mana . . ." He starts to apologize, but then he just straightens up and goes, "You don't have to be so cranky all the time when you get stressed."

"My mom is missing. How would you feel if your mother was missing?" The moment I say it, I feel badly, because I'm taking all this stress—and now this secrecy—out on him. None of this is Lyle's fault. Lyle is being kind and good, and maybe a little too excited, but still . . .

"Um, kind of happy." He shifts his attention to the very fascinating (not) ceiling. Another long light flickers and goes out. I want to hug poor Lyle now, and I give him what I hope counts as a sympathetic expression and mouth the word *sorry.* China laughs, even though he's pretending to be totally focused on some new map and database, and his fingers fly faster than imaginable over the keyboard.

"So, when are we going to start searching for my mom?" I ask, standing up. I've been listening hard to all the explanations, but it's disturbing to hear Pierce's thoughts all the time. I have to actively try to not pay attention.

"We need an actual lead, a place to look." China rubs his face against his hands. "Think, Mana."

I glance at Pierce. "I have been thinking."

Pierce stands up, too, in one beautiful fluid motion. There's something she isn't telling me . . . I can feel it.

"Go through what you know," she says. "What you've learned here and then what happened in the days leading up to the abduction. Something might jog your memory."

"Okay, once again." I sigh. " I know that China and my mom hunt aliens. And my mom is missing."

"Right."

"And she may have the thing you all are looking for and have hidden it somewhere, but she didn't do anything weird. Like, nothing at all. I can't think of anything different except not being at the game. So, she is probably kidnapped by evil aliens like Dakota. And there are other aliens who do *not* kidnap people, so those ones probably didn't kidnap her. There are some who just watch and observe. There are some who have lived here for centuries, like your people. Right?"

"Right."

Lyle peppers out. "Hey. The Rendlesham Forest incident? Was that real?"

"They were trying to show their strength, landing near two military bases like that," China explains. "Those were Mullys. Arrogant SOBs."

"That is so amazing." Lyle rocks back on his heels. "Everybody says it was nothing. The British were all, 'There is no security threat.'"

Pierce shrugs, but anger flashes in her, somewhere beneath the surface. "What were they supposed to say? 'Aliens are showing off, bullying us, but our presidents, our prime ministers don't even know because the military is too afraid to tell them?' That the military want to handle it themselves because they know how bad it could be?"

I swallow. "Really? Could it be really bad?"

Pierce touches my arm. Baldy, standing by the door, sneezes.

"Yes," she says. "It could be really bad."

Her fears flash inside my head. *Windigos everywhere. Corpses everywhere. People tortured. The planet overrun.*

"And if we find this chip? What is it going to do? It's just going to tell the president that this is happening? I don't get it."

"Okay," Lyle adds. "No offense, but I'm not really a massive believer in the intellectual prowess of our president."

"Big words," China snorts.

"Some of us have brains as well as brawn," Lyle retorts, pulling himself up straighter.

China eyes him. "What brawn?"

Pierce sends a thought at me: *Why must the males of your species always do this alpha-dog posturing?*

I answer aloud by accident. "I have no idea."

"Mana!" Lyle's face fills with hurt.

"That's not what I mean! I meant . . . I have no idea why you guys have to fight all the time," I try to cover.

"It's stupid," Pierce says. *Remember, you can*not *read minds.*

China grins. "I think they're talking about us."

"You wish. You two are so egotistical," I say, and smile to make it not so mean. Then I turn back to Pierce. "Can we just do one final rundown for the television viewers and move on? Okay?"

"Okay." She smiles like it's a relief. Lyle taps his foot, all annoyed.

I continue on. "You have a vested interest in what happens because Earth is your home, too. And for some reason you can't go back to your . . . your . . . home planet place. So you work with people like my mom and try to gather up information so you can inform the world leaders, like our lovely president, what is going on.

Because there is no way that kidnapping people is cool, right? And my mom has the chip that does what exactly . . . ?"

China and Pierce exchange a glance. I'm blocked out of Pierce's thoughts completely.

"It has the evidence to unequivocally prove that aliens exist, and that some are a threat not just to humans but also to other aliens existing currently on this planet," Pierce answers.

I resist the urge to blurt out the word *bullshit*, and instead hook my arm into Lyle's as Pierce suggests we take a tour of the facility. This feels pretty abrupt to me, like a massive change of topic and like a way to keep me from asking questions.

"Lyle . . ." I whisper.

"There's more than one room?! How cool is that? What do you think will be in the other rooms?" He smiles at me.

"Lyle, do you believe that stuff about the chip?"

He cocks his head a little to one side. "What do you mean? You think they're lying?"

I put a finger to my lips. We're walking so slowly Pierce has doubled back to us, so we abandon our conversation and speed up. The compound is all underground. There is a weapons room filled with cell phones and pens and regular old guns, along with netting. There are cages that are currently empty. They remind me of something out of the movies Lyle is always making me watch—all thick glass and bright lights.

"Can the spitting aliens get through those?" I ask Pierce.

"No. Acid-proof," she says, knocking the glass with her knuckles.

She shows us a room filled with lush plants and what must be artificial sunlight. It feels like a forest, a really lush, dense forest. The growth is somehow old, with tree trunks that require three people to hug. Lyle whistles in appreciation. I cannot believe he is whistling again.

"This is my room," she says, inhaling deeply. "My kind don't do·

well in man-made structures away from nature. So we brought nature in here."

"It is so beautiful," I whisper.

"It is," she agrees, and reluctantly takes us through the rest of the compound. There are rooms for guards like Brian and Aaron, guest quarters, a huge industrial kitchen, and even a pool, all underground.

"I expected this whole compound to be more Spartan," Lyle says as he stares longingly at the pool, "and smaller. I expected it to be smaller."

"Well, it *is* underground," I add. "I think that is a natural expectation."

Pierce doesn't say much during our exchange, and she is really professional throughout the tour. Lyle's enthusiasm is adorable—not even adorkable—somehow. But I feel like she's just playing tour guide while China takes forever.

When we're finally back in the main control room area, China says, "Did you show them their bunks for the night?"

"What?" I startle. "We can't stay here. We have to go find my mom."

"This is the best place to do that," Pierce says out of nowhere. "We can monitor things here, search for leads, and keep you safe."

"I do not need to be kept safe! What are you even talking about?"

"Mana, there were Windigos searching for you. A man shot at us on the road. Remember? Whoever has your mom is trying to locate you."

"Then I should be out there! Like a decoy! We could set a trap and snag them, just like in movies and stuff. Right, Lyle?"

Lyle's face reddens. "Absolutely not."

While we were on the tour, Brian's pain medicine for his foot seems to have kicked in. He's limping around pretty well now.

China explains that it is a mixture of alien technology and human toughness that is keeping him up, and acts surprised that Pierce didn't show us the medical room.

"It's his favorite part," she says, rolling her eyes. "He used to want to be a doctor, before he worked here. All the men in his family were, for generations."

"Hard to imagine that," Lyle says, and then we sit at a computer for a while, writing down everything we can remember about the past few days. China and Pierce read over our accounts and China keeps scowling.

"Nothing?" he says. "You remember nothing out of the ordinary?"

Lyle gets angry back. "Calm down, man. We're telling you everything we know, obviously. Mana wrote about twenty pages."

I did twenty-one, actually.

"I'm long-winded," I explain.

"Detailed," Lyle corrects, nicely, and I grant him a happy smile. He smiles back.

China makes a scoffing noise. "None of it matters. There has to be something."

He worries about your mother. A lot. Pierce's thought slides into my head. *He is not used to working alone. He depends on her.*

He is not the only one. I feel like I'm failing him somehow, but more than that, I feel like I'm failing my mother.

"Wait!" I stand up and pace. "I know there's something . . . something I'm forgetting." And then I remember. "The crank call. We got a crank call."

China whirls around and glares at me. He doesn't even say anything, but it is completely obvious that he thinks I'm an idiot. Not a big deal, because right now I'm thinking it, too. "We got this crank call in the middle of the night and I woke up—"

"And this is important *how*?" China's arms cross in front of his burly chest.

"She yelled. Mom yelled into the phone."

His arms drop to his sides. His hand seizes my wrist—not tightly, but in an excited way. "What did she say?"

" 'You better not try it.' " I tell him this as his fingers completely engulf my wrist and actually overlap. Our eyes meet.

"Try what? She never talks like that. Never yells. Not unless it's serious," he says.

"Exactly!"

"You guys are getting all excited about a prank call?" Lyle is still sitting at the computer. His face is stiff.

China ignores him and just keeps at me. "What did she say? Exactly?"

"Seriously. She just said, 'You better not try it.' "

"Anything else?"

"No . . ." I think for a second. What word did I just say . . . *seriously*? . . . It makes me remember. "Yes. She said, 'I am serious.' "

China tightens his fingers around my wrist and then seems to realize it, because he lets go of it completely and repeats, " 'I am serious.' "

I nod. Everyone stares at me. "What?"

"That isn't a normal thing to say to someone prank calling you. You say, 'Shut up.' You hang up the phone. Your mother would just hang up the phone and trace the call."

"She doesn't know how to trace—" I realize in the middle of my sentence that my mom probably knows how to do a lot of things that I would never expect. Like hunt aliens. "So, you're saying it was not a prank call."

"I doubt it." China whirls away, points at Pierce. "See if we can get a trace on all the calls to the residence within the last five days, just to be sure, focusing on that time frame, obviously, and seeing if there are any repeat calls from that number." He points at me now, and then at Lyle as if in afterthought. "You two, I want you to get some food, wash up, go to bed, and think about if there's anything else important you're forgetting."

"Wow. Thanks, Dad." I am snarky. I do not care. I already feel badly enough about not thinking the crank call was important and how I forgot it had even happened until right now.

"I'm not old enough to be your dad," China says.

"You *look* old enough."

He scowls.

"Mean, Mana. That was mean." Lyle drapes an arm across my shoulders and steers me out of the room.

When we're in the hallway, I finally say, "He just has such a superiority complex. I hate superiority complexes. And he is so bossy."

"I can hear you!" China yells through the open door.

"I don't care!" I yell back, acting like a five-year-old, but the truth is, I do care. I am so sorry I'm being such a brat, but I'm stressed and tired and worried, and being dismissed like a useless baby does not feel good.

"I think they have pizza," Lyle says. "I'm pretty sure I saw pizza and some of those pretzels your mom makes in the kitchen."

"Really?" I make a fist. He taps it; we explode them. Pizza and pretzels make everything better. Well, at least a little bit.

*I*n the kitchen, Lyle and I hash out everything that has happened during the day. He listens to me grump and whine and get sad and I ask him whether his mom is going to worry about him.

"I lied and said that I was going to Grayson Staggs's house," he explains. Grayson has ultracool parents who brew beer and have an annual Banff Mountain Film Festival party, and he is Lyle's guy best friend. Grayson would always cover for him.

And Lyle is completely cool and sympathetic and trying not to be too excited about the fact that extraterrestrial life is a reality, but I know he secretly is. He's just trying to tone it down because he's a good enough guy to know that the priority right now is finding my mom. And I love him for that, I really do.

After we have heated up pizza in one of the ridiculously large ovens, and after we have each eaten about half of an extra-large Veggie Delite, Lyle puts down his half-eaten piece and says, "Hey, you know I'm going to be here for you no matter what happens. Okay?"

The sincerity of it makes tears come to my eyes. "Okay," I manage to say, as he pats my hand across the kitchen counter. "Okay. Me, too."

"Best buds, forever, right?"

"Friends are friends. Pals are pals. But buddies sleep together," I respond.

He wiggles his eyebrows. "Awesome."

That night, I sleep in a bed I'm not used to, in a room that is just white walls. Lyle's room is next to mine. I miss him so much, but not quite as much as I miss my mom. Closing my eyes only makes me feel more disconnected from them and the rest of the world. How come sometimes the more you know, the lonelier you become? I mean, seriously, I'm not sure what I'm supposed to do when my world breaks apart and there is nothing I can do to stop it. I stare at the ceiling. I try to swallow down the horror of how helpless I am and how alone I feel.

The next day is more of the same. More lectures about aliens and the government. More conspiracy theories that are real. We all gather in the big computer room. The crank caller's number had been blocked, but they managed to trace it to an apartment near where my father lives, which they are excited about, I guess. Brian and Aaron want to go alone and recon the place, but China argues with them that their job right now is to protect the compound and Pierce and us, that *he* should go because my mom is his partner, and so on. This argument lasts for pretty much ever and I have to put my head down next to the computer, bored and tired of all the talk-talk-talk. We need to act, honestly. We need to do something. *I* need to do something.

A voice, not Pierce's voice, rushes into my head, interrupting my own thoughts. One word, angry and determined: *Now.*

Now?

The door to the room bangs open and freaking Dakota Dunham, who is so no longer attractive to me in any way, flies in, tearing at Brian with his hands, spitting acid stuff in his face, and taking him down before I can blink. Aaron shoots at him. The bullets sink in, but the alien/boy/thing just drops Brian, turns to Aaron, and smiles.

Another man appears behind him—blond, fair, and facially looking pretty much like a guy version of Pierce.

"Get out!" Pierce screams at me, pushing me toward the back of the room. Her hands are solid, forceful. Her hair whips around her head like it's alive. "China, take them!"

"But you—" he starts to say. His hand is on a gun. He is about to jump into the fight.

"I will handle this," she insists. She leaps over a row of computers and starts toward Dakota the acid-mouth boy. "The children are more important."

Children? She's calling us children?

Her thoughts are a blur of worry and anger. I can't get through them, but then one clear string of thoughts bursts through: *Must keep the girl safe. More important. Fight. More important. The weapon.*

How can we be more important? I back up. I want to run. I want to close my eyes and wake up in my bed, which is even wimpier. Instead, I lift up a computer monitor and heave it at Dakota's face. It makes a satisfying thumping noise as it hits the side of his skull. Dakota pivots toward me, all disgusting, gross face and acid tongue and evil eyes. How did I ever think he was cute? Seriously?

"You little jerk! Get the hell out of here!" I scream, in what is one of the worst threatening voices of all time, more of a squeak, really. I grapple for another monitor. "What did you do to my mother?"

"Mana." China yanks my arm, pulls me over a tangle of computer cables. Lyle is sprinting across the room in front of me, heading for a back door I didn't even notice during our tour of the compound. I guess they didn't actually show us everything.

Something/someone behind us yowls.

Something else shrieks.

Pierce! I scream her name in my head as China drags me toward the door.

Go, Mana! Do not let China know anything about you—anything strange. Hide it. Promise me!

Pierce!

"We have to help," I try to say, but China yanks me along so fast that I'm not sure if my words actually make it out of my mouth. I turn to try to see what is happening and if I can help. My bag is right in front of me. I grab it without thinking.

"Get down," China says, all commanding, ducking while he runs, and pushing me down, too.

"Why?"

"Just get down!"

Something green flies through the air above our heads, just barely missing Lyle, who ducks at the last second. The green liquid hits the wall fizzing and searing, and burns it. Lyle reaches out and wrenches open the door. He turns his head to make sure we're still with him, and his eyes widen with shock or fear. Something bad is going on behind us. I start to turn my head to see.

"Go, Mana. Go!" China pushes me through the door and then barrels behind me, pulling Lyle with him. "Move!"

He crashes his body into the door, slamming it shut. He bolts it and then touches a keypad. We are in a long hallway again, concrete. Closed doors leading to other spaces interrupt the walls just about every five feet.

"That probably won't hold him," he pants, motioning for us to run forward again. We do. "Keep running."

We get two-thirds of the way down the hall when China yanks open a door that appears to be the same as all the others.

"Get in. Get in. Hurry," he urges. His gun is no longer holstered.

Lyle and I bang into a room the size of an elevator. The walls are shiny metal, like cookie sheets or aluminum foil. It smells like popcorn for some reason, and for a hysterical moment I think maybe we are in a giant version of one of those metal Jiffy Pop popcorn bucket things that you cook over the burner of your stove, shaking it back and forth, back and forth.

"Mana? You okay?" Lyle's face is white with shock.

I shake my head no and he gives me a quick one-armed side hug. My bag smooshes in between us. China follows us into the room and presses buttons on a side panel. The door shuts. The room moves up like we're going to a different floor. I catch Lyle by his arm when we lurch sideways.

"Elevator?" I ask, panting or hyperventilating. "Are we in an elevator?"

China's face shifts into something serious. "Sort of."

I lean against Lyle a little bit. He's not winded, but I can tell he's upset, from the way he's standing so rigidly. "What do you mean, 'sort of'?"

China doesn't answer.

"China?" I am so not letting him off the hook.

"People tried to kill us back there," Lyle suddenly spurts out. "Or a thing tried to kill us, I guess. I guess that's more accurate. Right? In the past forty-eight hours I've been almost murdered twice. Twice!"

China nods at me. "You might have to slap your boyfriend. He's getting a little hysterical."

"I'm not hysterical," Lyle goes, just as I say, "He is not my boyfriend."

China just leans against the wall. "Right. So, it's like an elevator, but not. It's more like a transporter."

"Like on *Star Trek*." Lyle manages to sound normal again. I let go of his arm.

"Right." China straightens up and stands, legs apart, facing the door. "We're getting off just about now."

CHAPTER 13

Worry robs me of my ability to breathe. I think of Pierce, fighting there, alone with Brian and Aaron. I've seen what Dakota Dunham can do. They could be dead. They could be dying. I just met them and they are already gone. I don't even know anything about their lives or their families or their favorite kinds of ice cream or anything that makes them special or individual, or even if Pierce eats food or the nectar of certain rare flowers grown only in Switzerland. This lack of knowledge somehow makes their potential loss even more devastating.

I think all this as we wait for the doors to open.

"Any second now," China says, almost sheepishly.

Lyle gives me big eyes. I take his hand and squeeze it. He squeezes back.

"Really . . . Any second now." China groans. "It always does this. I always complain to Pierce and she says it's fixed. It's never fixed."

His voice breaks a bit when he says "Pierce." For a second, China has let his guard down. The door slides open. China barely surveys the scene to see if there are any evil acid-spewing drummers in sight. He just jumps out of the elevator/room thingy and motions for us to hurry after him.

We step out into a living room with a large, leather sectional sofa, a big flat-screen TV with three red Netflix envelopes in front of it, and a rattan-and-wire container that holds about one hundred old-fashioned CDs. A Bose stereo belts out Andrea Bocelli, this opera singer my dad's into.

"Where are we?" Lyle asks. He still holds my hand. It feels good. It's about the only thing that feels good as I take in my dad's apartment.

"You want to answer him, Mana?" China says. He grabs the thick, white remote for the Bose stereo system and turns the volume level down from thirty to a more decent eighteen. It's still loud, but you can hear people talk without having them yell. He takes a closer look at the display. "It's on repeat. It could have been playing for hours."

"Earth to Mana. Where are we?" Lyle lets go of my hand and pulls on my sleeve.

"My dad's apartment," I answer. "How . . . How did we get here?"

Lyle and I turn around and check out the door we just went through. The elevator is gone. "That's the door to my father's bedroom."

I yank it open. It's not metal. It's not shiny. It's just my dad's bedroom. There's a white down comforter on the bed. His razor charges on the outlet in the wall by the foot of the bed. There's even the ironing board he never puts away, just hanging out by the bureau.

"Explain this," I demand.

China straightens his spine, showing his exasperation in a somehow military way. "We were in a transporter."

Lyle whistles. Again.

At this point, I'm not even surprised anymore. "You transported us here? To my dad's apartment? Why?"

China doesn't answer.

Lyle does, all brave and calm and inquisitive. "Is Mana's dad involved in this, too?"

"No." China is rummaging through the remote controls. "He's not. But he's still close to Mana and her mom, and he has failed to appear at his workplace for two days."

Lyle crosses the room in a flash, gets ahold of China's collar, and waggles him, which is so totally out of character that I freeze for a moment and watch. "You knew this? You knew Mana's dad was missing and you're only telling us now?"

Lyle never grabs people.

Lyle is stoic.

Lyle is calm in a crisis.

"Back off, grasshopper." China shrugs him away like he's a fly. "I haven't exactly had a chance, have I?"

I slump onto the sofa. The leather is cold against the back of my head.

Lyle sits next to me and takes my hand in his. "Mana?"

I don't answer.

"I think she's in shock," Lyle says, dropping my hand, standing up, and tromping back over to China. "You put her in shock."

"And? You want me to elevate her feet or what? She's fine. She's much tougher than you give her credit for," China answers. He puts down the remotes, picks up my dad's phone, and starts pressing numbers.

Lyle comes back over and pushes my head down between my knees.

"I am not going to faint, Lyle."

His hand rubs my back in sweet, big circles. "I know. Just humor me, okay? You're looking pale."

"Both my parents are . . . gone." There is no other word for it. Gone.

I haul in a breath, smelling leather couch and fabric softener from my jeans. "They could be dead, Lyle." The realization hits me so hard that I hiccup. "I'm all alone."

His hand stops. "You're not alone."

My head snaps up. My body follows. "How do you figure that, Lyle, huh? Both my parents are gone."

He doesn't smile. He doesn't frown. He just says, "Because I'm here."

China turns around to face us. There is something guarded in his eyes, and he just stares for a second. Tension makes him stand a little taller. He pulls his coat around him, zips it up, and pockets my dad's phone. "We should get going."

"What? Why?" I stand up and pick up my bag from where I dropped it. "Why did we even come here?"

"I was hoping for a clue. Plus, the transporter was last configured for here, so it was easy," he says. "Do you think your dad would mind if we got ourselves a quick snack?"

He strides into the kitchen and pulls open a cabinet that has glasses in it. He shuts it, tries another. "Does your dad have any chips or anything? I'm starved."

I yank open a drawer near the refrigerator. "Crackers."

"Beautiful!" China takes the package from me. "Wheat Thins? Those aren't crackers. They're like fake chips mated with salt."

Lyle follows us in. "That's what I say."

"I hate them," China continues, opening the box anyway and shoving his hand inside.

"You guys are bonding over crackers?" This is unbelievable. "What about my dad? What about Pierce and Brian and Aaron? They could be dead."

"Hopefully, they aren't. Um, I'm going to use your dad's bathroom, okay?" Lyle asks.

"Sure," I say. Lyle moves closer to me. His hands touch my elbows and then slide up to my shoulders. "We will find a way through this," he says. He bends down and pulls me into a hug. His chin rests on top of my head. He smells so good—like comfort and strength with a side of smart thrown in. "We will find your mom and dad. We will be okay. Okay?"

"Okay," I mutter into his chest as he kisses the top of my head and lets go.

Once Lyle is safely away in the bathroom, China holds the box of crackers out to me. I snatch it away and say, "I'm serious. No crackers until I get some answers."

China meets my eyes. "We need to go because they could track us here. I need to get you to a safe location so that I can figure out what to do next, so you can figure out where your mom might have stashed the chip."

I nod. "What about Pierce?"

He walks toward the door, flings it open. "She's probably dead."

I catch him by the sleeve of his jacket. "What? Don't you care?"

"Of course I care." He doesn't pull his arm away, just examines me, glancing down while steaming. "What do you want me to do?"

"Mourn, maybe?" I shoot back. "Cry. Wear black. Act freaking sorry at least."

He puts his big, heavy fingers on top of mine. His fingers hide mine completely. I can't think of what to do, or remember how to move.

I gaze up at him. His eyes have lost the cocky crap that is usually in there. They soften into something else and then . . . it's gone. Just gone. He is hard and tough again. He moves his hand off of mine. He pulls his arm free of my fingers.

He says, "I'm sorry, Mana. We don't have time to mourn. Not yet."

"When will we have time?"

"When we find your mother."

"And the chip? And my dad?"

He is zipping up my coat for me. His hands seem big, like they could wrap around my entire circumference. I bet he would be a fantastic base, like Lyle. I bet he would never let me fall. This must be killing him—to be stuck with us. To not be fighting, with Pierce. To have lost my mom somehow. His eyes meet mine.

"And the chip. Not too sure about your dad."

After Lyle comes out of the bathroom, he's a bit ruffled, like maybe this is all starting to get to him. Maybe he only went in there so I wouldn't see him worry. I flash him an encouraging thumbs-up. He barely acknowledges it. China leads us through the hallways of Dad's apartment building. We move silently through the sterile, ugly, yellowing halls. Lyle says nothing. He doesn't even try to be encouraging. As we walk, we pass brown doors marked with gold numbers. I imagine Pierce, her amazing hair, the way her brain thought things so clean and steady, like she knew exactly what she was doing at all times. I am not sure what I'm doing at all times, or even most times. I would like to be more like her, like an alien. How odd is that? And now she's probably dead.

The walls of the apartment building seem to sway. China opens a door to a stairwell I never knew existed. As we walk, Lyle's silence begins to freak me out, because I seriously thought we had a moment back in the apartment. I soft-jab him with my elbow and say, "You're too quiet."

His head pivots as he meets my eyes, then he clears his throat.

"You really know your way around here," Lyle says, as China motions us through a door into the stairwell area. Flights of stairs reach up and down. "Why is that?"

China doesn't answer, just shuts the door and locks it behind us.

"That's a fire hazard," I say. "If there's a fire, people could get hurt. They won't be able to get into the stairway to get out."

China stares at me for a second, blinking hard.

"I don't believe you," he says.

"She's a softie," Lyle explains, jabbing me in the side with his elbow, just like everything is normal and we're just horsing around, tormenting each other like we do every day on our way to school, or at practice, or when we're just hanging out. I lean closer to him because it's so normal and familiar. He keeps soft-jabbing me. He smells a tiny bit like pine soap. My dad must have switched soaps in the bathroom. He's always been a lavender or mint Softsoap kind of guy.

"There's nothing wrong about being empathetic," I snap. "People always act like caring is a bad thing."

"Children! Children!" China interrupts, all mock authority figure despite his leather jacket and battle-fatigued face. "No more fighting. Play nice."

He starts thundering down the stairs and Lyle takes off after him, but I just stand there at the top of the staircase, because inside my head I am hearing something, hearing some*one*, and that something/someone is not me.

I wait. Everything is that ugly industrial white paint. The stairs go up above me. The stairs go down below me. The smell of old shoes, new paint, and stale air is totally not comforting. I stand there and listen really hard. Then I hear it again, and I absolutely, positively can identify this voice in my head. It's not alien at all, and it says, *Don't trust him.*

"Who?" I say. "Don't trust who? China? Lyle?"

But it can't mean Lyle . . . because the voice sounds exactly like him.

The voice doesn't answer. Someone jiggles the handle on the doorway to the staircase. It doesn't move. It's locked, but people can pick locks. Aliens can probably acid-breathe right through them. Imagine what aliens could do to flesh. My ankle throbs where the Windigo got it.

Panic hits me. I pound up the stairs instead of down before I realize what I'm doing, what a stupid choice that is, since China and Lyle went down, but it's all flight-or-fight in scary situations, right? We learned that in bio class. Right now, it's flight, up flights. I race up one flight, another, and then a man in a black suit bashes the door open. There's another guy behind him. They both step into the stairwell. I push myself back against the wall and take off again, leaping more than running, bounding up five stairs at a time like a cat woman. One more double flight of stairs and I'll hit the top. I hope to God there is a freaking door to the roof.

"You see them?" Man in Black Suit #1 asks, in this beautifully polished voice.

"No. I'll go down. You go up," Man in Black Suit #2 answers.

They separate. Man in Black Suit #1 takes the stairs army quick, like he's used to the stepper at the Y. Well, I've done my step machines, too, baby, and my squats and herkies, and I'm a freaking gymnastics/cheerleading machine. I sling myself up as quickly and quietly as possible. Five steps at a time. Seven. I use the railing to help propel me forward. Still, my heart races faster than my legs.

The door is right in front of me.

Lyle's voice sounds far away: *Don't trust him.*

Who? How are you talking to me this way? Are you an alien? Lyle?!

No answer.

I wish this telepathy thing were a little more controllable. I yank open the door. It says NO ADMITTANCE in big red letters that I totally ignore. Tumbling outside onto the roof, I hope suit man knows how to read.

The smell of heating units is what assaults me first: metallic, hot, heavy, and nauseating. The surface of the roof is completely coated with an inch of wet puddles and I slosh into it, soaking my sneakers. I pivot and slam my body against the door. I have to lock it, somehow, or else I have to run, hide somewhere on the top of the building. Nothing. There's nothing except the heating vent.

The guy is banging up the stairs behind the door, getting closer. His footsteps clank on the metal. Crap. Wind blows debris across the roof—pieces of paper, a McDonald's bag. There's nowhere to go and I know, I *know*, I am not big enough to keep this door shut against some guy's weight.

Crap. Crapcrapcrapcrap.

I lunge away from the door, slosh as fast as I can across the roof, and duck behind the heating vent. My dad's apartment building is on the edge of the Merrimack River. There's a curving asphalt walking path below me, surrounded by wet bushes. Concrete posts line it. It's too far down to jump. Eight stories down. Next to this building is another apartment building, one story smaller, one alley away.

There is no time. There is nowhere to hide.

I run as hard as I can—*Don't think, don't think*—and vault, launching my body forward. I squeeze my eyes shut. One word flashes through my mind and I'm not sure if it's my own word or someone else's: *idiot*.

Bam.

My feet hit something solid. I somersault forward and bang back up to my feet like I'm in some Olympic floor routine, ready to power vault into an Arabian. My eyes open. I'm on the other roof. Holy God. I did it. I smash toward the door that leads into the building just as bullets whistle over my shoulder.

"Don't shoot! Don't shoot!" I yell.

He doesn't listen. I dive toward the door, slip, fall. Water splashes wet and cold into my chest and on the front of my jeans. I force myself back into a standing position. My hand wraps around the cold metal handle of the door. Locked. Crap.

The guy is running across the roof of my dad's apartment building, building up speed. His tie billows over his shoulder. His gun hand is pumping for momentum. He's going to jump.

I yank at the door handle, kick the door. Nothing. It refuses to open. I glance up to see the Man in Black leave the apartment building roof. He flies through the air like he is doing some sort of parkour move. His legs scissor like he's still running, but he loses speed. His body slams against the side of the building, but it's too low. Just one hand clutches the edge.

I let go of the door and run over. He dangles there, his gun dropped. His head tilts up at me.

"Take my hand," I order him.

He does, clenching his fingers around my wrist. "You can't pull me up. You're not strong enough."

"Just don't let go."

Seagulls squawk in the distance.

"Believe me," he rasps. "I don't want to."

But I can tell, we can both tell, that he's not going to have much of a choice. I try to brace my legs against the little lip of the wall. My shoulders and arms quiver from his weight. "Just hold on. Your partner. He'll get here, right? He'll notice you're gone."

I can't see his eyes because of his sunglasses, but his voice shifts. He's resigned. He has already given up. "Mana."

"You know my name."

His fingers twitch around my wrist. "Mana. Don't trust anyone."

"What?"

"Don't trust the guy in the leather. If you have to, trust your boy-friend. Just not him."

"China?" I can't believe this. "No offense, but he's not the guy shooting at me."

"He's not who you think he is." The man's eyes stare into mine.

I lift an eyebrow. "Oh? Who is he, then?"

"Rogue. He and your . . . Dealing with something they don't understand. So dangerous." The man swallows. I can see his Adam's apple move. "Just don't trust him."

"Don't worry about talking right now. Keep holding on," I order him, but I'm buckling under the strain.

"The chip . . . If it gets activated, it is the end. Some things should not be unleashed. You can't control this."

And then he lets go.

CHAPTER 14

I n movies and those television crime drama shows, when
someone falls off a building, it is always in slow motion. The
camera focuses on the falling guy's face—yeah, it's usually a
guy. Women are too smart to fall off buildings. Women would
keep hanging on. Anyway, in movies the guy's arms windmill
in slow motion. His jacket flaps like a useless kite. His eyes register
shock and then fear, because he knows that he has no chance to
survive, and the person left on the roof watches, watches, watches
with the camera, noticing every nuance before the splat that is death.

That's not really how it is.

People fall fast.

And they don't fall just flat on their backs. They shift around as
gravity takes them. You can't see their faces for more than a second
after they let go.

And I have got to believe that is a good thing. That's the truth. I
have got to believe that is a really good thing as all the shaking in
my fatigued arm seems to spread across my entire body. Everything
shudders and wobbles and jiggles. And I back up and slump down
onto the snow, cross my legs, and just sit there.

That man just died. I was holding his hand and then he let go.
And he's gone.

He said I can't control the chip, that something would be
unleashed. What did he mean?

A seagull screeches and lands on the tip of the little concrete outcropping with the locked door. It's like my head moves in slow motion and I turn to stare at the bird, full-on. The snow makes him appear a little grayer than he should. His beak, though, is this brilliant yellow. He eyes me.

"I tried to hold on," I whisper. My breath comes out in cold puffs. The puffs disappear into the rest of the air, just kind of dissipate and vanish there.

The gull shifts its weight to one foot, hops a little, puts his other foot back down.

"Honestly," I tell it. "I tried. He let go."

My cell phone rings. It's buried in the pocket of my coat. My fingers fumble with my zipper, manage to get it down, manage, somehow, to reach inside the inner pocket and pull the thing out. I flip it open without even checking to see who is calling.

"Mana. Where are you?" China's voice, not my mom's, not my dad's, not Lyle's.

I don't answer.

The man said not to trust him.

The Lyle voice in my head said not to trust someone. Maybe him. Probably him.

He comes at me again. "Mana? You okay? You hurt? Are you compromised?"

"Compromised?"

"Are you a hostage?"

"Oh." My voice is a quiet whisper of fear. "No."

His voice calms down, loses its edge. "Tell us where you are. We will come get you. Are you still in the building?"

I swallow. "No. I'm on the roof of the building next door. The door is locked and I'm stuck."

"How'd you get there?"

"Long story."

"Okay. Never mind. Shut up, Lyle. She's fine. Didn't I tell you she'd be fine?" His voice is muffled and then clear. "We'll be right there."

"Okay," I say, but he's already disconnected the line.

The gull cocks its head at me.

I stand up, brush off my bottom, try not to tremble too much. "What? Who am I supposed to trust? He and Lyle are all that's left, okay? Give me a break, bird."

The gull lifts its cold wings, flaps once, and flies away.

"Whatever," I say. The edge of the building is just a few feet away. I wonder, if I tiptoe to it and stare down, what I would see. No, I know what I would see. A man who used to be alive, splayed out on a snowy alley, blood staining the snow. I would see someone dead, really dead, because I couldn't hang on well enough, because I failed and he let go.

Don't trust him, the Lyle voice says again. It's so far away that I can barely make it out. *Don't trust him, Mana.*

Who?

Don't trust him.

"Shut up," I snarl, and I turn away from the edge of the roof and go to wait by the door. If I can't trust Lyle, who can I trust? And Lyle is with China. So that is where I will go.

It's Lyle who lets me off the roof. It's Lyle who yanks me into a big old hug and says, "I thought they apprehended you. I thought you were dead."

My mouth tastes pine-smelling sweatshirt fabric. The heat from Lyle's body makes my mouth warm. I turn my head, press my cheek against his chest, and relax for about half a second, and then I pull away. I don't want to. I just know I have to. This is no time for random hugging.

"I thought I was, too," I say.

Sirens start in the distance. I want to ask him if he's talking inside my head, but I—something holds me back, some sort of gut feeling.

Lyle touches my face and says emphatically, "We have to get out of here. Okay? Get somewhere safe?"

"Okay." And then I realize something. He's alone, without the big bad bodyguard commando in leather. "Where is China?"

"He's trying to give the guys a bad scent. At least, that's what he said, which makes no sense." Lyle holds the door open for me and keeps talking after I shoot through and start down the stairs. "Bad scent? They're not dogs. Anyway, he's trying to lose them. He sent me up here to get you."

"That seems stupid. We should all stick together."

"He trusts me." Lyle is practically preening.

"That's quite a turnaround."

Lyle flashes a smile. "What can I say? I'm personable."

We clatter down the stairs. I turn to start down another flight. "Personable? That is such an old-lady word."

"Fine. Charming?"

"No better. You already got into Dartmouth; you can lay off the big words. You already took your SATs."

He laughs. He is just one step behind me.

"It's good to hear you laughing, Lyle," I say.

"It's not inappropriate? With your mom missing and everything?"

"Probably." We make it down another flight. Just a couple more to go. "But it's still good. Mom would say that it is our ability to laugh that makes us human. Even in the worst times, you know? We can still find something funny. And that gives us hope."

"Makes us human," Lyle says in a whisper. He's obviously a little freaked out by everything. So am I. "You haven't remembered anything more explicit about where the chip might be? We're alone now, so if there's something you've been too worried to tell anybody . . ."

"Nothing." I sigh. I am slightly amused that Mr. Runner seems more winded than I am.

"You're sure?" He touches my arm and huffs out the sentence.

"Sure." I stop for a second, stare at him. "Are you really out of breath?"

"Asthma."

"You don't have asthma."

"I know! I'm trying to joke."

"You had me worried for a second, man."

"You care so much about me." He smiles again, but it's forced. I don't like it, and I change the subject, walking again down the stairs.

"So where are we meeting China?" I ask.

We finally make it to the bottom. The big red EXIT sign hangs over a fire door. I wonder what we'll see when we open it and step outside. More alien freaks? A dead guy on the ground? Police officers in full body armor waiting to arrest us?

"We're meeting him at Martha's."

"Martha's?"

He nods at the door. "It's a diner. Are you going to open the door?"

I pause, waiting, trying to calm my nerves, and finally admit, "I'm kind of afraid."

"*You* are afraid? You're never afraid, are you? You do all that flying for cheerleading."

I squint at him, because all of a sudden he's acting fuzzy. "I'm always afraid, Lyle. You know that."

"Huh." He pushes the door open. "I thought you were the bravest girl I know."

"The bravest girl you know?"

"What?"

"You're talking like Mrs. Fuller, the librarian."

"Stress." He laughs again. It's a little too loud.

It doesn't take long to get to the diner, but it feels like ages that we're out there on the street, exposed, vulnerable. I narrow my eyes at every person who comes close, trying to figure out if they're human or just pretenders. While we're waiting for a table at Martha's, I lean against Lyle, because I'm tired and I know he'll let me. Not only does he let me, he puts his arms around me. It seems our ratio of touching versus not touching has increased as rapidly as his use of big words in everyday sentences.

I shift my weight a little bit, but he keeps his arms there. It should feel good, but it doesn't. It doesn't feel right. Lyle should be more awkward about this, because we aren't boyfriend/girlfriend; we're just best friend/best friend. His arms should be less tight, right? Or maybe it's me . . . Maybe all this stress, seeing the man die, is freaking me out.

"Tired?" Lyle whispers. His lips are so close to my ear. I swear they're almost touching my skin or one of my studs.

I half shrug.

"My dad . . . My dad, too . . . It's just so unbelievable." I can't think of what else to say.

"It'll be over soon," he says.

"You think so?"

A waitress motions for us to follow her.

"Absolutely."

"Absolutely?" I straighten up. He lets me go. "Yay for you, with the multisyllabic words."

"Multisyllabic is a pretty multisyllabic word itself," he says as we sit down.

"Thanks," I say to the waitress, as she hands us some laminated menus. I thank her again, but Lyle doesn't.

I think about that for a second. Lyle always says thank you. Lyle is polite to a fault.

I eye him. "What are you getting?"

"Breakfast all day. So . . . a sausage breakfast sandwich on a bagel." He puts down the menu and smiles at me.

Everything inside of me shudders and freezes.

I force myself not to react. "That was quick."

He just keeps smiling.

I make myself smile back.

The thing is: Lyle is a vegetarian. That's why we had veggie pizza instead of pepperoni and pineapple, which is my favorite.

"So," I say, putting my menu down, too. "Do you think China will be here soon?"

"Probably." Lyle sips his water. His Adam's apple slides up and down just like it normally does. Maybe he just likes sausage now. Maybe danger has made him into a carnivore. I blink hard, trying not to imagine him having one of those acid tongues behind sharp *Tyrannosaurus rex* teeth.

Our waitress takes an order at the next table. A kid at another booth starts whining while his mom orders a meatloaf special. I make myself tune it out and focus on Lyle. There are the same wide eyes, the same shock of maple brown hair. There is the Lyle smile, with normal, human teeth. But maybe the eyes aren't quite the same. Maybe there are talons behind them, something sharp, unknowable, un-Lyle-able. And he smells like pine. Maybe my dad didn't get new soap.

I decide to take a risk, a calculated question. I pick up a sugar packet and start fiddling with it. "So, your mom was so nice about everything the other night."

"Yes," he says. His fingertip traces a line down the side of his water glass. "She's pretty understanding. She likes you."

"She's always so calm. I wouldn't have imagined anybody's mom would be so calm when stuff like that happens."

"Your mom would be," he says.

"Oh, she's not as mellow as your mom," I lie. "Nobody is as mellow as your mom."

"True." Our eyes meet.

I try a new tactic. "I think I'll get a coffee. You want a coffee?"

"Good idea."

Lyle knows I don't drink caffeine. I press my lips against each other, try to be calm Mana, cool Mana, nonpanicking Mana . . . try to be more like Lyle normally is, actually. I lean forward across the tabletop. "Listen, I really have to pee. Will you order for me if she comes while I'm gone?"

"Sure." He focuses all his attention down at the menu in his hands. "What do you want?"

I'm already getting up, hauling my bag with me, and moving past the waitress, who is still negotiating the order at the table behind us. I toss the words over my shoulder. "Blueberry pancakes."

He repeats it. "Blueberry pancakes. And coffee. Right? Why are you taking your bag?"

"Um . . . uh . . . girl issues," I whisper, and try to make a really embarrassed expression.

His eyebrow raises. Just one of them. I make one last effort. "Plus, Mr. Manateeman is in there. You know how I am about manatees."

Penguins. How I am about penguins.

"Yes. Such a soft heart." He points a fork at me. "Don't be too long."

"Just one sec. I swear." It's all I can do not to run full throttle past everyone sitting in their comfy upholstered booths. It's all I can do not to scream and panic and hyperventilate. It's all I can do to just carefully walk back to the restroom. I pull on the door. Locked.

"One minute," some lady calls out in a happy singsong voice.

"Sorry." My answer is automatic, polite.

I stare at the picture of a woman on the door and at the braille dots beneath it. I clutch my arms with my hands. I will not glance back at the pseudo Lyle. I will not glance back.

I glance back.

He's watching. His face arranges itself into a smile and he waves.

"Someone is in it." I mouth the words and point at the door with my thumb.

Lyle rolls his eyes. He makes hand motions like banging on the door. I fake laugh and gaze away. Everything inside me trembles, swirls in on itself, barely hanging on, barely staying in place.

What is going on? Has he been hit on the head? Lost his memory? Is he brainwashed? Controlled by some sort of alien force? A robot? Maybe he's a robot! An android? Is that what they call them? All I know is he's not normal Lyle. I have no idea who he is, or what he is, but he is definitely not normal Lyle.

Lyle would not let me have caffeine.

Lyle would not eat meat or smell like pine.

Lyle would not just be like, "Oh, of course you love manatees," when I love penguins.

Lyle would not say his mother was *mellow*.

I wave at him again. He fake yawns. He seems normal. Maybe I'm imagining things.

But no, I know I'm not. He was out of breath on the stairs, going *down* the stairs even. He runs distance. He got recruited to an Ivy for running distance. He never gets out of breath.

Someone flushes. Then there's the sound of running water, someone pulling paper towels out. The door unlocks and opens. A waitress scoots out and I scoot in, lock the door, examine the place.

It's a tiny bathroom. Used brown paper towels lay abandoned by the stained metal basket. One of those water-stained drop ceilings makes everything seem dingier. There is no window and therefore no escape.

"Crap," I mutter.

I double-check the lock, take out my cell, and type in Lyle's number. It makes a funny noise and the display reads NETWORK BUSY.

"Oh my God."

I try my dad's number, even though I know he won't answer. I get the same thing. Network busy. My fingers tremble and I try 9-1-1. Network busy.

It's no use. There must be a block on my phone. The whole thing is pointless now. I toss the phone in the trash with all the wet, crumpled paper towels. Someone tries the door. I scoop my cell back out because, honestly, if I do find my mom again, she is not going to be happy with me throwing away something so expensive.

"One second," I say.

There is no way out. No window. Just four walls and a ceiling.

A ceiling.

I vault up onto the sink and push at the ceiling tiles with my hands. I get one out and to the side. Gripping the edge of the supporting wall that separates the bathroom from someplace else, I yank myself up in a perfect pull-up, which we practice at cheering, and—boom!—I'm through the hole. It is not pretty up here. I barely fit between the wires and the wall edge. I cram in, fetal, pathetic, my bag shoved in with me. This is the first place someone will search. I push the tile back in place. Light leaks through the tiles, for which I am thankful, and I can see just enough to manage.

The wall edges north and south and then connects with another wall. I creep along it, dragging my bag, figuring that maybe I can get to another room, move another ceiling tile, and hop down into an office. It's stupid. It's the best I can do.

Someone pounds on the door.

I skitter faster and get to the spot where the walls meet. I move beyond that, trying not to sneeze from the dust and the ceiling particles that swirl around like dirty snow. Then I lose my balance. My foot shoots into a ceiling tile and breaks through. The rest of my body, unfortunately, follows. I scramble, trying to get a hold on something solid, but I'm not quick enough. I fall, belly first, but I tuck forward and turn. Bam. I hit the floor, feet first at least, in a good stuck landing, just like at the end of a particularly difficult tumbling run.

"Holy sugar diabetes!" a woman in a white apron swears. She drops the pitcher of pancake batter in her hand.

"Sorry. Sorry." I try to actually use some observational skills. I'm in the kitchen. Things steam on massive metal grills. There are bowls and spatulas everywhere. A guy stares up at me, away from the steel counter where he is chopping onions with a massive knife. My heart beats so hard that I can feel the pulse of it even in my fingers. I manage to stand up straight. "Sorry."

The woman bends, starting to wipe up the batter. "Holy Gobsmackers, what are you doing?"

I give her some paper towels, trying to fight the urge to just run away.

"My boyfriend . . . he's out there." I force my voice to sound panicked. It is not a hard fake. "He's . . . he's really mad at me. He hit me this morning and he said he won't let me go back home and I . . . He scratched up my ankle."

I pause.

The man with the onion stares at me, basically flabbergasted. That's a word my mom would use, but it's perfect: flabbergasted.

"Oh my glory." The lady taps my wrist to make me stop wiping at the gooey batter. "We have to call the police."

"No. We . . . His dad is a cop." I am turning into such a good liar.

"That doesn't matter," she says. The pancake batter oozes into a pumpkin shape.

The guy with the knife goes, "Oh, yeah, it does, man. Those cops protect their own."

Nobody says anything. Something on the grill sizzles. The room smells of onion and grease and eggs. It's a comforting smell. I gently move my wrist out of her grip and stand up. "I am so sorry. I am really super sorry about the mess. I just, I just have to get out of here. Is there a back door or some window I can go through?"

The woman nods and stands up, too. The man gestures toward the back of the room. There is a tiny metal door squished next to the giant stainless steel refrigerators and some piled-up cardboard boxes. "Right through there. You want me to go out there and talk to him, honey? A guy who hits don't deserve a looker like you."

"A guy who hits doesn't deserve anyone," the woman says. She blows hair that has escaped out of her bandanna, trying to move it off of her face without actually touching it. "And no fighting, Billy. You're on probation."

He brings the knife down, slicing the onion into two parts. "It'd be worth it."

"No," I say. "I'm good. Thank you, though."

I start through the kitchen and almost get all the way to the door, rushing without rushing, if that makes sense, before I remember to say, "Thank you for being so nice. I am so exceptionally sorry I broke the ceiling."

"No big," Billy says. "Stuff happens."

Yes, it does.

CHAPTER 15

A couple minutes later and I'm fast-walking down River Street, getting sicker and sicker to my stomach with every freaking step I take. Aliens. Mom is missing. Probably my dad is missing, too. Someone—some*thing*—was impersonating my best friend, or has brainwashed him, or whatever. And I have nowhere to go. I check my cell phone. Nothing. No signal.

The world is dreary, and suddenly way more dangerous than it seemed two days ago, when I was just trying to deal with crappy classes and a computer-science question that was totally beyond me because it was about binary and I missed school the day we originally did binary, which should be the easiest lesson of all. That doesn't matter now.

The guy on the roof said to trust Lyle and not China. Was that because they had already done something to him or with him? Was it all just a big trap, and was Pierce in on it? What the heck?

I wish there were still pay phones around. I could call Seppie, even though Lyle and I didn't want to put her in danger by involving her—if that was even Lyle. Wait. When did Lyle *stop* being normal? Did he eat pizza with me as normal Lyle? Did he run through the compound? Comfort me at Dad's apartment? Because I totally thought we had a moment there. Was that even him in the back of China's truck? I think . . . I think it was . . . Right? I try to remember when things started to seem off.

It doesn't matter. Or, it does, but I can't dwell on it. Right now I need to figure out a way to get help. Seppie will think I am completely whacked at first, but I'm sure she'll believe me eventually, and she'll have advice. She always has advice. So how to reach her? My cell is obviously being blocked. Probably traced, too. Okay . . . I need a stranger . . . a random, nice stranger who would loan someone covered in ceiling dust his or her phone.

Today in Nashua, New Hampshire, seems like the kind of day when families and single people sort of straggle about and do errands. They go see movies and buy groceries for the week. They do home-improvement projects and make trips to the hardware store. They go to dance lessons. These are the people I pass by as I trot away from the diner and deeper into this little city. Normally, I would trust any of them. Just locate a sweet-seeming mom type person and ask for help. But how do I know who is one of them?

People stare at me funny. A man in a yellow windbreaker lifts his chin at me like I will contaminate him somehow. These guys in skater clothes jostle each other with their elbows and whisper. Their eyes are right on me. I must look like a survivor of a zombie apocalypse.

I round the corner, shivering, and come out onto Main Street, and there he is, standing by the entrance to Apple Tree Books. His hair is all mussed from the wind and his cheeks are red. Lyle? Not Lyle? Crap. I pivot and run back the way I came, but he's seen me. His feet pound on the sidewalk behind me.

"Mana! Wait up!"

I do not wait. I rush forward, sprinting as fast as I can. My arms pump to get up speed. Lyle races after me, yelling, "China! I found her! I got her!"

Don't trust him. The memory of the warning echoes in my head. Don't trust who?

Lyle gets my arm, because he's always been a faster runner, the fastest runner ever. I whirl around, angry, scared. I pound my hands into his chest. "You are not Lyle."

"What?"

"You are not Lyle," I scream. "Get away! Get away from me!"

He wraps his arms around me, pushing me against him, for some reason. Maybe to keep me from hitting him, maybe to keep me from running away. His chest is hard against my face. His T-shirt smells a little sweaty but not like pine—more like mint. The zipper of his coat pokes at my ear.

People have stopped walking. A twentysomething woman in a camouflage coat has whipped out her cell, which I totally could have used three minutes ago. She's probably calling the police.

"Mana. Mana! She's—it's okay," he says as I flail. "It's me. It's Lyle."

Stopping the struggle because I'm not getting anywhere, I still myself and say softly, "How do I know?"

"What?" His voice is an exasperated confused question.

"How do I know? How do I know you're Lyle?" My heart pounds against my chest—a thousand beats a second, it feels like.

He loosens his hold a little bit so we can really examine each other. His eyebrows lift high. "Mana. *What* is *up*? You know I'm Lyle."

I shake my head hard, over and over again, like I'm trying to get it off my body. Then I realize I'm doing it and how weird it must seem. "No, you're not. Lyle is a vegetarian. Lyle does not try to impress people with big words, because he is not pretentious like that, and Lyle knows that his mother is not mellow, and he doesn't get winded, and he smells good."

"Of course I'm a vegetarian."

Footsteps pound up behind Lyle. I peek. China's face is ruddy and worried. His eyes close a little as he glowers at me and demands, "What is going on?"

"She doesn't think I'm me, or . . . I'm not sure what it is," Lyle says to him. "She ran from me."

I struggle against him, try to force my way out of his arms.

"Let her go," China commands him. "People are watching."

At the same time that Lyle lets go, China opens his arms up like a man surrendering. His voice comes out solid and calm. "Can you tell me what happened?"

I back up a step, scrutinizing him for clues. "How do I know you're China?"

"You don't." He says this like it is totally normal, all flat-toned and passive. I have no idea how Mom can stand to work with him— he's so blah and cocky all at once.

"Great," I mutter. A siren starts up again. A bus rumbles down the street.

A woman yells, "Miss! You okay?"

I can't think of how to answer her, the nice woman who wants to help but can't. Nobody can. I'm alone.

"She's fine!" China uses his authoritative military voice. He walks toward the woman and flashes his wallet. There must be a badge in there. "She's a runaway. All fine now. No worries. Move on. Thank you for your concern."

The woman and a couple other people stare at him, then nod and walk away slowly, checking over their shoulders as China returns to Lyle and me. A UPS truck rumbles by. Some cars slosh up the wet rainy-snow mixture on the road. It splats on the sidewalk.

"I can prove I'm Lyle," Lyle says. His arms cross over his chest and he hops on the balls of his feet. Everything about him appears, quite frankly, adorable. But so did Not Lyle. And this could still be Not Lyle. But he's not winded, this one. Whichever one it is says, "I have no idea why I have to prove it, but I will."

I nod. "Go ahead."

"Okay . . ." He thinks for a second. "I love *Doctor Who*."

"Anyone who has gone in your room knows that."

"Okay . . ."

"We need to hurry up," China says. He checks all the windows above us, then the alleys, just like a cop in a TV show would. "It's not safe out here."

Lyle snaps at him. "I'm thinking! Shut up. Give me a second. Okay. Oh! I used to sleep with my sonic screwdriver, and one day you came up to me and asked if you could be my TARDIS."

"What?" China snorts. "Who is that?"

"*Doctor Who*'s time machine thing," I tell him, but I am studying Lyle. "You remember that?"

He blushes. "I remember lots of stuff about you."

"You do?"

"Absolutely."

China grabs Lyle's arm and mine. "Great. Let's play violins and sing the love song later. I've got to get you two somewhere safe." He points at me. "And *you* have to figure out where your mom would hide that chip."

I lock my knees so he has to drag me along Amherst Road. "Nope. No way. I am not going with you. How do I even know you're good?"

"What?"

"I'm serious. How am I supposed to know if you really are my mom's partner? She never mentioned you."

Lyle cocks his head. "Mana?"

I can feel the anger coming off of China. It is waves of heat and impatience. It is a clenched fist, a kicked-in door.

"What?" he manages to sputter.

"Mana," Lyle starts. "He hid us from the Men in Black. He brought us to the headquarters and everything."

"I know . . . but maybe those Men in Black aren't bad." My voice falters. "Um . . . although one did actually shoot at me on the roof. Then he warned me about China. So shooting me would not be a nice-person thing to do, and he probably wouldn't just change his ways to be nice and warn me, so the warning was probably a deception to tell me not to trust China and to trust Lyle instead, because they had already made a duplicate you or brainwashed you, and um . . . okay . . ."

Crap.

Lyle swears and China whips around to take both my arms in his. "Are you managing?"

"Yes," I say. "I think so. It's just . . ." I sigh. "Agh . . . This is so strange. My head hurts from thinking. It just hurts so much."

Lyle moves China out of the way and pulls me into a Lyle hug, which is what Seppie and I always call them. It's like a bear hug but skinnier. "Okay, Mana. You're going through a lot, but think about it this way: Dakota Dunham was a total ass who shot acid at you, right?"

"Right."

"So, you don't trust him. China captured him. That's a bonus point for China's trustworthiness. Right?"

I say it again. "Right."

Lyle keeps on hugging me. "And then the Windigo thing in your house obviously wanted to kill us. Bad. China helped get us away."

"Sort of after the fact."

"True, but still," Lyle says persuasively.

It makes sense. "But we never saw the Men in Black do anything."

China grumbles like this is all getting on his nerves. "Your mother said you were smart."

Lyle lets go of me. "She *is* smart."

"Then why isn't she acting it?"

"Because it's a lot to handle!"

They square off. Lyle does a lot of finger-pointing and China's hands are loose and fluid, as if he's not really threatened at all, or is trying hard to seem superior and too macho for any of this. But that muscle twitching in his jaw is pretty revealing. I'm sure that he's at least a little pissed. Even though he isn't puny at all, Lyle is so much smaller than China in the muscle-mass department—runner body versus steroid body—but right now he gives the impression that he is just as dangerous and angry. He's angry for me.

"It's okay," I say. "It's . . . I'm not telling you something."

Even though my voice is quiet, they both hear me, and they both turn to face me. Lyle's face softens, but it's China I address. "Before the man on the roof shot me, I heard a voice in my head telling me not to trust you."

"You did?"

"Yes. And he told me to trust Lyle, not you, but the voice sounded exactly like Lyle's voice. And then in the restaurant . . ."

I don't finish. I wasn't supposed to tell China about the voices. That's what Pierce said.

China doesn't even flinch. He just says, "What happened in the restaurant?"

I tell them about Not Lyle. I even tell them about the workers in the kitchen. I tell them everything except for what Pierce said.

When I'm done, China grimaces. "This is my fault."

We're still standing on Amherst Road, but we've moved to a doorway. Its granite recess blocks us from most of the cars that go by. You would have to really be studying the entire area, and possibly squinting, in order to see us.

"How is it your fault?" I ask.

"I went to the wrong roof." He sighs, rubbing a hand through his hair.

"The roof next door," Lyle elaborates. He shudders in the cold and runs his hands up and down his arms. "The original roof at your dad's apartment building. He went there and realized we were both missing. Then he backtracked and found me in your dad's bathroom."

"Wait. What were you doing in there?" I take this information in. "Why did nobody call me?"

"They blocked your cell signal."

"So they *can* do that." I was right about that, at least.

"Half the time you get 'network busy' signals, that's them. I knew we were in trouble when I couldn't get through. They obviously wanted you to doubt me and trust Lyle, because they had already copied him."

"Copied him?" I stutter. "Not just brainwashed? I mean, I know I sort of understand this, but part of my brain is just imploding as I try to think about it."

"Didn't you two read the alien species files? You sat there for hours." China's lips are thin.

"How did they copy me?" Lyle asks. "I wish I could have seen that."

"With perception filters and a shape-shifting alien. They're the Wores. Very dangerous. They knocked you out in the bathroom, copied you, must have tried to use telepathy on Mana here," China explains. "You read the file."

My jaw tightens. I feel like there's iron in my bones. "I hate them."

China nods. "That's normal."

"We have got to get that stupid chip," I say. "We have got to get it now. This is bigger than just my mom, and it has to end. We cannot have eight hundred million Lyles running around and my cell blocked so nobody can text me."

China starts laughing.

"What?"

"You." He snorts. "Texting . . . Eight hundred million Lyles . . . You crack me up. *Bigger than your mom.*"

Whatever.

CHAPTER 16

I basically know three things at this point:

1. We have absolutely no idea where the chip is.
2. It is impossible to not worry about your missing mother, especially if she has been abducted by aliens or their minions. Add your dad into the equation and your heart rate increases to twenty-five thousand beats per minute.
3. Being with China and Lyle is driving me absolutely insane.

Oh, sorry. There is another thing I now know:

4. Once you see a hot guy spit acid, get chased by a Windigo, read aliens' thoughts, leap around like a parkour hero, and meet an evil doppelgänger of your best friend, it is easy to accept that anything is possible.

China buys a new car at a local dealership, hauling out a massive wad of cash from some inner pocket of his leather jacket.

The Jeep salesman basically drools all over his bright yellow tie, which is way too short to be professional-looking. Poor guy. He flips through the cash. "Is this legal?"

"Absolutely," China says. He flashes a confident-man smile, like he's some sort of movie star or real estate tycoon. The Jeep salesman totally buys it, although, to be fair, he does keep giving me these peculiar side glances.

"It's because your pants are soaked," Lyle says. "Are you cold?"

"Uh, a little . . ."

"You're not okay, are you? You're just trying to be okay." Lyle cocks his head to the side, seeming very much his normal, attractive self.

"Pretty much." I'm glad he was still him at the compound and at my dad's, at least before the bathroom altercation. And I'm glad he wasn't actually hurt, just unconscious. I'm glad that China found him. I'm glad he was the one who chose to hug me so many times, to hold my hand, to . . . Are those stress responses? Or does he like me? Like me in a way that's not as a best friend?

I wonder for a minute what he would do if I just tried to kiss him. If I just took his hand, instead of him grabbing mine.

We prop ourselves against the chilly wall of the showroom while China and the salesman bend over a big, iron desk, filling out paperwork in a tiny side office. There's a giant window, so even when the worker is at his desk he can see the cars on the showroom floor, and any potential buyers. The cars are so shiny compared to the dingy, gray, wet world outside.

Lyle takes my hand in his just as I'm thinking about taking his, which feels awkward and perfect. His fingers are much thicker than mine and they bend so that his fingertips touch the skin on the back of my hand. I shiver.

"See?" he says. "You *are* cold."

That's not actually the kind of shiver that I was shivering, but I don't say anything because he keeps right on talking.

"I want this to all work out okay, Mana."

"Me too."

I wince. Of course I do. What an inane thing to say.

"I'm going to help you, you know. We'll find your mom and then we'll get that chip thing and the world will not be invaded by aliens and . . ." He pauses. "Um . . . and then something good will happen. Something we can think forward to and get excited about."

"Like what?" I squeeze his hand, just a little.

He thinks. "A *Doctor Who* marathon?"

"Lyle!"

He laughs.

"A world without an alien invasion?"

"How about something simpler?" I stare up at him. His eyebrows are raised up a little bit. Damn, they're so cute. Wait. I think eyebrows are *cute*? The stress is obviously getting to me, or maybe it's just because I'm super relieved to have Real Lyle back and Not Lyle gone. *Kiss me,* I think. *Kiss me.*

"Like what?" he says, and his voice is hoarse and low.

I make myself not think about all the girls he's dated.

I make myself not think about all the times I've seen him making out at a party or at a dance.

I make myself not think about the fact that we're supposed to be just friends, because seriously? We might not even survive all this craziness. What if I never take the chance and therefore never get to kiss him, or see if he wants me to like him that way, or potentially even likes me back that way, and instead just die not knowing?

Crap.

Crap.

Crap.

I can do this. I am fearless and tough and I can do this.

So I make myself go up on tippy toes and I kiss him. My lips push against his lightly.

He tugs his head away, just an inch, not too far. He makes my name a question. "Mana?"

"Please, Lyle."

And then he doesn't hesitate. His lips come right back, brushing against mine. And it doesn't matter that we're at a Jeep dealership, standing in the middle of the showroom floor, and it doesn't matter that I have voices in my head, or that we both need new, nonsmelly clothes, or that the world is full of aliens, or that China is making a joke about us to the car salesman. All that matters is the way our lips touch each other, the way his hand is all curled into my dirty hair, the way he feels so solid skinny against me, and how his arms are lifting me up, off the floor.

"Don't let me fall, Base," I whisper against his lips, laughing.

"Never, Flyer. Never." He kisses me again. He breaks away to say the words. "I'll never let you fall."

Twenty minutes later, all the paperwork is filled out and we're tooling around in a brand-new Jeep. I try not to keep touching my lips and instead pump the heat up all the way. China and Lyle argue incessantly, for freaking ever, about what the right thing to do is. Lyle votes for telling the regular police. We decide that Mom would never keep the chip on her person.

"The more I think about it, it's against her nature. If she was kidnapped, or if she was worried, she would hide that chip because she'd know that if it was on her? Well, aliens do pretty good searches. They'd do it right away," China says and we agree. China votes for going back to my house and searching for the chip, and then China says we don't even have a say, because he is the expert and in charge and blah blah blah.

"It's got to be there," he says for the five hundred millionth time. "I can't think of any other place she'd put it. Can you?"

"No." I smoosh my legs into the heated seat and tuck my backpack beneath my legs.

Lyle leans forward between our seats. "It's too dangerous to go back there. That's what they expect. It's too obvious. They were waiting for us at Mana's dad's apartment. They'll be waiting for us there. They might even be at my house now, or Seppie's. They're not stupid. To go back is to play right into their hands."

China scoffs. "We can handle whatever they try to do."

"We almost lost Mana! Do you even remember what happened at the compound? With Pierce?" Lyle's face reddens. "Have you even checked in? Do you know if they are okay?"

"Of course I've checked in." China's cheek muscle twitches.

Lyle leans forward a bit. "And?"

"They haven't responded."

"Is your seat belt on?" I ask, trying to decrease the tension with the first thing that I can think of, which is kind of a dumb thing, I guess. "Lyle, is your seat belt on?"

He fake glares at me. "Yes, Mom."

"Do not 'Yes, Mom' me. Just because you're pissed that I don't think we should go to the police, either," I say. "You are totally taking it out on me."

"No, I'm not," he says. He makes direct eye contact.

My insides get a bit melty, but I insist, "Yes, you are."

China nods. "You are, dude."

Lyle's hands lift into the air. His knuckles knock on the roof. "Don't call me dude."

China does this little side-glance thing, where he keeps all his attention straight ahead but for one second acknowledges the object in his peripheral vision. That object is me. He has got just one hand on the steering wheel, hanging over the top, all casual. "The kid's really cranky. Is he always like this?"

"No," Lyle and I say at the same time.

"Only after kissing you?" China snarks.

An awkward silence descends. I lean forward, touch my nose to my legs, try to not have a heart attack of anxiety right there. What if me kissing him made Lyle an ass? Was it bad? I thought it was amazing. But what if—

"The kiss was good," Lyle says sheepishly. "That's not why I'm grumpy. Please don't think that's why I'm grumpy, Mana."

China taps his thumb on the steering wheel. "Not well played, dude."

"Do not call me dude. I am not a dude," Lyle says, and then adds, "please."

"Dudette?" China asks.

"Look, I have no idea why you have to put me down, but we have bigger things to worry about, so can you lay off?"

"I have an idea!" I say. "The chip is obviously not at the house. The aliens searched it; you searched it, too, right, China?" I ask.

"Right."

"So Mom had to put it somewhere safe or with someone safe. She normally goes where after work? The grocery store and the gym," I say. "We should look there."

China drives us to the grocery store first. All the food aisles and people make it seem pretty impossible. Disheartened, I throw up my hands. "How can we possibly find it if it's here?"

"It would be a good hiding place," China says, starting to walk straight toward the organic produce aisle. He really does know my mom. "She wouldn't put it in any of the front items because they could get purchased."

He starts knocking boxes off the shelf. Cups of organic kimchi soup, Annie's macaroni and cheese, and additive-free fruit gummies topple to the floor. Lyle gasps. "What are you doing?"

I answer for China. "Looking."

"You're making a mess!" Lyle glances around, embarrassed and horrified. A crowd has begun to gather. They all make faces.

"It's the fastest way," China says, without even looking up. He's just moved on to the Thai packaged food. People stare at us, and I've never felt so disconnected from the rest of humanity as I do right now. All these people, who must think we are beyond deranged, staring at us like we're the bad guys, like they are better than us, while simultaneously they are scared by us. Even with China and Lyle right here, I feel so alone.

I rush off. I have to look all around the front of the store before I find it: the fire alarm. Yanking it down, I sprint back to the aisle.

There's a second of delay and then the lights begin to flash and the alarm sounds—a horrible blaring noise that hurts my ears.

"Good job," China says. "You take after your mom. Quick thinking."

I smile and start searching. "We don't have much time before the fire department gets here."

"About five minutes," China agrees. "We can get through this in five minutes if Lyle helps."

Lyle throws up his hands, giving in, and then begins dumping food products into the aisle even as a red-shirted Hannaford's worker yells at us to evacuate. China doesn't even look up.

"Sorry!" Lyle yells. "Important business! Trying to find the right box of organic oats."

We don't find that or the chip. But we manage to leave the store via the storage room's back door just as the fire department barges through the front door.

We don't fare any better at the gym, but much to Lyle's relief, we don't make a mess for the employees there to clean up. We just casually peruse all the equipment, touching the bikes, the treadmills, the weight machines, the rower. I search the locker room even though Mom doesn't have a locker and just brings a bag and changes. We can't find anything anywhere.

"We're just not thinking of something," China says as we get back in the truck, but unfortunately, none of us comes up with any great ideas. "I think we should just go back to the house. It's the most logical place. She probably—"

My cell phone rings, interrupting him. We all jump. I panic and clasp it to my chest, but don't answer it.

"Who is it?" China demands. He moves into the passing lane to get around an old lady driving a copper-colored sedan.

I read the display. "Seppie. I was supposed to meet her at the Y today. How did her call get through?"

I flip it open, trying to figure out how to get out of the fact that I was supposed to meet Seppie a half hour ago. She always knows when I'm lying.

"Hey Sep . . ."

"Mana?"

I try to think fast. "I am so sorry that I'm—"

She talks right over me. "Mana, listen, Lyle's—"

She's gone.

"Seppie?"

Nothing. I glance up at China. He mouths, "Everything okay?"

I mouth back the word *no.*

"Seppie?" I try again. I can hear noises in the background.

The next voice I hear sounds like it's being digitized by a computer, mechanically disguised or something. "Mana."

"What are you doing to Seppie?" I demand. "Who are you?"

Lyle leans in toward my shoulder. "What's going on?"

I put up my free hand to make him stay quiet. China swerves the Jeep into the slow lane and then into the breakdown lane—so there's no extra noise, I guess. He puts on the hazard lights. I put the phone on speaker so everyone can hear.

The voice comes back. "Seppie is fine. For now. But I need you to bring the device to me."

"What device?" Does he mean the chip?

"Don't play stupid, Mana. You're not stupid. I know you're with your mother's partner. I know you have the device."

I turn to China for help. He nods vigorously.

"Right. Right . . ." I watch China scribble something on the back of the bill of sale receipt for the Jeep: *Pretend we have it.*

"Right, okay, the device," I lie.

"If you want your friend to live, you need to bring it to me."

Lyle curses.

"Alone," the voice goes on. "No Lyle. No China."

"How do you even know about Lyle?" I ask. I clutch the phone so tightly that I accidentally push a button. It beeps obnoxiously—a long tone of nothing, in an unfortunate pitch.

As soon as the tone stops, the voice says, "I know everything about you, Mana."

"But—"

China gives me a warning look. A logging truck drives by and the entire Jeep jiggles in its wake.

"I'm going to text you the address," the voice continues. "Do not attempt to call back on this line. Do not bring anyone else. Just you. Just you, or she dies."

He hangs up.

"Crap," I say.

A text message comes through.

"Where's the meeting?" China asks.

I can't believe it. "The animal rehabilitation place?"

"A zoo?" China repeats. "Is there even a zoo here?"

Lyle answers for me, because I'm still staring at the phone. "Yes, but it isn't a zoo. It's more like an animal refuge, but they've got lions and moose and monkeys and emus."

"Lyle loves it," I manage to say. "He volunteers there in the summer. He's the softie, honestly."

"Good." China almost smiles and starts up the car. "You might be useful after all."

CHAPTER 17

The animal refuge looks exactly the way you'd expect a wildlife refuge to look at the end of autumn, when it's closed because there aren't enough people around to justify keeping it open. The workers only come in at dawn and dusk to feed the animals. Cold metal cages pen up mountain lions and bobcats and wolves. Some grazing, herd-type animals huddle in corners by stumps of trees. Some stare as I walk by. Some sleep in the fetal position, like this world and its cold is just too much for them. The dirt trail that meanders past the monkey house and the llamas is covered with a light dusting of snow. It's naked of footprints, except for mine. A wolf howls. The mountain lion paces back and forth in her little cage as I go by. The place smells of wet fur and helplessness, with a nice after-aroma of predator poop.

I wonder if these animals ever knew what it was like to be free, or if they think this is it—the sum total of their existence. A cage, food and water, people staring. And I wonder if people are like that, too. We go around thinking that our lives are somewhat planned and vaguely understandable. We're born. Most of us go to school. Some of us make the sex, have a baby. We die. We watch online videos, gossip, love each other, worry, eat, drink, study, work. That's it. But if the last forty-eight or so hours have taught me anything, it's that this idea of a life is just a cage, really. There are so many things we don't know, don't even know that we don't know. We are those mountain lions, and sometimes someone opens up one of our cage doors and the reality we've been basing our existence on just cracks.

I make my way to the caribou field. This is about an acre of land at the far side of the refuge, surrounded by a metal fence. Caribou and bison roam around in there. The caribou resemble reindeer, like happy little promises of good gifts to come. I keep trudging toward them, too hyped up by fear and adrenaline to shiver any more. Finally, I spot some footprints. Two sets. One set, hopefully, is Seppie's.

I pull out the little silver tool that China gave me. It looks like just a mini flashlight, but it zaps right through metal somehow. It's how I broke the lock on the big wooden front doors and got into the refuge. It's how I break the security lock on this fence, too.

If I get out of this, I'll have to make a donation to the refuge to cover the costs of the locks. Ahem. Right. *If I get out of this.*

My feet smoosh into the three inches of snow. Some leaks into my shoes and melts into my socks, making my feet cold again. For the last two days, I have basically been nothing but cold. I tighten up against it. It doesn't matter. What matters is saving Seppie. What matters is finding my mom, and probably finding my dad, too, assuming he really is missing and not just on some weird work assignment with no cell signal.

A raven circles in the sky above me. Some sort of animal moos, which makes me jump. It's probably a cow. I'm not sure. Do they have cows in animal refuges?

Following the footsteps through the field, I spot them. Two figures. One is a little bigger than the other, a little taller—and has a gun pressed to her head. But she's not cowering. She is beautiful and angry, standing up straight. That's my Seppie. Even though I can't see their faces yet, I recognize her stance. I get closer. My heart beats panicky hard. My fingers twitch into themselves. I don't know if I can do this. I don't know *how* to do this. What am I doing here?

Then I gaze up again, stop worrying, start thinking. I will save her. I have to. And to do that, I have to assess the total asshole who is holding her hostage, willing to kill her to get what he wants. I stare. I stop walking.

"Mrs. Stephenson?"

She moves her shoulders up just a little bit. Some muscle in her cheek twitches.

"Mrs. Stephenson?" I repeat.

She says nothing. A caribou traipses downfield and bends his head down to poke through the snow, graze, search for something that he can eat, something that is green and makes sense in a world that has suddenly gone white.

I look at Seppie. "It's Mrs. Stephenson? Mrs. Stephenson kidnapped you?"

Seppie nods. She crosses her arms in front of her chest. "I think when aliens do it, it's called abduction."

I just stare at her.

"What are you talking about? Mrs. Stephenson, what is going on?" I adjust my backpack straps so the weight isn't so heavy on my back. It suddenly feels like I am going to fall over backwards and not be able to get up. God, is she really so angry that I slept in Lyle's bed? We didn't even do the nasty. She is so out of control.

Mrs. Stephenson nudges Seppie forward. She's still got the gun—which I now see is sort of weird and shiny—pointed at the side of Seppie's head, but at least it isn't pressed into her hair anymore. Seppie is trying not to cringe, and to be all brave cheerleader toughie, but it is so not working.

"Mrs. Stephenson?" I say it again, like saying it will suddenly make this whole scene make sense. It doesn't work.

Instead, she just stares at me while her mouth moves. It's the only part of her body that does. "I need that device, Mana. That chip."

That's when it registers. She's here for the chip. Lyle's overprotective, churchgoing, wide-hipped mom is not here because she's angry and has gone mental about the whole finding-me-in-bed thing. No.

She is freaking kidnapping my best friend because she is somehow a part of this whole dealing-with-aliens thing.

I try for jokey. "Mrs. Stephenson? You don't even like chips. 'A moment on the lips, a lifetime on the hips' is what you always say."

"I'm not talking about Cool Ranch Doritos here, Mana." Not even a smile.

"You have no sense of humor." I put my hands on my own, sadly nonexistent hips, and glare at her. "I do not have the chip."

"Of course you do," she says. "Your mother said she was going to give you something."

"You talked to my mom?"

Her face shifts into something more Mrs. Stephenson–like. "Right before she . . . vanished. She told me to keep an eye out for you, said that she might have to take an abrupt business trip. I knew what she was saying. She just didn't know I knew. She said that you were her baby girl and she loved you, and she wanted me to make sure that I kept an eye on you. Who else would she give it to, honestly? It has to be you. You're not smart enough to know better. You're too focused on your own little world of cheering and boys and school to know that your neighbors—your own mother—aren't who you thought they were."

"That hurts," I manage to say.

"She's just jealous," Seppie says, "because Lyle likes you."

Mrs. Stephenson laughs. "That can't happen. Alien never mixes with human well. My people won't allow it anyway."

Alien and human? Her people? Aren't people her people? I try to focus. My whole brain shifts. If alien and human can't mix, that means either Lyle or I is an alien. If she is saying her people won't allow it, that probably means her people are not people. That means Mr. Stephenson is some kind of alien, too. It means that *Lyle* is, too. It means . . . I am not? Even though I can hear voices? Or maybe I am, too, but Mrs. Stephenson, despite her know-it-all attitude, doesn't actually know it all. Either way, it means my mom didn't know about the Stephensons.

"Does Lyle know?" I ask. I don't specify what I'm talking about, because open-ended questions usually make people talk more. I learned that from Mom's after-party interrogations of me.

"About our nature?" She smiles, and now I know for sure. He is an alien. She is an alien. "Not yet. He will soon, and then he'll drop you like a hot potato—if you aren't dead already, obviously. He drops all his girlfriends. You know that, girls. You've watched him. They last . . . what? A week, at most? Do you know why? Humans are inferior. That's why. Dull and inferior and unworthy. Lyle doesn't even know he is different yet, but he can still sense it."

Whoa. I kissed an alien. My male BFF is an alien. And a really good kisser. And, more importantly, his mom is an alien. No, even *more* importantly, his mom is an *evil* alien. Somehow, this makes complete sense.

None of this matters. She's just trying to hurt me and distract me. Back to the heart of this: I need to get Seppie safe, to get away from Mrs. Stephenson and her irrational eyes and her damn gun. I need to find out what she knows about my mom.

"Why would my mom tell you to keep an eye on me?"

"She knew they were after her."

"Who? The Men in Black?"

"Not just them." She gazes around us nervously, clears her throat. "There are some alien factions who really don't want the world to continue this way. People are destroying the world. True, some alien races aren't much better, but we all are tired of this . . . this hiding. Colluding with militaries for safety. We want an end."

I think for a second. "The man I talked to, one of those guys in suits, he said that if they didn't get the chip, then it would be the end. What did he mean? What would end? He used the word *unleashed*."

"If that chip is activated, the world will end. Or at least the world as you humans know it. Those Men in Black, part humans and part shifters, the whole group is a mess. They don't want the chip activated, but they still want it intact. Probably for the same reason your mother did," she says. "This world is no good for us as it is. Do you know what would happen if the masses realized that we are already here? Some of us, like that Pierce, trapped here for centuries?"

"Total concentration-camp-genocide scenario," Seppie says.

Mrs. Stephenson pulls the gun away from Seppie's head a little bit. I guess she figures Seppie is a sympathizer and not as much of a threat. People never think cheerleaders are much of a threat.

"You're sympathizing with her?" I ask Seppie, making my voice angry.

"No." Seppie shrugs. "She's an ass and she has crap taste in music. She made me listen to show tunes in the car. Show tunes! God. But I can see where she's coming from."

She never shuts up, does she? Mrs. Stephenson says in my head. I force myself not to react. I can't give away that I hear her thoughts. Why can't I hear Lyle's? Or did I? Was he telling me not to trust himself when he had been knocked out? Maybe his subconscious reached out to me, tried to warn me, even though his own conscious self didn't know what was going on.

I have to focus. I inhale, try to still myself, and ask, "Mrs. Stephenson? I get what you're saying, seriously. But I don't understand why that makes it okay for you to hold a gun to Seppie's head."

"Mana. You don't understand how serious this is."

"Oh, really? I don't? I saw a guy die today. Someone shot at me. My whole house is wrecked. My mom is missing. She's probably dead, you know, *and* my dad is missing, and now you're telling me *I don't understand this is serious*?" I'm shrieking. I swallow down the extra words I want to yell. My shoulders shudder from the weight of it. "Do not tell me I don't get it. I am not stupid, okay?"

The caribou closest to us gives up his grass hunt. He lifts his long neck and examines us, slowly moving, watching the craziness, I guess.

"We are aliens." Mrs. Stephenson sighs. "Because of this, we're not safe, Mana. Not just because of the chip. Because of your mother and her little partner, because of the Men in Black, because of human ignorance and fear and the inferior and pathetic nature of your species." She rolls her eyes—not literally, although with aliens, who knows what they can do. "Your mother is part of the genocide. Don't you know what she does?"

"No," I say, lying. I know what they do. I just want to hear her say it.

"They hunt aliens down and kill them or contain them, locking them up forever. What gives them the right? Why should we have to hide ourselves to live on this world? Why should we have to play by human rules?"

"Because it's our world," Seppie says, sounding pretty pissed off.

"It's about sharing. When we came here, we thought we could share."

"Then maybe you should leave." Seppie gives me an expression like *Can you believe this lady?*

"We don't want to leave. This planet is lovely. It's situated in a peaceful part of the galaxy with a minimum of threats, isolated. It's adorable. An adorable planet." She glares at me. "But your mother wants us gone."

"But you're an alien and she didn't do anything to you," I protest.

"Your mother didn't know my nature."

That's why Pierce didn't want me to tell China that I could hear thoughts, I bet. She didn't want him to know I was an alien. She wasn't setting me up, I don't think. She was protecting me. But is it really possible that I could be one and my mom wouldn't know? I am so confused, so ridiculously confused.

"Why is Pierce safe from getting locked up, then?" I ask.

"Because she helps them. They trust her. She's been here for centuries, so they don't deem her a threat."

There's something she's not telling me. Her thoughts are blocked. My instincts tell me that means she is lying somehow.

"And my mom? My mom would hunt you and Mr. Stephenson and Lyle?"

"Yes. Yes, she would. She doesn't care that we're neighbors, Mana. She just wants us gone."

My head whirls. "I cannot believe Lyle is an alien."

"Oh, I can," Seppie teases. "I mean, he does have those freaky eyebrows and he runs so fast, really fast, without even sweating most of the time, and you do remember . . . the eyebrows."

"Shut up."

She gives me this look. Her face says, *Just hold it together. One more sec. Hang on.*

I know that look from doing planks at practice. I know that look because Seppie is my best friend. And yet, that look is not helping me out.

I start hyperventilating. I know! I know! I've gone through all this stuff, all this horrible, horrible stuff, and it's only now that I am engaging in total freak-out behavior. There has got to be a reason for this breathing issue, this anxiety and fear, but I don't know what it is. I just don't know.

Well. Yes I do.

I wheeze in and out, trying to get enough breath.

"He"—wheeze—"can't"—wheeze—"be"—wheeze—"an alien."

Gasp.

Gasp.

Wheeze.

"Oh, crap," Seppie says, jamming Mrs. Stephenson with her elbow. "She's hyperventilating. You've made her hyperventilate, Mrs. Stephenson."

Mrs. Stephenson's eyes go all big and shocked. She starts striding toward me. "Mana, breathe slowly. Big breaths. In and out. In and out."

I glance up at Seppie. She's a good distance away from Mrs. Stephenson all of a sudden. I try to will her to run. She does not. Instead, she starts walking toward me, too. Without stopping to think about it, I reach out and snatch Mrs. Stephenson's gun arm. She's so shocked that she actually drops the weapon in the snow. I dive for it.

"Run, Seppie!" I am screaming it the best I can, but I'm hyperventilating, so I'm not so sure how it's going. "Seppie! Run!"

I grab for the gun. Gasp. It feels like my lungs are broken, like my heart is broken. Gasp.

"Mana . . ." Mrs. Stephenson's voice, coming from a long, long way away. It's a plea and a hope.

And then the world goes white.

eppie shakes me into consciousness, jiggling my hands, shoving my shoulders back and forth. "Mana, baby. You've got to stop with the hyperventilating routine."

"I can't help it. Too much emotional stress. And my heart was beating so-o-o ridiculously fast; it was painful," I say, rolling my head on my neck, trying to stretch out the muscles. I must have fallen weird. Then I remember what's happening. "Mrs. Stephenson!"

I sit up with Seppie's help.

"I took care of her." She shrugs. "All that karate stuff since kindergarten actually paid off."

Mrs. Stephenson is sprawled on the ground. "Is she . . . ?"

"Dead?" Seppie gets all offended. "No. I don't kill idiots. I just knock them out. But maybe I would have if she wasn't Lyle's freaking mother. You know she put a gun to my head? That takes a lot of nerve."

"It makes no sense."

"Tell me about it." She takes me by my shoulders, stares into my eyes, and I stare back into hers. We are connected, best friends. The brown of her eyes is so deep and familiar. She's a tough cookie, Seppie. And I can trust her. I know I can trust her.

"It's all so weird. And what about my dad? Where is he? And how can my mom be an alien hunter? And Lyle is an alien."

She points over her shoulder. "See that hut over there? There's a space heater and some grain in there."

"So?"

"There's also some duct tape." She laughs, but a painful laugh—the kind of laugh you do when you really want to cry. "I think we should tie her up while you fill me in on what the hell is going on. Good?"

I nod. "Good." Then I throw my arms around her and say, "I am so glad you're here."

"Don't know how to kidnap your neighbor without me, huh?"

After we've dragged Mrs. Stephenson over to the shack and turned on the space heater, I fill Seppie in on the whole China/ Mom thing.

"Is he hot?" she asks.

"Seppie!"

"Well, he should be. All alien hunters should be hot."

"My mom was an alien hunter."

"Is. Don't make her past tense." I swallow hard. Seppie puts her arm around my shoulders. "Don't stress. We'll find her, okay? Your dad, too."

I nod.

I think I love the space heater. I keep turning around in front of it, its coils glowing a ghoulish orange, while Mrs. Stephenson sits in the chair with the duct tape over her mouth and around her wrists and ankles.

"You tied her up pretty well," I say. "You think it'll hold?"

"It's duct tape. Remember when we duct taped the principal on the wall during Spirit Day? It held his body weight, and he's, like, two hundred pounds."

"Easily," I say. Mrs. Stephenson's eyes are still closed. "She will wake up sometime though, right?"

"Right." Seppie blows on her hands. "So, can you explain to me what's happening here?"

I chew on my fingernail. They're all totally broken at this point—like that matters, though, when you're dealing with aliens and kidnappings. Quickly, I get Seppie up to speed with what's been happening.

She shakes her head, amazed. "Wow."

"I know, right? This is what we've been dealing with."

"You're amazing. That's a lot to deal with."

I shrug off the compliment, but it kind of makes me feel good inside. "I am totally confused about the Men in Black, by the way. Are they government workers? Humans? Aliens? Alien sympathizers? I think China said they were part of the government. But they ransacked my house. If my mom was a rogue former agent, that would make sense, but not them working with Dakota, who is most definitely an alien. But were they even working with Dakota?"

"Whoa, whoa, whoa . . . Captain Hotness is an alien?"

"He was the acid-spitting alien," I say.

"Did that make him hotter or less hot?"

"Way less hot."

She stares at my fingernails, holding my hand in hers. Then she curls my fingers under, like it's too painful for her to gaze at a hand in need of a manicure. "Does it matter what the chip does and what it's connected to?"

"What do you mean?"

"I don't think it matters. Whatever it is, it's dangerous and it sucks."

Mrs. Stephenson twitches in her sleep. We don't say anything for a second. The space heater whirls warmth toward us.

Finally, Seppie says, "So, where do you think your mom put it?"

"No clue. I mean, we don't think she'd have it on her person because that would be dangerous. That means she stashed it somewhere simple, but somewhere nobody would expect. The best place to hide things is out in the open, right? The hardest target to acquire is a moving target—"

All of a sudden I get it. I mean, I finally get it. I smack my forehead with the palm of my hand. "Oh my God. I am such an idiot."

"I tell you that all the time."

"Shut up."

I rip open my backpack. I pull out my assignment book and my extra body shield for cheering. And then I get to the container of pretzels. I point to the happy penguin sticker on it. "See this?"

"The penguin sticker? Cute."

"I know. But this is a *new* sticker. My mom put it on there the day she disappeared."

Seppie's eyes squint and she moves closer.

"I think she hid it behind the sticker."

We both stare at Mrs. Stephenson. She hasn't moved, except for the earlier twitching. The heater makes a popping, sizzling noise. It's getting toastier in here.

"Do you want to unpeel it?" Seppie whispers. I put one of my fingernails underneath the sticker. It hits something hard. I pull the sticker away, and there it is. A tiny, circular, black piece of metal plops into my hand. The symbol I saw at Pierce's compound is emblazoned on the side. It doesn't look exactly like a chip to me, honestly, but it definitely is something.

"Holy—" Seppie starts.

"Crap." I finish. "Holy freaking crap."

We stare at each other. We turn to peek at Mrs. Stephenson. Still out.

"What do we do?" Seppie whispers.

I close my fingers around the little piece of salvation. "We get my mom back."

know that Lyle and China are at the animal refuge, staking out the place, hidden over by the monkey house. I also know that China probably put a tracking device on my clothes and in my backpack and another one in my cell phone, because that's what any good covert agent would do.

"I have got to ditch this stuff," I say, tossing them down. I slip the chip in the front pocket of my jeans and check for tracking devices in my clothes.

Seppie breathes in through her nose. I know this because her nostrils flare. "You're just going to leave that stuff here?"

"Kind of."

"That's littering."

"Dude, the fate of the world is at stake."

"If we destroy the environment, we destroy the world," she says, pretty freaking adamantly.

I squat down near Mrs. Stephenson, who has started to moan a little bit. "We'll take her cell, instead."

Seppie's hands go to her hips and she straightens up like we're in a performance cheer. The judges are so into posture. She scrutinizes me down on the floor and says, all argumentative, "And you don't want Lyle and the China guy to know what we're doing because . . ."

"Because China might just want the chip. That might be his

priority, not my mom. He's such a soldier, he would sacrifice her for the quote-greater good unquote. I know he would. Plus, he said not to trust anybody, not even him."

"Cold." Seppie has a way with words. She means China's attitude is cold, but it makes me think of Mrs. Stephenson, who is unconscious on the floor.

I find Mrs. Stephenson's cell phone in her jacket pocket, stash it in my own, and say, "We should move the heater closer."

Seppie lifts up the heater by the top handle and says bitterly, "Of course. We don't want Mrs. Abductor to freeze to death."

"She just wanted the chip to keep Lyle safe."

"To save her own ass, is more like it."

"Hey, that's Lyle's mom, you know."

"His mom, the alien."

I cock my head, studying Mrs. Stephenson. She's kind of pasty, and super stressed, judging by the furrows in her forehead. Dark half-circles have made homes under her eyes. "No matter what she said before, she looks pretty human to me."

"Trust me, she's not." Seppie shudders.

I jerk up. "What? How do you know? Did she do something?"

"She flew."

"What?"

Seppie swallows. "Seriously. She flew me here. Didn't you notice there was no car? Not that many footprints in the snow? She just picked me up and landed here. It was insane and cold and scary as all hell, like nothing in those romantic vampire movies. Not that I would ever think of Mrs. Stephenson that way."

I fall back against the shed wall. The whole building wobbles. "You're serious."

She raises her hand. "I swear."

"Oh my God."

This is too much. Maybe I'm the same kind of alien they are.

Maybe all that leaping around in the locker room was like gearing up for flying. Maybe Lyle runs so quickly because he's not truly touching the ground? It's all so big and overwhelming.

Finally, I manage, "So if she flew you here like Superman, then there's no car to bring us back."

"Bingo."

"Crap."

The heater makes a clicking noise. My heart makes the same damn noise. "So, what are we going to do?"

"You really don't want to have that guy help?"

"No." I stomp back and forth. "I just don't completely trust him. He says he's helping, but . . . and . . . It's just . . . these . . . these voices in my head kept telling me not to trust him."

"One. Stop pacing. There is not enough room in here to pace. Two. Let's talk about the voices in your head thing. How do you know you can trust *them*? Three. Hasn't he been helping you all along? So, either way, who do you know you can trust?"

"One. Pacing is exercise and exercise is good. Two. I am freaked, too. Three. Yes, he has, but I don't want him to help because he just wants the chip. I mean, I think he cares about Mom and everything, but his main goal right now is to get this chip." Seppie leans back, crosses her hands in front of her chest and thankfully doesn't lecture me on trust issues. I trip on the heater cord and the whole thing clanks over backwards. I kick it back into the right place. The heater stops glowing. It turned off when it fell over. I twist the knob to get it going again. "You. Lyle. Mom. My dad."

"And our goal here is to find your mom, right?"

"Right."

"And you have a plan to do that?"

I think about that for a second. "We are going to have a controlled meeting, at our location and on our own terms. Wow. I sound like China. We're going to Walmart, where we can get weapons like knives and crossbows. We're going to have a little exchange." Seppie takes this all in stride as soon as I say it, which she deserves mad props for, honestly. She just trusts me. *I* don't even trust me. Seriously, I heard those voices in my head, alien voices. Humans can't do that. But I might not be human. I swallow hard and stare at Seppie's beautiful face. "Do you think I could fly?"

"Well, you are the freaking flyer, aren't you?"

"I'm not talking about cheerleader flying," I say.

"I know you're not." She puts on a fake, cheesy-white-person-in-a-bad-eighties-movie smile. I love that I don't have to explain that I'm worried, that there's a possibility that I might be alien, too. I love that this isn't a thing. I love that she just says, "Buck up, little camper. Let's go see."

We walk toward the door, but then she stops and says, out of nowhere, "You don't have an acid tongue, do you? Or Lyle?"

"Not that I know of."

She inhales deeply. "Good . . . good . . . But Dakota Dunham is really an alien creeper."

"He is absolutely an alien creeper."

"Damn, what a waste. He was so hot."

"I know."

We don't have much time before China and Lyle will come searching for us. Seppie boosts me up onto the roof of the shed. She makes a big *oomph* noise, like she doesn't lift me up all the time in cheering, but I let it go because, let's face it, it's not every day that your best friend's alien mom abducts you.

It's slippery on the roof, all slanted and slick with snow. I try to get a good position.

"You look like you're surfing."

"Shut up."

She smiles. "Okay. You going to try it?"

"I think so."

I don't move.

"Mana?"

"Yes."

"You okay up there? You know, you don't have to try this. We could hot-wire some car somewhere."

I glare at her. "You do not know how to hot-wire a car."

"And you don't know how to fly."

The monkeys are making a big ruckus to my right, squealing and screaming. I can see the tip of the roof of their house, just past the hill. Lyle and China are right around there somewhere. I need to hurry.

"Did Mrs. Stephenson do anything special?" I ask.

Seppie thinks for a second. "She just sort of squatted and lifted up." She demonstrates.

"Like I'm going to make a really big jump?"

"Exactly."

"Okay."

I squat. I lift my arms up over my head in a T reach.

"Like this?"

"Perfect." Seppie jumps back and forth on her feet. "Mana, are you really sure that you want to do this? We could—"

I jump.

"Mana!" she shrieks, running closer to the building to catch me. Her long dreads flutter out behind her, snow filling them. She swears.

I reach up and reach up.

I am off the shed.

I am off the world.

I am flying.

Sort of. I mean, I'm leaping up and up.

And it is so-o-o cold.

And so-o-o cool.

But mostly cold.

And then I land on my feet, easy, and bounce up again. It's not exactly like Superman. More like giant leaping with significant air time.

Seppie is running around in a desperate circle below me, chanting, "Holy crap. Holy crap. Holy crap."

I land again.

Her arms fling open wide, like at the end of the "Defense" cheer. "You are smiling so big," she screeches.

"It's freaking amazing!" I screech back. "It's so cool. Like being a kangaroo mixed with a bird, but um . . . not quite. But it is *so freaking cool*!"

I turn around and motion for her to climb on.

"Piggyback?" she mutters. "You want to give me a piggyback?"

"I'm not strong enough to fireman carry you," I say. "And we have to get supplies, weapons . . ."

"But . . ."

I growl at her. "I know you're used to being the base and lifting me up and making sure I don't fall, but it's my turn. Got it?"

"Okay. Fine."

I bend over a little bit, loosen up my knees. She leaps on. I stagger forward. And we are up.

"I can't believe you can do this," Seppie yells into my ear, as we jump up so that we're at the level of the middle of pine trees, heading straight for Walmart. The wind smashes against us as she clutches my shoulders.

"Me either."

I adjust my arms under her legs. Seppie leans forward a little and we buzz past a gaggle of crows that had been roosting on a middle branch of a big maple tree. They caw and cackle, taking to the air.

"We pissed them off," Seppie says. The crows flutter away. I cannot believe I'm doing this. Flying! Me . . . My heart soars and falls.

"I can't believe I'm an alien," I say.

"What?"

"I can't believe I'm an alien!"

For a second, Seppie doesn't answer. Then she goes, "Well, believe it. At least you don't have tentacles or an acid tongue or anything. That's good."

"Damn good." Although to be fair, while gross, an acid tongue is a pretty amazing weapon.

Walmart waits up ahead. We've been following Route 101—not directly, obviously, but over to the right of it, just out of sight of cars (hopefully). I don't want people to see bounding cheerleaders and think they've gone insane. I know that would have freaked me out, last week. I would have set up an appointment with a mental health expert immediately.

Walmart is huge from the air. It's a big box of gray surrounded by acres of impervious surface full of shoppers' cars and blowing plastic bags.

"Disgusting," I say.

"Can we land for real soon?"

I nod and find a good place in the back parking lot, by the loading dock. We thud down. Seppie hops off the moment my feet touch the trampled snow. She's shivering from the wind and cold. A plastic bag blows into her leg and she kicks it away as she tries to rearrange her hair. "That was amazing," she says. "But let's go get my truck at the Y next, okay?"

"You don't like my kangaroo-style flying awesomeness?"

"Sweetie, I'm sure I'd like your flying just fine if it wasn't so damn cold, or if you were, like, a hot vampire," she says, and starts fast-walking around the building, toward the front doors. I have to trot to catch up. My body feels achy, like I've had the flu. I wonder if that's a flying side effect.

We round the corner and see the front doors of Walmart. The dull gleam of the giant yellow smiley face greets us. People push their way through the doors, into the massive room of merchandise covered by a layer of dust and grime. Our shoes squeak on the dingy, off-white linoleum floor.

"How can you not want to be an alien when you see this?" Seppie whispers.

"Maybe box stores are alien inventions," I whisper back, glancing over my shoulder, half expecting Acid Dakota Dunham to show up, or maybe more of those Men in Black. The only people behind us are an angry man in a big, flannel shirt and duck boots from L.L.Bean or Carhartt or whatever, plus someone that he probably calls 'his woman,' who is slumped forward, from the weight of her life, I guess.

It is so sad. This entire place is sad, all merchandise and materialism, but you know . . . you know . . . It would be worse if it didn't exist. It would be worse if that lady slouching behind us never had a chance to straighten up her shoulders because of some stupid alien–government conspiracy, because the chip I have stuffed into my pocket somehow got into the wrong hands.

We step farther inside, into the false warmth blowing out from the heaters.

A lady in a blue bib waits by the Sale rack. She's got a roll of yellow stickers in her hand. She smiles at us. "Welcome to Walmart."

Seppie takes a sticker as we walk by and plops it on my nose.

"Nice," I say, ripping it off.

"I don't want you to get too cocky, now that you have superpowers."

"Shut up."

"No, you."

We do our annoying-kids-in-the-car routine. It's comforting somehow.

We walk past the extra-large women's bras and toward the back of the store, where the electronics section is. Seppie holds my hand and squeezes it, just a little bit.

"I know you're worried about your mom," she says, "but we'll get her. It'll be okay."

"Of course we will, without a doubt, and everything will be perfectly fine," I say back, but the truth is, it's not that easy to believe.

Once we have everything we came for, we kangaroo fly to go get Seppie's car and drive to my house so I can leave a note.

Chip for my mother. Meet us at the high school gym. No tricks. Even exchange. 3 P.M.

I leap out of the car. Leaving the door open, I run as quickly as I can to the front door of my house and tack up the note. The wind blows the yellow plastic tape against the porch. It's this one spot of color in a world that's otherwise just snowy white and shadow. I rush back to the car again. I'm sure the house is watched and I'm sure the people or aliens monitoring it are the ones who have Mom, plus a few extras, I bet.

I yank the door shut behind me and Seppie squeals out of the driveway.

"Think anyone saw?"

"No clue."

She speeds down my road while I'm still trying to get my seat belt on. I can't seem to get it to buckle. "I can't latch it."

She glances over. "That's because your hands are shaking."

She swishes on the windshield wiper. The truck fishtails around the corner, the whole back section zigzagging on the slick road.

"We should probably slow down," I suggest, in what I think is a perfectly normal voice for someone who is terrified.

Seppie doesn't answer.

"Or maybe play music. I am kind of freaking out here."

"Did you get your seat belt buckled?" she asks.

"Yes."

"You liar. Just try to calm down, okay, Mana? And buckle your damn seat belt."

"Yep. Mm-hmm. Okay."

I try again. It clicks in. I stare at Seppie's face. Her jaw is rigid. "You're freaking out, too. You're just pretending to be calm."

"Of course I'm freaking out," Seppie says. "How can I not be freaking out?"

She turns right onto the road. There are hardly any cars out. Slush covers the normally well-defined lanes of the street. Snow piles up on the edges, from when the plow last came through.

"This is going to work," I say.

The wipers whisk the snow to the right and left, back and forth.

"Of course it will."

We're just sitting there when "Jingle Bells" starts blasting out of nowhere.

Seppie jumps. The truck swerves toward a snowbank. She gets it back into the lane. "What the hell is that?"

"Mrs. Stephenson's cell?" I say, after a second of thought. I dig it out of the backpack and stare as the stupid, incessant ringtone keeps going on and on.

"Who is it?"

"It says it's my mom's cell."

"I thought *you* had your mom's cell."

"I gave it to Lyle."

She makes a face. "You should probably answer it."

"I know."

It stops ringing.

Seppie groans. "Mana . . ."

"If I talk to him, I'll end up telling him what we're doing. I don't want him hurt."

"I know."

"You know?"

"Honey, I know a lot of things you think I don't know, actually."

"Oh, really? Like what?"

"Like Lyle likes you."

The phone rings again. Same ringtone. Same number.

I admit, smiling, "He does not . . . but we kissed."

She screams and slaps my thigh. "Shut up! Was it good?"

All I can do is nod super emphatically.

"Holy . . . wow. Answer the phone."

Lyle's voice cracks when he speaks. "Mana?"

"Hey, Lyle . . ." I pick at my jeans. There is a hole in one of the knees. I must have done it when I fell earlier. I didn't even notice until now.

"Are you okay? We found my mom in here. She's pretty messed up. She won't tell us anything. Somebody duct taped her to a chair."

"That was me."

"What?"

"She kidnapped Seppie. I'm . . . well. . . . I'm not sure how to tell you this gently, but . . . Lyle, basically she's an alien."

There is a pause. This pause is long, and I instantly regret how abrupt I was, explaining this.

Finally, he says, "My mom?"

"Yes. And I'm really sorry, Lyle, and I'm sure this is a lot to process and is beyond hard to hear, but probably your dad, too, because your mom is antihuman in a big way. She's really bigoted. I don't think she'd marry a human."

Again, the pause is long. I add, "I wish I could have done this face-to-face, but I didn't want to risk her hurting you."

"So that means that I—"

"Pretty much," I interrupt before he can say it. "I don't know how China feels about aliens, Pierce being the exception, so maybe you could not tell him that you probably are one, too. Maybe you could pretend like you're adopted."

There is a big silence on the phone as I try to think of what to do.

"Maybe you should put China on the phone, actually," I suggest.

After a second, his voice comes through in an exasperated rush. "No. No. I'm just processing. How is Seppie?"

"She's okay. I'm with her now."

"And you're okay?"

"Perfect," I say, as Seppie pulls into the high school parking lot. I motion for her to go around toward the left side, where there's an auxiliary parking lot. "We should go in the back."

"Go in the back where?" Lyle demands.

"Um. We're okay, Lyle. I'm sorry that we didn't come out and get you, but . . . I . . . um . . . Well, I don't know if I can trust China, and—"

"Holy crap. You found the chip, didn't you?"

Seppie parks. I stare at the solid brick side of the building. Right behind it is the gym. There's an emergency entrance here.

"Yeah, Lyle, nice announcing it. I have to go, okay? I'll give you a call back in a little bit."

"Mana. Do. Not. Hang. Up," he says. "What are you doing? You found the chip? Are you trading it for your mom?"

"What do you think, Lyle?"

Seppie motions for me to hang up.

"Mana. You can't do that without us. It's dangerous."

"I know. That's why I'm not telling you where we are. Duh. No offense. Sorry, that sounded mean . . ." I peek over at Seppie, who gives me a *do not be an idiot* face.

Lyle keeps talking, but not to me. "Holy crap. China. She found it. She's doing it. Mana, where are you?"

I hang up and silence the phone.

Seppie turns the key in the ignition and pulls it out. "So?"

"Does he really like me? Lyle?"

She pockets the key. "You just said his name unnecessarily, which he does all the time to you. That's a pretty big sign." She smiles and opens up her door. It starts dinging because the lights are still on. She peers back in at me and flicks the headlights off. "Think you can manage the whole seat belt thing, Little Miss Love Bug?"

"Shut up. You are such a pooper scooper." I jump out with that brilliant insult.

She reaches into the back of the truck and pulls out the two mechanical bows we bought at Walmart. We're too young to legally buy guns, but they let us have these killer bows, thanks to the magic of Seppie's credit cards.

She sticks one of the accompanying quiver things in her belt. I do the same. Then, carrying the bow beneath her arm, she stomps over to my side of the truck.

"You ready?"

"You look like the female Rambo."

"Who the hell is Rambo?"

"He's this warrior guy from the eighties."

She presses her lips together and then says, "You are as peculiar and as obscure as Lyle. Don't try to deny it."

"It's why you love us. We just make you feel more normal."

We stomp through the snow, over to the emergency fire door. Using the lock destroyer that China gave me earlier, I fry the door open.

"Brilliant." Seppie nods approvingly.

"Thanks."

I turn the doorknob as she says, "You really think I seem all badass?"

"Oh, absolutely one hundred percent badass."

I hold the door open for her and she smiles and says, "I've always wanted to be badass."

The gym smells like Febreze and basketball trainers and polish. Our wet shoes squelch across the floor.

"Thank God the custodian left the lights on in here," Seppie says, "because it would be so freaky if it were dark."

"We would just turn the lights on." I adjust the bow.

"Oh. Right."

We stand in the center of the gym, on the red center court line where they do all the basketball tip-offs, where I land my tumbling run at halftime.

"It's creepy being in here alone." Seppie shudders, then stands up all straight. "Waiting for aliens. It's so quiet. Sometimes, when we're cheering, I want everyone to just shut up, for it to be silent, but now . . . Well, I could use a good, riotous basketball crowd right now."

I touch her arm. She jumps.

"You don't have to do this with me, you know."

Her hands go to her hips. "What kind of friend would I be if I made you rescue your mom all alone?"

"A sane friend?"

She snorts. "True." She weaves her arm around mine. "I'm not leaving you. I am an official badass. Got it?"

Something sticks in my throat. "Got it."

We wait.

We wait.

We wait some more.

"You think they'll see the note?" she asks.

"They'll see it."

"Do you think waiting in the center of the gym is a good idea? Should we go put our backs up against the bleachers?"

Ack. "Yeah," I say, because suddenly the thought of being surrounded by aliens seems really plausible. "It's stupid to wait out here. We need to be strategic."

We hustle over to the bleachers. They're wooden, all folded up right now. When they're stacked on top of each other like this, they're probably fifteen feet high. We stand beneath them, silent for a few minutes. My mind races with scenarios that get more terrifying with every minute that passes.

"I hate waiting," Seppie says.

"I know."

"Your mom is going to be okay."

"Uh-huh."

"You think the aliens will—"

"Seppie. I am so sorry, and I know this is going to sound mean, and I don't want to sound mean, because I love you and you are the best friend and base anyone could ever want, but could we not talk for a minute?"

"Of course," she says, and presses her lips together like she is holding stuff back. But she can't do it, and she goes, "Why?"

I lift my hand to stop her. I whisper, "I think I hear something."

"What?"

"Aliens."

"You hear the aliens?"

"Sh-h-h . . ."

"What are they saying?" she asks, voice hushed now.

There's no time to tell her, just time to order, "Get out your bow! Now!"

It's freaking Dakota Dunham again, now also known as Acid Tongue Boy. He skims across the ceiling, darting through the metal girders and straight at us. He comes across as barely human. He's not *any* human. He spits.

I shove Seppie sideways. The acid splashes against the wood bleachers, right where her stomach was. It hisses, eating through the old wood.

"Crap! Crap!" Seppie fumbles with her bow, voice rising. "Was that the acid? Did he really just spit acid?"

"Totally acid."

"Damn, I wish you could do that."

"It would be handy."

Dakota takes another run at us. I pull the compound bow up to my shoulder, trying to remember all the hunting lessons my dad taught me. Steady. Let the pulleys do the work. Aim.

The arrow soars and hits him in the ankle. He squeals and tumbles, head over heels in the air, smacking down in the center of the room.

"I am so not into this kind of alien." Seppie rocks backwards into me. "Even if he was a hottie, like, three days ago."

"We can't all be cute and cuddly like me." I put my bow down at my side. "*If* I am an official alien, that is. Still confused about that."

"You can actually shoot that?" she says, motioning toward the bow.

"My dad taught me when we went hunting."

She nods. Her eyes glaze over a little. "You never told me."

"It was sort of a secret from Mom, because she was always so antiweapon, antifighting, which makes no sense at all now. Plus, it's not exactly cool!, knowing how to shoot a compound bow. It doesn't fit with the cheerleader image."

Dakota moves a little bit. Seppie takes a step forward. I touch her arm with my free hand. "Do not go near him."

As if to prove my statement, he sits up and glares at us. He yanks out the arrow, hobbling up to a standing position.

"Crap," Seppie mutters.

"You need to think of a better swear."

She's shaking, but says, "Are we going to have to shoot him again? Because he's looking pissed."

I bring the bow back up, get out another arrow. "I know. I know. Watch out for his spit, okay?"

"Okay."

Dakota limps forward. One step. Another. He stares me down. He is an alien. I am an alien. He is a freak. I am a freak. And he is alive, and that means he's dangerous.

Another step.

My hand trembles.

"Mana!"

I aim.

Something smacks into him from the side. I twitch my hand. There's still an arrow there. I didn't shoot him. Something else did. And not with an arrow. A gun.

Men in Black swarm inside the gym. There have got to be ten of them, at least. Two capture Dakota, haul out a cell phone, just like China did so many days ago, and disappear. So Men in Black and acid aliens are not allies. Good to know.

Seppie staggers backwards and hits the bleachers.

"Holy shit," she whispers.

"Much better swear."

She doesn't answer, just stares. I stare, too. A final man comes in. He has his hand on a woman's arm, hurrying her along. It's my mom. My mom!

Joy surges through me, and I let it sit there in my heart for a second before I start frantically surveying her, checking to see if she looks obviously hurt. I want to run to her and hug her, yank her out of that guy's hand. It's so hard to be cautious, but as I look her over she just seems pale. There are circles under her eyes, like someone dipped their thumb in charcoal eye shadow and just fingerprinted it on there.

"Mom."

I start forward, but Seppie grabs my arm, holding me back. "They've got guns. Remember the plan."

"Whatever." I shrug off the plan and run across the gym floor. Love and relief fill me.

Mom gasps and yells, "Stop. Mana. Don't come closer."

I slip on the gym floor, which is wet from all the shoe slush. "What?"

"They'll shoot you."

The man holding her arm nods.

Stopping, I look from one man to a woman next to him to another man. They all have the same intense, take-no-prisoners expression, so I cross my arms. "Fine."

One of the men steps forward.

"How do I know you won't kill us?" I demand.

"You don't."

"Great."

He smiles a slow, crooked smile. Then he shrugs.

"You are no Will Smith," I say.

"We're nothing like that stupid movie."

I cock my head. "Really? So you don't have any morals at all?"

"Of course we do." He gestures toward my mother. "It's you all that have it wrong."

"Right."

Seppie scoots up toward me. Her hands raise in the air. "No shooting, okay? Nice human cheerleader here. Does not want to be shot." When she gets to me, she says, out of the corner of her mouth, "Can we cut with the talking?"

I try to keep her a little behind me, where it is safer by, like, two millimeters. "No." I bend over and pull up my sock, then I make a big deal of adjusting the bow on my back, plucking at the arrows.

"Please tell me you didn't actually bring it, Mana," Mom says.

The man next to her glares at her but doesn't hit her or anything. I take that as a good sign, and also as a sign that I don't have to murder him. Yet. "Mom, I had to. I had to get you back."

"This is bigger than me, Mana."

I nod. "I know."

I put my hand in my oversized pocket and pull out a Coke can and the tiny chip.

"It's so tiny. So easily destroyed," I say.

I count to three.

One.

Two.

Three.

Nobody moves.

I take a deep breath and nod. Seppie twitches next to me. I can't read her mind, but I don't need to. We are connected, in this to-gether, best friends for life, which may not actually be for very long. I flip the pop-top of the can. The carbonation makes it all sizzle, threatening to foam over. Just a little jiggle and things could get messy. Instead, I take a sip. It will make me look casual, like I am just so confident that I can take a moment and hydrate.

Mom gasps. "Mana! Don't!"

The man holding her clamps his hand over her mouth. She bites it. He swears and adjusts accordingly, while blood drips down to the floor. Wow. I hope she's up to date on her hepatitis vaccinations and everything, because yuck. Contagion much?

I try to ignore all that and just talk. "If the point is to make sure the chip doesn't get into the wrong hands, it seems like it might be a good thing for me to just destroy it, right? Then nobody would be after it anymore. Everyone would stay alive. Good aliens would be able to go on acting like humans. And the bad aliens could keep on mutilating and abducting in exchange for technology, right? And humans could just keep on keeping on, all oblivious." I take another sip. The Man in Black closest to me—the leader, the one who actually talked?—his finger twitches on his gun. I can see his shirt move when he inhales.

I meet Mom's gaze.

"But that's not really your goal, is it?" I take another sip. Coke is tasting pretty good right now, sweet good in the middle of all the bitter bad. My mom never lets me have it. She's never let me have any caffeine. I suddenly realize that was all bull. You can't be aller-gic to caffeine, can you? What does it do? Raise your heart rate? Maybe that's what she didn't want. Maybe raising my pulse makes me hear aliens? Or maybe being near the chip is doing that? Maybe the caffeine makes me stronger, too, more acrobatic. There are so many questions that I need answers to.

"Miss?" The closest Man in Black reaches out his hand, the hand that isn't holding the gun. "Why don't you give me that chip and I'll give you your mother?"

"Are you going to destroy it?"

He nods. "Of course."

Seppie blinks hard, once. That's our code. It means he's lying. She's so good at reading people, but to be honest, I kind of figured this one out already.

"Send my mom over first," I say.

"Under no circumstances," he answers.

"Listen. I'm not an idiot. We're completely surrounded. You have guns trained on us. We're, what? Two girls? Two cheerleaders? What are we going to do? Escape with our pom-poms and bows? Dematerialize in the middle of a toe touch? Get real, okay?"

He raises an eyebrow like some sort of cool, unemotional villain in one of Lyle's graphic novels.

"Fine," I say, tipping the Coke can. "I'll destroy it now, then."

I tilt the can more. Someone gasps. I move my chip hand under the can, right in the path of where the soda will flow out.

"Fine," the Man in Black with the twitchy gun finger says. He snarls a little. He turns to the one touching my mother. "Let her go."

He lets go.

Mom scurries across the floor toward us.

I move the chip out of the way and spill a little Coke on the floor. Everyone stops. The entire gym is still.

"Oops." I bob my head from side to side like a total ditz. "My bad."

Seppie makes a guffaw sort of noise. Mom starts across the gym again. She moves past the Man in Black and says, "Excuse me, Jacob."

He nods.

My head is buzzing hard and funny. It's like the whole thing is vibrating. It must be the caffeine. I am absolutely wired.

My mother gets to my side, which is exactly where a mom is supposed to be. I hug her. She's soft and strong and smells like snow. She sniffs in my hair and murmurs, "Oh, honey . . ."

As much as I don't want to, I pull away a little bit. "It will be okay."

Her voice is a warning. "Mana, we cannot give them the chip. The moment you hand it over, they will kill me, and probably you and Seppie as well, but that's not what matters. My partner and I have only just determined that this chip is really a device that activates a weapon that will kill humans indiscriminately. That's what it's for. It's part of a—"

The Man in Black, the one in charge, holds out his hand, interrupting her. "The chip?"

"Everyone? All humans?" I blurt out, horrified. "Just randomly."

"The chip," the Man in Black insists.

This is it. The moment. This is all me, and everything that happens next will be because I decided to do what I am about to do. Nobody can catch me if I dismount poorly, if I make the wrong choice. All the responsibility is mine. So, for one more second, I glance at the metal circle in my hand. I glance at the Coke can. There's no choice. I drop the chip into the hole you drink out of and I toss the can to the lead Man in Black. "Catch."

The moment I do it, the gym explodes with activity, but to me it's all slow motion. Men in Black are diving for the Coke. They're lifting off their heels. They leap. They lunge. Their faces are twisted with determination. Other Men in Black are aiming at us. Gunfire rocks the place in a slow rumble, a roar. Seppie screams. My poor, sick-looking mom grabs for a bow. Both of them will be too late to defend themselves.

A bullet hits Mom. She staggers back. Blood leaks through her coat.

I hold up my arms. My fingers splay out. They vibrate and buzz. I scream. It's a noise louder than a gunshot. It's a feeling bigger than a caffeine buzz. My hands agitate with some sort of power that whips across the gym like a bluish-white wind, and suddenly everyone, everything, except for my mother and Seppie and me, drops to the floor.

Bullets clatter harmlessly onto the court. The Men in Black splat down. Their faces smash into the wood. Blood comes out of some of their noses. The lights that hang from the rafters drop and shatter all around us, but somehow, miraculously, none of the glass hits us. *Nothing* hits us. There's a three-foot circle all around us and nothing gets in—no bullets, no men, no glass. Silence takes over. Just silence.

"Holy crap," Seppie says after a couple seconds.

A basketball net loses its hold on the backboard and flutters to the ground.

"Did I . . . ? Did I just . . . ?" I lower my hands, shaking, and freaking scared to death of what just happened, what I just did.

Terror twists Seppie's face. The door to the gym opens up. Mom, wobbling and unstable, tries to lift the bow, but she's too weak from whatever they've been doing to her, and the bullet. I wrap her up in my arms and then think better of it and try to get to the wound, to stop the bleeding. Finding it, I use a hat to apply pressure. The blood still leaks through my fingers.

"You need to sit down," I tell her.

"If I sit I won't get up, honey," she says, proving she is the toughest woman ever.

Panic surges through me, but my voice is calm as I order Seppie, "We need to get the car and get her to a hospital."

Just then China leaps into the room, with Lyle following behind him. They're both holding machine guns. *Lyle* has a *machine gun!*

Another net falls.

In a split second, China takes in the scene. He gazes across the gym at me and Mom . . . and smiles. "She had caffeine, didn't she?"

"Yes . . ." Mom nods, falters.

She really has always known—always known I was something different. And China? He knew, too. He must have always known. The secret he's been guarding has to do with me.

"The device?" he asks.

"She put it in a Coke can," Mom says. China hauls in a breath, leans against the wall. "She was saving . . ."

I wrap my free arm around her just before she passes out. I catch her, the way everyone has always been catching me.

CHAPTER 20

Before he leaves, China and I stand outside the hospital emergency room entrance. They are already working on my mom. I pace back and forth, back and forth, but China is motionless, just observing everything. He gives me a tiny flashlight, kind of like the one that lasered through the locks. Only this one has a laser that kills.

"Just in case," he says. "I don't want you to . . . It's not like you'll need it. Not now that the chip is gone, but . . . I can trust a cheerleader with this, right?"

"I'm not just a cheerleader. I mean, that's not what defines me."

He smiles enough to show he has actual dimples; I haven't seen them before. This must be his real smile. "I know."

"And where are you going?" I pocket the laser and cross my arms in front of my chest. "You're just leaving?"

"I have work to do."

"What about my mom?"

He runs his hand through his hair, then stuffs the hand away in his back pocket, acting all casual, trying too hard. "She'd want me to continue doing what we need to do."

"Which is?"

"Search for your dad. Catch more aliens."

So that's it.

"Like me?"

"Not you. You're not an alien, Mana. You are human. You're a special human who can't have caffeine, but I promise you that you are human." He reaches out his hand. I shake it and stare at him with my mouth wide open. I thought . . . I was sure I was an alien. I'd come to terms with it and everything. I thought that Lyle and I were both aliens, that we were the same.

I don't even know how to ask him what that means or how he knows, and he just shakes my hand like this is a normal thing to reveal. We stand there for a second and then he lets go. He reaches up and musses my hair. "I swear to you, she'll be okay."

And then he just gets in his illegally parked Jeep and drives away. Seppie, Lyle, and I watch him from the waiting room windows outside the emergency room wing. He really just drives away into the sunset, like he's some sort of stupid hero, which he is not. He's just an attractive covert agent in a leather jacket who has dimples and an attitude. That's all.

And we stay. Well, Lyle and I stay. Seppie has to go home, eventually, but she comes back over and over again, switching shifts with Lyle to keep me company.

Clutching Mr. Penguinman, I let myself take one last glance at my mom, who is still unconscious in the hospital bed. The doctors say she had internal injuries that happened before she came to the gym. They had tortured her. There is evidence.

Even with the Coke, I'm not one hundred percent sure how I managed to knock all the Men (and Women) in Black to the ground, yank the bullets out of the air, and keep us safe without even moving. I've tried for hours to figure out what happened. Lyle, Seppie, and I all think it has to do with the caffeine and my heart rate. We're still not sure where the mind reading and leaping came from.

The doctors have chemically induced a coma so that Mom can heal. Tubes stick out of her arms. Monitors beep by her side. Everything smells like blood covered up by bleach, like chemicals trying to hide the truth. The entire ICU room resembles something out of Lyle's sci-fi movie collection.

Only it's real.

I tuck Mr. Penguinman in next to my mom's side. I kiss her cheek. Her skin is cold.

"I'm going to go do the right thing," I whisper. "Lyle is going to stay with you, okay? Keep you safe."

I straighten and walk away. My sneakers must still be wet, because they're heavy, hard to move.

Lyle has already pulled a chair up by the door and settled in. Our eyes meet. His long legs push him into a standing position by the door. His eyes linger on mine. "You sure you don't want me to come?"

"Of course I want you to come."

"I will."

A gulp sticks itself in my throat. The monitor beeps. I whirl around, but it's just a beep, not an alarm.

We haven't kissed again. We haven't talked about the kiss. We act like everything is the same, when everything has changed. Lyle and Seppie and I are all tied together now, more than we ever were before. It's not just what happened that ties us together, it's the knowledge of what *could* happen. The knowledge that Lyle isn't human and neither am I, exactly. We got my mom back, but his parents have vanished. Well, his mother has been taken by China somewhere, and we think his dad is on the run.

"I'll be okay," I manage. I play-poke his chest. "Thanks for standing watch."

He stands up out of the chair and puts his hands on my shoulders. "Mana . . ."

"I'm good. Don't worry." I poke him again, trying to be all tough girl. But I'm not. Not really. "You are the best friend ever. You know that? Seriously."

"I don't want you to go." He yanks me in, hugging me. He smells like the spaghetti sauce he had for lunch, and beneath that is his normal minty smell. He's the best of me, I think, the good and solid best of me, and it doesn't matter if he's human or alien, or if his mom kidnapped Seppie and threatened me. What matters is that he is Lyle—beautiful, strong, sexy, geeky do-gooder Lyle. I am so terribly lucky to have him in my life.

"I'm worried about you," he says. "I don't want anything to happen . . ."

He doesn't finish his sentence. He doesn't have to.

I repeat, like doing that will make it true, "I'll be okay. Don't worry."

"Like I'm not going to worry."

I nestle in for one second, just one second, because that's all I can spare. "Take care of her, okay?"

He inhales so deeply that my head moves with his chest and his breath and then he says, "I promise."

Before I can blink, really, I am on my way to the airport.

In the taxi I pull the card out of the front pocket of my backpack. I found it there right after China left.

PATRICK KINSELLA
SPECIAL AFFAIRS
323 East Capitol Boulevard
Suite 42
Washington, DC.

I flip it over to read the writing again: *Come anytime.*

I push the card into the front pocket of my jeans. It gets a little stuck.

"I hope you know what you're getting, Mr. Kinsella," I murmur.

"American Airlines?" the cabby asks me again.

"Yep."

"That's terminal B. Just another three minutes."

"Great, thanks."

I nod. I close my eyes. I wait.

*T*he whole flight, I have this massive urge to tap on the window and wave at the clouds. That's when it happens. I'm just sitting there next to a guy whose khakis strain against his super-muscular thighs, imagining *Twilight Zone* scenarios, missing Lyle and Seppie, missing my mom, wondering about my dad, wondering about China, wondering about what it means to be human, a special human in love with an alien boy, when I give in and let myself cry.

The big, anonymous guy next to me puts down his copy of *Sky-Mall*. He puts his hand on top of my hand, which is resting on that ugly plastic foldout tray that comes down from the seat in front of you. I stare at his fingers.

"You okay?" he asks. He has a good, mellow voice.

I sniff in. "Is this the part where I cry and then gaze deeply into your eyes and we fall in love forever because we're soul mates who are destined to be together and you help me fight the evil aliens who spit acid and shift form and then we make mad, passionate love for hours but it turns out you aren't human?"

The plane starts to go down.

His hand twitches but he doesn't move it. I have to give him that. Instead, he goes, "Did you lose your pills, or did you take too many?"

I sort of snort, and this makes me guffaw, which then makes me laugh pretty hard.

He laughs, too, and he holds my hand in his big one for the rest of the trip. And I think about how humans can be so kind to each other, even when we don't know a thing about each other. We can still reach out and touch someone's hand, knowing we will never see it again, knowing there is nothing in it for us, because we will be stepping off a plane, going to different lives. Still, we do it. Still, we reach out.

CHAPTER 21

The taxi ride into DC takes forever, but eventually it drops me off near the White House. I tip the cabbie way too much and climb out of the cab, saying good-bye to the smell of sweat and myrrh incense and hello to the smell of winter cold and engine exhaust fumes.

I cough.

Welcome to DC.

All the buildings in this section of the city are gray marble, appearing as though they aspire to be the homes of the gods in ancient Greece. It's grand, I know that. But it's also pretty impersonal. People hustle around, giving the impression that they're all identical, with their briefcases and long, dark overcoats. I move with them, stepping in slush, feeling a little bizarre in my dark-purple coat, my bright winter hat.

I do not fit in.

Of course, I will probably never fit in again, just because I *know*, or because of my status as "special human." Whatever that even means. Maybe this Kinsella guy has some answers. I want answers.

So I slosh through the slush, searching for the building. The taxi driver let me off two streets down, as close as cars are allowed to go to the White House. But then I find it: 323 East Capitol Boulevard.

The large square of the building just sort of looms over everything. It fits in with the other squares, grounded on the road, one after the other, like giant molars, ready to grind and chew.

"Lovely."

A man bumps me and mutters, "Sorry."

He keeps moving by. Everyone is progressing across the street, up and down sidewalks. I'm the only one standing still.

I take the steps two at a time, the stupid chip burning a hole in my pocket.

A woman at the front desk, who is wearing one of those hands-free cell phone headsets and a lot of bracelets, takes my name and calls up.

I can hear her voice in my head: *She's not from here. Not with that coat.*

Obviously, since I can hear her in my head, neither is she. I wonder how many aliens there are out there, like Lyle, some knowing, some not. I smile at her.

"Yes, thank you. I'll send her right up," she says to someone on the other end of the phone line. She disconnects, nods at me. "He'll see you now. Take the elevator to your left, go to the third floor, cross toward the left and then take the first hall to your right."

I cock my head. "Um?"

She flashes a smile that is just politeness. There is no depth. She pushes something on her keyboard. "There'll be signs."

There *are* arrows directing people to suites, just like in hotel hallways. Suites 20 to 40, go left. Suites 41 to 60, go right. That kind of thing. I follow the arrows down a hallway full of mahogany doors and brass nameplates that list numbers and occasionally departments, but never names.

Suite 42 is one of the first doors. There are no noises coming from behind it. Nobody walks through the halls. Security cameras that flash little red lights are the only signs of life. One of those automated spy drones, the kind they always show on CNN—they're about six inches wide and resemble dragonflies—well, one of those flies by me. Creepy. It buzzes around me and then moves down the hall.

Since they know I'm here anyway, I knock on the door.

"Come in," says a male voice, rough, lowish. "It's open."

My hand slips on the brass knob. I'm sweating, I guess. I wipe it off on my coat. Try again.

The man sitting there pulls his legs off of the desk. He stands up and smiles. "Mana."

He walks around the desk, leans in, shuts the door, smiles some more.

"You're . . . You're . . ." I can't find the right words. "You're in a suit."

He nods, and his lips turn up in an amused smile. "I am, indeed."

He motions for me to sit down.

I sit down.

"Where's Patrick Kinsella?"

He thuds his chest.

"*You* are Patrick Kinsella?" I search around the room for some sort of evidence.

"I'm Patrick Kinsella."

"Huh. Okay, right . . . I'm glad your real name isn't a country, I guess. I kind of thought that was a little weird." I cough nervously and stand back up. There are pictures on his desk. One picture is of him, younger, with two sweet-seeming parent-type people. There's a big lake behind them and a big fishing pole in the dad's hand.

"Moosehead Lake," China, aka Patrick Kinsella, says. "We had a summer place there. It's in Maine."

"Uh-huh."

I pick up the other picture. It's China the way I know him. He wears a leather jacket. No happy smile graces his features. Same goes for the slim woman next to him. Mom.

He taps the photo. There is a cut on his finger. "We'd just pulled off a monster case. You know that acid-tongued alien?"

Dakota. I nod. I remember to breathe. Mom seems so proud there, so proud and unhurt and alive. But she's wearing a leather jacket. Totally not her style.

"We'd just hauled in twenty of them. They'd been wreaking havoc all over Argentina, slaughtering cows, terrorizing villages. God, I hate those aliens." He stops himself, unfists his hand, and turns to me. His voice gets softer. "How's your mom?"

"I called Lyle after I got off the plane and he said the doctors say they're 'cautiously optimistic.'" He probably already knows that. He probably already knows everything.

I rip my gaze away from the picture, force myself to study China/Patrick. He tilts his head. "Mana . . ."

I hold up my hand to stop him. "Tell me what the chip or device or whatever is. What it really is. I know I've only been getting half-truths. I want whole truths."

He eyes me. I meet his gaze and don't back down, not for a second.

"Mana . . ." He says my name all sternly, but I can tell his resolve is weakening.

"The chip is gone. It can't hurt to tell me the truth now. It wasn't some master alien list, was it? We believed you about that at first, but then we thought it would kill all the aliens. Then we learned that it would kill all the humans."

The air in the room is stale and stagnant.

"It would have killed you, your mom, me," he says. "It would have killed all us humans."

"Okay." I step backwards and end up against the wall, next to a picture of an American flag. I am not shocked, but to hear him say it just makes it more real.

"The chip is part of some kind of a machine, a key part to a machine that's been developed by aliens. It does not discriminate between good or bad. It just kills all."

"And the Men in Black?"

"Wanted to use it against the aliens somehow. I think they know more about it than your mom and I do, honestly. We were still trying to figure out exactly what it was when we plucked it out of Dakota Dunham's locker. Anyway, the Men in Black . . . They're tired of merely picking away at aliens. The mutilations and abductions are increasing. More and more humans are starting to understand that something bad is going on. Many segments of formerly peaceful alien species feel threatened. It may be our home, but they want to evict us."

I can understand that. I can. But . . . "How do you feel about aliens?"

He swallows hard. "I've always thought aliens were parasites. But Pierce isn't. Lyle isn't. Christ, how many more kids like him are out there? Not even knowing. How many adults?"

"But me?"

"What about you?"

"You said I was a human, a special human. But what does that even mean? How can I not be an alien when all of a sudden I'm hearing aliens and leaping? What about what happened at the gym? Why can I do this all of a sudden? *How?* I am an alien, right? You were lying before . . ."

"Human. You are human."

I lift an eyebrow. "Seriously."

"Seriously. You're human with enhancements. You're a weapon, Mana. That's what you were meant to be, at least. It happened without your mother's knowledge, believe me. It happened when you were young."

"*What* happened?"

"Experiments."

"What kind of experiments?"

"I think you know."

My nightmares. Is this about my nightmares? Were they real? Sickening dread makes a home in my stomach, but I push through the panic of it and say, "I obviously do not know, which is why I am asking you. Why? Why was I experimented on? Who did it?"

"The aliens wanted to fight fire with fire, infiltrate the humans from within. So they came up with a plan. You were a baby. Your mom found the lab and rescued you; she kept you and raised you as her own."

"What?"

He repeats it all over again, calmly, but I'm anything but calm. Inside me is one sentence, one question, repeating over and over again.

I am not my mom's.

I am not my mom's?

"But—I—I—I look like my dad. Sort of . . ."

"Your dad is just a cover."

"What?"

The world spins in a very bad way. I grab the edge of the desk as China continues, "Your dad was advised of the situation. He agreed to be your father, pretend to have once been married to your mother. She was the best person available to keep you safe, hide you, raise you like a normal kid until—"

It takes me a second to realize he's broken off his sentence. "Until what?"

"Until it was time to use you."

"Use me?"

"Against the same people who made you. Not against humans. But against *them*. The aliens. The twisted, sick aliens who stole a baby and warped her DNA for their own purposes."

I stagger backwards. "I have to sit down."

"Your parents love you. You know that, right?" He tucks a seat underneath my butt, grabs a water bottle, and forces it on me. I gulp it down because I don't have any idea what else I should do.

I am a weapon.

My parents love me.

My parents are not my parents.

My whole life is a lie, a story.

I am a weapon.

"Why is it all acting up now?" I finally ask. "I was normal before. I mean, I was good at tumbling and everything, but I was normal."

"It has to do with your heart rate and adrenaline," he says, confirming the theories Lyle and Seppie and I had. "If you're upset, your extra abilities are activated more easily. We honestly weren't sure if you would ever manifest anything. For a while we thought it was a failed experiment."

"*It* was a failed experiment? You mean *I* was a failed experiment. Nice. You know how to talk to a girl, China, also known as Patrick Kinsella. You really do."

He has the decency to redden. "I suck at this. I know that. I'm sorry. It's a lot to process."

He closes his eyes for a moment, as if it's just too much. I won't push him on this now. I will later, though. That's for sure.

I nod and grab the door. "Thank you for telling me. When did you find all this out? Pierce said not to trust you."

"I figured out part of it the moment I saw you leaping in the locker room. I had heard rumors of a baby, a stolen baby, but I never knew. Your mom protected your identity even from me. Pierce, though, obviously recognized you immediately. She was there on that mission; she saw the baby. She could tell it was you from your thought patterns or something like that, I'm sure. She didn't tell me she had figured it out, but I noticed you two communicating in a way that made no sense, so it had to be telepathically. And she took such an interest in you. She spends most of her time bored—helping us, but uninterested. Her determination of your identity made me realize it, too."

I have so many more questions, like if I have any more abilities that will manifest (he has no clue, but possibly). If I will get an acid tongue (he doesn't know), and how my dad would ever agree to this, and where he is now, and if the aliens have figured out who I am now (he doesn't know, he doesn't know, and again, he doesn't know).

He stops my questions with his deep voice. "Mana, the threat isn't over. We think that the machine that chip is meant to activate still exists and that there are parts of it scattered throughout the world. We hadn't destroyed the chip because Pierce thought we could use it somehow to track down the other pieces, as well as the aliens who were masterminding this plot. Turned out that was a bad call."

He makes a little scoffing noise, as if he is ashamed to admit he was stupid.

"But they don't have the chip," I say, turning to stare at his worried, cranky face.

"I know you destroyed it, but I'll bet they're already working on producing another one. In order to be safe, to be really safe, we have to find and destroy the other parts of the machine, go after the aliens who are trying to kill us all."

I think about this for a second, and then just say it. "I brought the chip."

He twitches. "What?"

I pull it out of my pocket. I had put it in a Ziploc bag to keep it safe. I hold the bag by the edges and it just dangles there. "I brought the chip."

"But it's . . ."

"I honestly cannot believe you thought I would really destroy it. I'm not that stupid. If it's something my mom spent all that time trying to protect, I'm not just going to throw it in a freaking Coke can." I'm only half kidding. The other half is annoyed. "People have no faith in cheerleaders."

"People have no faith in anything." He smiles really slowly.

"Except processed cheese. I think people have faith in processed cheese. And Spam. And Snopes. And the Internet."

He doesn't respond, just leans across the desk. We stand there for a second, staring at each other, and suddenly everything becomes awkward and I sort of cough. And he straightens up and takes a step backwards, and I go, "Well . . ."

"Well what?" He pulls out a gun.

"You're going to shoot me?"

"Put the chip on the floor, Mana."

"No."

"Mana, I am not kidding around. Put the chip on the floor."

"No. You need it. You said you need it to find the other parts of the machine."

"We'll find them the hard way." He pulls the trigger. The roar of the gun is massive and deafening. I gasp, but there is no time to move, to do anything, to think. And then the bag in my hand is gone. The thing is obliterated.

"You shot the chip!"

"It needs to be gone. I can't believe you trusted me like that."

"I did not trust you," I say. "I thought you were going to shoot me."

"You . . . you . . . are risky, and amazing, and . . ." He flusters around like he is going to swear at me, but instead all the tension leaves his body and he says, "How about you help me find the other parts? Just till your mom's okay. I don't work well without a partner."

"You're lying," I blurt.

"What?"

"You're just trying to keep an eye on me, or protect me. But this is not about you being lonely without a partner. You are not the sort of man who gets lonely."

He lifts an eyebrow. "Does it really matter why?"

"No. It doesn't matter at all."

When I finally get back home, Lyle's waiting for me in the hospital. He's bent over his iPhone, watching some sort of grainy UFO footage on YouTube. There are white lights in the sky. I wonder if it's real. My mother is still unconscious, still in the bed. Monitors beep to tell us she is alive.

My feet are soft as I step into the room, but he hears me anyway.

"Mana?" His voice is a whisper. He puts his phone on a nightstand, next to a bottle of water, and stands up. His eyes are big and brown and soft. I rush into his arms, hug him tightly to me, and his arms encircle me without hesitating. He smells like minty soap, even in here, where everything smells like hospital.

"I missed you," I whisper.

"I missed you too." He breaks our hug the tiniest of bits and gazes down into my face. "So, judging from your texts, we're going to save the world, huh?"

Watching his face, which I know so well, I say, "You decided?"

"Yes." He smiles and grabs his coat, shrugs it on. It's not leather. It's a dark overcoat, long. He puts his arm around my shoulders. "But you have to swear not to have any coffee."

"Not even one tiny sip?" I tease.

He yanks open the door and turns to flash me a heart-stopping smile. "And don't even think about ordering a Coke."

ACKNOWLEDGMENTS

I would like to acknowledge and shout out my gratitude to the following people who make my life and this book possible:

The Earth, because without you, there's no any of us. I'm sorry we treat you so poorly. Thank you for letting us live and die on you anyway.

All my high school friends who used to look at the night sky with me and imagine weird things—and kind of believe them—and freak ourselves out. This means Jackie Shriver, Joe Tullgren, Karin Raymond, Chris LaSalle, David LaFleur, Brandon Constant, Shawn Young, and Christine Allard Bristol. Thank you all for making me weird.

Melissa Frain, the editor who has so much patience she can't be human. Thank you for making this book possible and being so out of this world in a good way. Many thanks to the rest of the intergalactic Tor team, including (but not limited to) Amy Stapp, Kathleen Doherty, Ali Fisher, Seth Lerner, and Linda Quinton! Thank you for flying this book into the world and being such stable bases that I'd recruit you into any cheerleading team, any time.

Edward Necarsulmer IV, for always waving the pom-poms, even when I am out in space, floating aimlessly, which is a lot.

Dwight Swanson, for his invaluable contributions to this book and for his ability to double-dog dare, so I had to put him in here even though he didn't actually do anything.

Mike, Lynne, and Grayson Staggs, for being the best kind of new friends possible and for creating instant community among so many people. And to everyone at poker. Because . . . poker.

Steve and Jenna Boucher, who have volunteered to be family since I have lost so much of my own.

Nicole Ouellette, Maryanne Mattson, Lori Bartlett, and Laura Ludwig Hamor, for their exceptional kindnesses.

I have lost my mom and my dad since my last book, and the support and love of people like the ones listed above, plus the Bar Harbor Fire Department, have meant a great deal to me.

So, the most thanks go to Emily Ciciotte and Shaun Farrar, for being my gravitational pulls and spotters. Without you two, the me that I am would be lost to space. I love you.

CPSIA information can be obtained
at www.ICGtesting.com
Printed in the USA
LVHW111910260819
628963LV00004B/396/P